The Isla Vista Crucible

September 1969-June 1970

Reilly Ridgell

Savant Books and Publications
Honolulu, HI, USA
2012

Published in the USA by Savant Books and Publications
2630 Kapiolani Blvd #1601
Honolulu, HI 96826
http://www.savantbooksandpublications.com

Printed in the USA

Edited by Zachary M. Oliver
Cover by Dennis Krull

13-digit ISBN: 9780983286165
10-digit ISBN: 0983286167

This is a work of historical *fiction*. As such all names, characters, places and incidents should be considered fictitious. Every effort has been made to make non-fictional elements as accurate as possible; however, there may be mistakes, both typographical and in content, and the non-fictional elements are current only up to the print date. In summary, this work should be considered a work for general entertainment, and not used or cited as a source of factual or historical information.

Acknowledgements

I wish to thank the handful of people who read this book before publication and offered their advice. I particularly would like to acknowledge Malcolm Gault-Williams for his book "Don't Bank on Amerika," a history of the Isla Vista riots, which was invaluable in helping me keep events in their proper order. I also would like to thank Gregory Desilet, author of "Burning Banks and Roasting Marshmellows" for his help in obtaining information for me that I would have had difficulty obtaining myself.

The Isla Vista Crucible

Introduction

The following is an account of the lives of three college roommates during the tumultuous school year of 1969-1970 in Isla Vista, the student community next to the University of California at Santa Barbara.

Chapter One

SEPTEMBER 1969: Serendipity, Blind Faith, and the Nature of Political Inquiry

Music albums making the charts during September1969:

James Brown—It's a Mother
Judy Collins—Recollections
Creedence Clearwater Revival—Green River
Miles Davis—In a Silent Way
Donovan—Barabajagal
Love—Four Sail
John Mayall—The Turning Point
Moby Grape—Truly Fine Citizen
Santana
Tammy Wynette—Tammy's Greatest Hits

Reggie looked forlornly at the bulletin board filled with a dizzying array of cards and notes advertising for roommates. A number of students waited in the real estate office, some in small groups around the two desks talking with the two visible employees, others waiting their turn. Reggie stuck his hands in his UCLA Lacrosse jacket, tried to disguise the look of consternation brewing inside of him, scanned the board once again hoping for inspiration, and waited. There was time yet. Classes wouldn't start until the last week of September. He had all day, and if necessary he could come back up again from LA in a few days. Still, a slowly building sense of desperation began to manifest itself. He really wanted to get his living situation settled. Besides, the waiting was increasing his anxiety.

He felt a tap on his shoulder and turned to see a thin, short-haired, red-headed student wearing glasses nodding at him. He may have been slightly older, maybe mid-twenties, or perhaps only looked older. Reggie was 22.

"Looking for a place to live?" the student asked bluntly.

"Yeah, I am. You got one?" Reggie asked.

"Sure do, and I need a roommate to make it work."

"How much per month?"

"Your share would be about $80 per month," he responded. "It's a small one-bedroom in the middle of I.V."

Reggie sighed. It was more than he had budgeted for, and he had really wanted his own room, but he didn't know his way around and, after all, a bird in the hand..."Looks like you got yourself a roommate."

"Well, wait a minute. Let's go outside and talk a bit."

"Uh, okay," was all Reggie could manage.

They stood outside on the sidewalk next to the real estate office sizing each other up. Traffic passed by slowly. Everywhere there were people, mostly young, walking to stores or shops or riding their bikes. There was a vibrancy to Isla Vista that Reggie normally would have found fascinating. Not right now, though. First, he needed to take care of business. Reggie looked at the student, wondering what the problem was.

"Before we decide to share an apartment, we should know some things about each other. I love music. I have a large record collection and a very expensive and sophisticated stereo system…"

"Hey, I like music, too, and I won't touch your system if you don't want me to," Reggie interjected.

"What kind of music do you like?" he asked Reggie.

"Well, rock, of course. All kinds of it, actually. Don't you?"

The would-be roommate let out a sigh. Gesturing with his hands in front of him, he began to explain. "I like mood music. I listen to it all the time, from the minute I get home until I go to bed. I read by it; I study by it; I eat by it; I even have it in my car. I have to have it on all the time."

"Mood music? What's that? What do you mean?" Reggie sputtered.

"Beautiful music. Easy listening, semi-classical. Like Mantovani and 101 Strings."

Reggie was stunned. He'd never known anybody his age who actually liked mindless, monotonous elevator music. Muzak was the worst, and the kind of music his parents always played. There might be good tunes in there, but they were drowned in syrup, extinguishing any possible spark of creativity. They were offensively inoffensive. The thought of living with someone who listened to it all day long was downright frightening. It would be like being trapped in an endless hallway with no doors to get out.

"Uh," Reggie began, "maybe you don't have a roommate. I don't think I could handle that. Thank you for the warning. Guess I'll keep looking."

The Muzak-lover smiled and nodded in agreement. Obviously, he'd been through this before.

Reggie headed towards the campus on Pardall. He thought he remembered seeing some real estate offices on the other side of the loop, at the business center of Isla Vista. Two parallel streets, Embarcadero del Norte and Embarcadero del Mar, defined the business district, curving slowly toward each other, joining and completing a loop at the end. He took a deep breath. The sea air felt cool but there was a noticeable oily smell to it. There had been an oil spill nearby earlier that summer.

A car slowly passed, music blaring. To his relief, it was "Soul Kitchen" by the Doors, from their first album that had come out two years before. Maybe the guy in the car had an eight-track system, or maybe there was at least one good radio station around. Morrison's plaintive plea to be allowed to sleep all night in someone's soul kitchen faded when the car turned the corner and disappeared. Reggie smiled. It was going to be a good year.

There are times in one's life when serendipity takes control. Sometimes it's obvious, like when Reggie unexpectedly got accepted to grad school at UC Santa Barbara. Other times, it's just a string of small, unrelated decisions and events, each unimportant, but, taken together, ended up leading to a particular situation that wouldn't have happened if any one of them had been different.

On the other side of the loop, on Embarcadero Del Norte, he saw a small real estate office, and walked in. There was a woman behind a desk. Two young guys stood in front of the desk talking, but not to her. They stopped and looked at Reggie. He nodded and approached.

"I'm looking for a place to stay, but I'll need a roommate."

The woman looked up and then at the two guys. One of them was tall, about six foot four inches, with shaggy blond hair and chiseled features. The other one was shorter than Reggie, with a mop of curly black hair and a scraggly goatee.

"Wanna live in a beach house?" the tall one asked.

"A beach house?" Reggie asked, definitely interested.

"Yeah, we got a place on Del Playa, but we need one more roommate. We've been waiting for someone to walk in who needs a place and looks okay. You look okay. How about it?"

Del Playa! He never thought he'd have a chance to get a place on Del Playa, the street that fronted the ocean.

"How much is it? I can't afford very much."

The taller one looked Reggie in the eye and smiled. "It will cost you $93 per month. I'll actually be paying twice that because I don't want a house full of people. I'm also taking the two small bedrooms so you'll have to share the big bedroom with him." The young man nodded at his companion.

Reggie's heart sank. "I don't think I can afford that…"

"Don't make up your mind until you see it. I've got a good feeling about you. I really think this house is the place you want to stay." He held out his hand to Reggie. "I'm Trent, Trent Foster." Trent exuded a combination of confidence and studliness, but wasn't the least bit threatening, and he didn't seem to be making any effort to con or unduly pressure Reggie. Reggie, in turn, felt honored that the guy liked him.

Reggie took the fellow's hand and looked into his eyes. God, but they were blue! His shoulders were so broad, he probably turned sideways just to pass through doorways. "I'm Reggie Blake."

"And I'm Donnie Johnson," the short one said, nervously extending a hand.

Reggie ended up following them in his old Ford to Del Playa, where they turned right, and headed away from campus. They drove parallel to the beach for almost a mile. Apartments and a houses lined both sides of the street. Cars were parked anywhere and everywhere. The houses and cars thinned as the three traveled farther. About three houses from the end of the street, on the ocean side, sat a one-story, wooden house with a two-car, covered carport and paved parking space for two or three more cars. A small wooden sign on a post near the driveway entrance read "Windward House."

Reggie fell instantly in love with the place. The room he was to share was huge and had its own bathroom. He could deal with not having his own room to live in a house like this. A smaller bedroom faced the entrance; another extended out from the back of the house and faced the ocean. The hallway between them led to another bathroom. The living room was small, but had nice carpet and a fireplace along the outside wall. A huge. sliding glass door led outside to a deck that filled the "L" space formed by the ocean side bedroom and the living room. There was a bit of yard, ending abruptly at a cliff edge. Twenty feet down was the beach. Waves lapped a few feet out from that. The finishing touch was the flagpole next to the deck.

In the distance, some of the Channel Islands were visible, which, was the reason the area was called Isla Vista, Spanish for "Island View." The only thing that marred the beautiful view was an oil platform about a mile out off Devereux School to the right. But Trent was correct. Reggie had to live there.

The three walked out of the house to the bluff's edge to take in the view. The morning light lit the sky with a crispness making everything below seem clean and hopeful. A pelican flew into view a few yards off the shore. Suddenly, it turned, dived, and appeared to crash into the sea. A few seconds later, it popped up, flapped its wings, kicked its feet, ran along the surface of the sea, then lifted off into the air and flew away. Reggie wondered if the pelican had caught anything.

The three turned and looked back at the house. On the side facing Devereux was an empty lot. On the other side of that lot was a two-story, mushroom looking cement and glass house. Next to that house was another, the last house on Del Playa. On the opposite side of Windward House from the vacant lot was an open field, extending at least for a couple hundred yards in the direction of the campus, before another house with a raised deck revealed itself off in the distance. He thought he saw some female forms on the deck, looking over at them.

"It's gonna be expensive for me, too, but my parents can swing it," Donnie said. "You know what's cool? Yesterday was my birthday. This makes a far out present."

"Yeah?" Trent asked, "your birthday, huh? Yesterday was what, September 14? How old are you?"

"All of 18. I'm an incoming freshman," Donnie replied.

"Lucky you," Reggie added. "Now you can legally fuck and get drafted, but you still can't vote or drink booze, *and* if you fuck someone too young, you can be put away for a long time."

"No shit," Donnie noted.

"Well," Trent said. "I'm a 21-year-old senior, almost finished with my math degree. And you?" he asked Reggie.

"I'm 22 and in grad school," Reggie answered. "I finished my bachelor's degree at UCLA last June. Hey, how did you guys find this place?"

"I knew the students who leased it last school year. They actually kept it until, well, last week, I think. A couple of months ago I put my name in for it, and when the real estate lady called me up late yesterday evening, I came in early as I could this morning," Trent explained.

"This is just too cool," Reggie observed. Serendipity was definitely at work. If he hadn't been turned off by the Muzak-lover, he might not have walked into the other real estate office when he did, and somebody else might have met up with Trent and Donnie. Not only his decision to come in today, but even the time he had left LA played a part. It was almost too good to be real.

"Well," Trent asked, "what do you think? Can you manage it?"

Reggie looked at the house, looked back over his shoulder at the ocean and the islands offshore, and then looked up the cliff line to the other house where the girls still seemed to be watching them. "Well, it pretty much chews up my savings and the student loan I got. But yeah, I'll figure it out. You're right. I've got to live here. Where do I sign?"

An hour later, copy of lease in hand and checkbook pretty much wiped out except what he needed for fees, Reggie walked onto campus. UC Santa Barbara was much more compact than UCLA. And it had almost no hills, which also was nothing like UCLA. Isla Vista, the student community right next to it, was flat, too. Reggie decided it would be best to buy a cheap bike to go to campus and back. That should work pretty well, and he wouldn't waste gas or time looking for parking close to campus. In a pinch, he could walk, though their house was about a mile out.

He soon discovered that all of his classes would be in the same building located about in the middle of campus. That was good. It wasn't too far from the library, where he may need to spend some time. He walked over to the student center and liked what he saw. The back was a sloping lawn leading down to a small lagoon separated from the ocean by a hilly strip of beach. It looked peaceful. Though classes hadn't started yet there was a smattering of students sitting here and there on the lawn. Some were eating as it was near lunchtime.

Fees paid, and with no other pressing business, he decided to find the recreation center. After some explanations to staff, he was ushered into an office. A dark haired man probably in his late 20s or early 30s sat behind a desk.

"So," the man began, "you're interested in lacrosse?"

"Well, yeah. I played last year, my senior year, for UCLA. It's only a club sport, not varsity. But I enjoyed it and when I was preparing to come here for grad school someone said UCSB was going to start a lacrosse team. So, are you?" Reggie asked.

The man leaned forward, put his hands on his desk, interlocking his fingers, and looked straight at Reggie.

"Do you want to start a team?" he asked.

"What, me? You mean start the team?" Reggie paused, thinking of the implications. "I'd what, have to organize everything, run the team, all the stuff associated with that?"

"Yeah," the man answered.

"Well, will I get paid, is there any money in it?"

"Maybe. Do you qualify for work-study? I can hire you on work-study, but you would have to qualify and you'd only get a limited number of hours at minimum wage, $1.60 per hour."

"Yeah? Work-study, huh. I don't know if I qualify, I've never applied for financial aid. If I did qualify, and I started the team, how much support could you give? I mean, we'd need uniforms, gloves, sticks, balls, helmets, goals, and a place to practice and play. Can you buy or provide that stuff? Otherwise, never mind."

"Oh, I believe I can squeeze a little out of my budget for equipment. But I need someone committed to do the legwork of setting this team up. How about it?"

Reggie sat, deep in thought. He was here to get his master's degree in political science, not play lacrosse. Certainly not to spend all his time trying to organize a new team. But he needed money. Maybe he'd qualify for work-study, and that would justify his effort.

"Okay, if I qualify for work-study, I'll do it."

After another hour, he was back on the road for home, listening to the Stones' "Between the Buttons" album, one he thought underrated. "Connection" was a great short rocker, and "Something Happened to Me Yesterday" was interesting. He hated, however, their "Satanic Majesty's Request" album. It was the Stones' piss poor attempt to achieve the kind of psychedelic symphony the Beatles had managed quite effectively with "Sgt. Pepper." If the Stones weren't careful, they'd fade into irrelevance, though many people liked "Beggar's Banquet."

He did have some Dylan to follow up the Stones, popping into his eight-track probably "Bringing It All Back Home," or, perhaps "Highway 61 Revisited." Maybe he'd listen to both, trying to make sense out of the lyrics to "Desolation Row" or "Mr. Tambourine Man," which somehow formed vivid images that worked only when Dylan did it. Then, for a change of pace, he might throw in some old Creedence. He loved the earthiness of their sound.

Anyway, he had enough to make it all the way back the two hours it would take to get to his family's home. Maybe if he'd spent less on eight-track cassettes, he'd have more money for school. Of course, most of his stuff was a bit old. He hadn't been able to buy anything new, and there was always something interesting coming out. With regular albums going for $3.50 to $4.00, it was just too expensive to keep up with it all. He hadn't even been in a music store in over a month.

He had found a house and a job, scoped out the campus, and pretty much liked everything he saw. His '50 Ford, a flathead V-8, purred along. He slowed as the freeway turned into a surface street that traversed about four or five blocks through the city of Santa Barbara. There the ubiquitous hippy backpackers stood by the stoplights to hitchhike, holding up signs detailing their desired destinations on the constantly traveled corridor between LA and the Bay Area. He looked somewhat like a hippy, with his hair nearing his shoulders and his headband, but he didn't pick anybody up. Clearing that, he'd hit open freeway, pass by Ventura, drop down into Oxnard, then take the coast highway past Point Magu, through Malibu, past the Palisades, and finally into Santa Monica and home. Soon, he'd return to Isla Vista for good, bringing his meager possessions of a few clothes and not much else. Then he'd settle in and start what he was now confident would be a very good year.

A few days later, the three new roommates, now settled into their new home, were sitting around the table, discussing nothing in particular.

"Go ahead, take a look. The waterbed is huge, man; it takes up almost the whole room. That's why I need two rooms. One room for sleeping and fucking, the other for study and work," Trent explained. Shirtless, he leaned back in his chair, perfectly relaxed.

"But," Reggie asked, nursing a Coke, "how can you afford it, paying double and all?"

"Easy, I'm rich. Well, actually, my parents are rich. Not Rockefeller rich, but I've never wanted for anything. My dad pays my fees and gives me enough for double rent and spending money," Trent explained.

"You said you're from Balboa in Orange County, right?" Donnie asked. "Are your parents conservative? Mine are. I mean, they love me and all and they're supporting my education, but their politics are just extreme. We have lots of arguments about that. How do you handle it?" Donnie finished, doodling with a red pen on a napkin.

"Yeah, they're conservative. It doesn't bother me, though, I'm apolitical. By intention, too. I just want to have a good time; I'm not a crusader."

"But," Donnie continued, "we all have the war staring us in the face. All expense paid vacation to the beautiful tropical paradise of Vietnam. A II-S will only keep you out so long. Man, I don't want to get drafted. That's enough for me to get political."

Trent shrugged. "If I get drafted, I get drafted. It's just the way it is."

"Hey Trent," Reggie asked, "what is that you have on the stereo? It's interesting, very bluesy."

"Oh, it's a new group, Blind Faith. It's a super group, really, Eric Clapton and Ginger Baker are in it and so's Stevie Winwood. This album came out last month, haven't you heard of it?"

They all sat and listened for a few moments. "Can't Find My Way Home" was playing, and Reggie decided he really liked it. The guitar and vocals went together so well.

"I thought Clapton and Baker were in Cream," Reggie injected, feeling guilty about talking over the music.

"Cream broke up, a few months ago I think. And Winwood was the lead singer for the Spencer Davis Group and then Traffic, he's a really good keyboardist and singer," Trent added.

"Yeah, yeah, I thought his voice sounded familiar," Reggie offered. "But did Traffic break up? I didn't know that."

They stopped talking and listened to the remaining cuts on side one. As the last cut on the first side was finishing, Trent reached over and grabbed the album cover that had been out of sight of Donnie and Reggie.

"Hey guys, check this out. Haven't you seen this around? It's the album cover."

"Damn," Reggie said as he took it in.

"Far out!" Donnie added.

On the cover was a young girl, maybe only 10, 11, or at the most 12. She was naked, but visible only from the bellybutton up. Her breasts looked like they were just starting to grow. She held what looked like a shiny, silver, toy airplane. She looked at the camera with this natural expression that seemed to indicate that her lack of attire was completely irrelevant.

"Whoa," Reggie uttered. "They've got to get in trouble for this. It's almost perverted. I can't believe this passed the record company censors."

"Why do you think it's perverted?" Trent asked. "I think it's one of the most artistic album covers I've ever seen."

"Look, she's only 12 at most. And it's a sexy pose. They shouldn't be making sexy poses with a girl so young. I mean, I like it okay, but it makes me feel guilty because I'm wondering what she looks like below the bottom of the cover where we can't see. It's just weird. Like I almost want to fuck her, but I know it's wrong."

"Well," Trent replied, "I wouldn't mind seeing her in the same pose say when she's 14."

"Fourteen will get you 20," Reggie observed.

"I didn't say I wanted to fuck her at 14, just see her in this same pose," Trent explained.

"Actually," Donnie added, "Trent's right. It is artistic. Look at how the background really sets her off and draws you to her. The grass of the hillside is so green, and the sky so blue with the white clouds. The colors are so clean. Then she is there, completely natural, her straw blond hair hanging down to her shoulders, and it's all balanced by the only unnatural thing in the picture, a silver airplane model, also very clean. It's really an excellent composition, artistically speaking."

"Wow, Donnie, that's pretty good," Reggie said. "But I still say they're going to get in trouble for it. I mean, the way that airplane looks, except for the wings, it's really phallic."

"I don't think that's the point," Donnie countered, "I really think she represents the natural and the plane represents, I don't know, maybe technology. Something like that."

"Actually, you know what," Trent offered, "that looks like a hood ornament from an old Oldsmobile. I think it's chrome, not silver, and I think it's supposed to be a rocket ship, not a plane. But I agree with Donnie, it's about balance between the very clean, pure, innocent, and natural girl and the equally clean and pure fabricated object."

"Then again," Donnie offered, "maybe she's really a very young looking 25 year old model with tiny tits."

"In that case," Trent spoke, "I WOULD want to fuck her."

They all broke out laughing, Reggie almost spewing his coke.

"See," Reggie sputtered, "it is a sexual picture."

They all continued laughing as Trent set the controversial cover up on the fireplace mantle so they could look at it as they finished listening to the album. Clapton's guitar was perfect as usual, and Winwood's vocals were high and uplifting. Somebody had once called him a white Ray Charles, but Reggie couldn't hear it.

Trent moved over to the couch that was against the wall and Donnie moved over to the only easy chair in the living room. The album finished, but nobody moved to put on a new one. They stared out through the sliding glass door, watching the swells roll in on a steel gray sea as overcast skies had muted the colors.

"So Reggie," Donny asked, "are your parents conservative?"

"Uh, well no, actually," Reggie explained. "They've always voted Democrat; they supported the Civil Rights Movement; they believe the government should help the poor; they loved FDR and Truman, but weren't too fond of JFK until after he was killed. But, and this is a big "but", my dad hates the anti-war protesters. Can't stand them, especially the flag burners and the ones who denigrate America. That drives him up a wall. He's a vet. Landed at Omaha Beach and survived, obviously, and I'm grateful for that. Fought the Nazis so we could be free, and the anti-war protesters now equate the U.S. to Nazi Germany. He can't accept that at all."

"But what about you," Donnie asked, "you look liberal with your longish hair and nifty headband. You can't think the war is right. You have to know it's imperialism, a vestige of the European colonial era, and completely illegal, since no war was declared by Congress, and immoral. The establishment capitalist war mongers are just making good money off it, the war has improved the economy, and that's why it goes on."

Reggie smiled and stretched. "Well, Donnie, you sure have a good start at getting the rhetoric down pat. With such conservative parents, how did you end up a radical?"

"I'm from Reseda in the Valley, but in high school I hung out with the liberal kids, many of them Jewish. I seemed to fit in better with them. And they had the anti-war information that just seems to make so much sense to me," Donnie explained. "I mean, Ho Chi Minh won against the French and then got cheated when the Americans helped partition Vietnam and elections were never held that would have unified the country under Ho. That's why the Viet Cong took up arms. You can't blame them."

"Well," Reggie began, "not so fast. Ho was an open and avowed communist who defeated the French with the help of many groups in Vietnam which were not communist. After winning control of at least North Vietnam, Ho purged all the non-communists. Some were killed, some jailed, and some fled south. Now consider that there is no free speech in North Vietnam, that only one political party is legal there, and they want to impose their system on the rest of Vietnam. And there are many in the rest of Vietnam, including those who fled from Ho, who don't want that. They've asked for our help. Add to that the problem that there are many third world countries around Vietnam which could also fall to communism, considering the communists use any means to win, including assassination of village leaders opposed to them. It's not that clear of a picture, it's not black and white. It's a mess, really. We should have never let the French come back in after World War II. And by the way, did you hear? I think Ho Chi Minh just died recently."

"That will just make the North Vietnamese more determined. You don't actually support the war, do you?" Donnie asked, a tone of incredulity in his voice.

"Actually I used to, very vociferously. I believed in the domino theory, and I believed in the Munich analogy. Stop them now over there so we don't have to fight them later in Santa Monica. It made sense for a long time. But after Tet, and as the damn thing kept dragging on and on, it kinda stopped making sense. I don't know what I believe now. But I don't want to get drafted."

"Can you keep a II-S through grad school?" Donnie asked.

"Uh, I think so. As I understand the rules, as long as you're making progress toward a degree, you're okay. But I heard they're thinking of changing those rules, only allowing you to finish the semester if you get drafted. I'm waiting for the lottery in December, and then I'll see. I think I can hold them off long enough at least to get my master's, and then if I get drafted I'll try to get into the Air Force Officer Candidate School," Reggie explained.

"Well," Donnie continued, "I think the war is a complete mistake. It's a civil war, and we're interfering. You can't tell the pro-American peasants from the pro-VC peasants, and our troops take the same hills over and over. The South Vietnamese government is a joke; it's not democracy. It's just a bunch of corrupt upper class trying to hold on to their wealth or rip off even more people for more wealth. And who knows how many innocent civilians we've killed with indiscriminate bombing and burning of villages."

"Like I said," Reggie answered, "it's a mess."

They went silent. After a few moments, Trent got up to put another album on the stereo. Sensing a need for a change of pace, he chose Joni Mitchell's "Clouds" album. Reggie always found Mitchell's voice interesting. It wasn't as pure as Joan Baez' or as clear as Judy Collins', but she seemed to do more with it. He wondered if those three singers would be considered "beautiful music?" As he listened and watched the gray ocean through their door, the morning wore on, the cloudiness obscuring the point at which it morphed into afternoon.

Farther to the south and later that same afternoon, in the high desert town of Lancaster, Charlie, a Los Angeles County Deputy Sheriff, turned off the short gravel road that ran past his house and pulled into his driveway. His modest home sat nicely on the desert a few miles outside Lancaster in a small neighborhood of four or five other houses spread out along the gravel road. There was plenty of space here, the brown desert stretching out in all directions with the iconic Joshua trees, limbs raised in supplication to someone or something, dotting almost evenly across the landscape. Charlie got out of his car in uniform, secure that all his neighbors knew he was a cop already, and entered the house.

"Susie, I'm home," he announced, taking off his gun and putting it up high in the hall closet where he always kept it.

His wife came out of the kitchen, smiling that smile she always had when he came home from a shift safe and sound. She had a cooking spoon in one hand, but threw her arms around his neck and gave him a kiss and hug. He loved the feel of her and silently thanked God that they had found each other all those years ago, and that she was still with him.

"Dinner is in about a half hour. Sit down and relax a bit," she said, her eyes looking him over longingly. He loved her eyes, too. Maybe they'd do something tonight. She returned to the kitchen and he went into the bedroom to change. Returning to the living room, he looked through his albums next to the stereo system. Sinatra. Had to be Sinatra. The best of the best. He only had five Sinatra albums, but he picked one of his favorites, and soon the voice that mixed smooth with power was filling the room. He sat down in his easy chair and looked out the picture window to the desert and the mountains beyond.

"Hi Dad," came a voice from the hall.

"Hey, Tommy, what's up? How was school today?"

"Pretty bad," the nine year old said, flopping on the couch. "And do you have to listen to that stuff, it's so boring."

"Hey, don't knock Sinatra. And why was school so bad?"

"Oh, you know, I don't like it when the kids talk about cops. And Dustin was teasing me today like he always does. Keeps 'oinking' when I walk by."

Charlie tensed. The pig reference annoyed him to no end.

"What did you do?"

"Nothing, like you told me. Just ignored him. Dad, why did you become a cop? Seems like nobody likes cops, except other cops."

Charlie sighed. It was the dilemma of his profession.

"The truth is, and I want you to understand this, I became a cop because I want to help people. That's how I see it. Hey, over 90% of the people obey the laws voluntarily. They want to be good citizens. But society needs police to take care of those few percent who don't want to follow the rules. You have to have police. I enjoy going to work each day not because I want to give people a hard time, but because I want to help keep us all safe. And that's the truth. Do you understand?

"Yeah I think so," the boy said softly. "But the kids at school don't understand that."

"Somewhere down inside they do. Everybody, except hardened criminals, knows cops are necessary, that the police are a good thing. Everybody knows that, really. Everybody."

A few days later, Reggie was on his bike cruising smoothly along Del Playa heading for the first class of his graduate career. The bike ride from Windward House to the campus was actually refreshing as the sea air, albeit still a bit oily smelling, rushed through his hair. Isla Vista was a pretty unusual community. About 75% of the residents were students, mostly at UCSB but also a number who drove all the way down to Santa Barbara to attend Santa Barbara City College. Most of the students were young. A few older people lived in I.V., but usually at the far end away from campus where there were more single-family houses than apartments. Near Windward House, actually. Some were professors; some had other jobs on campus. Some worked at Devereux, the private school on the other side of I.V. that was primarily for disabled or emotionally disturbed kids.

The loop area of I.V., however, was right next to the campus and contained all the shops, eating places, and other businesses for the half square mile community. It was always full of people. Reggie turned at Taco Bell and followed the road as it became a pathway onto the campus. Reggie loved college campuses. They had a certain feel to them that made him never want to leave. Perhaps it was, again, the youth of the place. Some 90% of the people on a college campus were between 18 and 25. They were thus sheltered from both kids and older adults. And a college campus seemed both informal and important at the same time. There was a sense of adventure, of intellectual stimulation from classes as well as discussions with fellow students, of the outstanding social life possibilities with all the good looking young people wanting to have fun. And, of course, that ultimately meant sex. And Reggie anticipated lots and lots of great sex.

Up ahead loomed the Storke Tower, UCSB's signature piece of architecture. It reassuringly overlooked the entire campus and was visible from almost everywhere, looking like a white, elongated, squared tube rising up from the center of campus. He glanced up to the top, wondering if anybody ever went up there, and thought it might be an interesting place for a fountain. A minute later, he was at the bicycle racks for the building housing the political science department and his graduate education was about to begin.

Reggie filed into the seminar room with about 10 or so other grad students. He immediately noticed a black girl sitting across the circular table from him. She wore a baggy sweater, but it didn't begin to conceal the considerable bulk of her bosom underneath. Her ample breasts bounced and jiggled ever so slightly every time she moved. And, she had the blackest skin he'd seen in a long time on an American. She wore her hair in a big, round afro. Then the professor came in, moved to the head of the table, and, with a big welcoming smile, sat down. He was Dr. Gupta, from India, and his skin, too, was very dark. The class was called *The Nature of Political Inquiry*, a theory class. That's okay. Reggie had been through some theory classes before.

But not like this. The good Dr. Gupta, still smiling, looked around the room at each of them. In his clipped Indian accent, he began.

"First of all, I would like to welcome you to this semester and this class, *The Nature of Political Inquiry*. I know some of you are brand new to UCSB, and it will take some of you time to get adjusted. I understand that and believe me, I sympathize with you."

That was all Reggie understood. From there, Gupta took off on a discourse on understanding political theory that was on some plane that Reggie didn't even know existed. He couldn't believe it. He found Gupta's dialogue almost impossible to follow, and he had no idea how to take notes. Gupta went off on some tangent about Thomas Hobbes. Reggie's mind wandered. His eyes scanned the room trying to find something to keep him awake.

He saw the black girl's arm lying across her notebook paper. The contrast was incredible. Her skin was so black, almost like the deep, shiny blue-black that some Africans possessed, and the paper so white. Her lips were full and puffy, her nose broad but short on her face. He thought he heard Gupta saying something about John Stuart Mill. How could that be? What happened to Locke? Or did they both write at about the same time? And it was only the first hour of the first class.

Moving his eyes across the ebony skinned beauty, Reggie began having sexual fantasies, wondering what it would be like to kiss her, to have her luscious lips moving up and down on him. He felt a stirring in his pants and he shook his head to clear his erotic images, stopped looking at her, and tried to focus back on Gupta. But the professor was so far gone on some tack Reggie was completely lost. He looked again toward the black girl, but she was focused on Gupta, occasionally taking notes.

It was not a good start for him. His two rules for success in college might not be enough. First was the rule of always attending classes. In four years at UCLA, he had never cut a lecture. He'd cut some "quiz" sections with TA's, but never the main class. He always figured why go to college if you weren't going to go to class? His second rule was to always do all the assigned reading. This was much harder to keep. In political science, a lot of the reading was mind numbing. He could read 50 pages and realize he'd been thinking about basketball or girls, and didn't remember a thing of what he'd read. But he believed that following those two rules guaranteed at least a "C" in any class. However, this was grad school, and a B average, 3.0 or better, was required to qualify for the oral exams. And if you couldn't understand the lectures…

He exited the class next to a tall, skinny kid who was just shaking his head. He turned to Reggie.

"Did you get any of that? What was he talking about?"

"Not sure," Reggie answered. "Just when I thought I understood where he was going, he'd change directions. I don't think my notes make any sense at all. What will his tests be like?"

"Don't worry too much," came a voice from behind. Reggie turned to see the buxom black girl just behind them. "Gupta comes on like that, but his tests are reasonable and he really likes students. He won't give anyone less than a B unless they skip too many classes or don't really try at all. I've had him before. He's very understanding."

"Well," Reggie answered, "thanks for that piece of information. That makes me feel a little better. I'm Reggie," he held out his hand. The other student by this time had taken up a conversation with someone else and had moved on, leaving Reggie and the black girl alone in the hall.

"I'm Vicky," she answered, taking his hand lightly. They walked together to the elevator and on outside, talking about Gupta and the UCSB poli sci program. She was tall, only an inch or two shorter than Reggie, and just seemed to exude power together with sexuality. Or maybe they were one in the same. Anyway, she had long legs to complete the package and give him even more to think about. They exchanged basic information about where they lived along with a few other details. But once outside, she waved at a couple of male black students.

"I've got to go," she said. "I'll see you next class."

"Bye," he said, and went to his bike. He got on, wheeled it around, and saw one of the black students looking at him as she talked to the other. He began pedaling to head home, and the black kid's eyes followed him a bit too much for his comfort.

Back in I.V., he decided to stop by the music store to see what new stuff he'd missed. He walked in and some unfamiliar Creedence was playing.

"What's this?" he asked the clerk.

"It's the latest Creedence Clearwater Revival album. Called, umm," he picked up the album cover, 'Green River'."

Reggie listened to the new Creedence as he poked around in the different bins. They still had their unique sound, and were still doing creative things with it. They hadn't fallen into a rut. Their music still sounded fresh and worth listening to. He looked around. So much he wanted to buy. The Blind Faith album was there, little girl and all. Dylan's "Nashville Skyline" was an interesting departure. It was a country sounding set of love songs. Nothing greatly political and no rambling, wigged out images. A tight album.

The Who's "Tommy" was there. Reggie liked the Who. They didn't try to copy either the Beatles or the Stones, and did their own really creative work. He wasn't sure he could get behind "Tommy," though. The concept of a deaf, dumb, and blind pinball player was strange. Still, "Pinball Wizard" was a good song. And he loved Keith Moon's maniacal drumming.

The Crosby, Stills and Nash album was there. He hadn't warmed up to them, probably because he really didn't care for "Marakesh Express." But "Suite Judy Blue Eyes" had caught his interest, and he knew he'd eventually have to pay more attention to this album. Besides, he had really liked both the Byrds and Buffalo Springfield, from which Crosby and Stills had, respectively, come. He was quite wary, however, of Led Zeppelin. He had the thought they were just a hard rock, heavy metal band with loud substituting for good music. Suddenly, he noticed the Creedence had ended and the clerk had put another album on. Reggie turned and went up to the counter.

"What's this?" he demanded.

"You like it? Listen carefully, see if you notice something."

"Yeah, the sound is very distinctive. It's rockin' blues but also kind of delicate. What am I supposed to notice?"

"Just listen," the clerk said.

Reggie listened. He heard harmonica, a flute, an acoustic guitar, and some interesting vocals. Then he realized it. There was a bass guitar, but no drums.

"There're no drums," he announced. "Who is this? How does he get so much power without drums?"

"Pretty good, huh? It's John Mayall's latest band. The album is called 'The Turning Point'. Just came out."

John Mayall, who the hell was John Mayall, Reggie thought to himself.

"Wanna buy it?" the clerk asked.

"Yes, I do, but I can't. Unless I want to give up lunch for next week. Man, there's just so much I want to buy. I need to be rich."

The clerk shrugged his shoulders. Reggie left the music store. Maybe going there was not such a good idea. He could never buy every album he wanted.

He walked into the door at Windward House and saw Trent with a girl in the living room.

"Hey Reg," he called, "come on over here, I've got something to show you."

Reggie walked on into the room and sat at the table, dropping his notebook with some emphasis.

"What's wrong?" Trent asked.

"Oh, just a professor who's too smart and therefore unfathomable and music that's too good, but too expensive. Who's your friend?"

"Sorry, this is Shirley," he said.

"Sheila," she corrected, a bit of a hurt look on her face.

"I'm sorry; damn, that was bad," Trent said, his eyes focused only on her. He put an arm around her. "Can you forgive me? That was pretty cold. Of course I know you're Sheila."

Reggie watched the little drama unfold. The girl was pretty. Had long, tanned legs, long blond hair, and a decent set of boobs. He was amazed at how quickly she forgave Trent and melted right back into him. If Reggie had done something like that, the girl would be out the door. He watched Trent kiss her, and everything was okay again.

"What were you going to show me?" Reggie asked, looking out past them to the ocean. It was a bit breezy and white caps were visible.

"First," Trent explained, "we need to smoke this. You okay with that?" he held up a joint.

"Yeah, sure," Reggie answered, "is it any good?"

"Sir," Trent put his hand on his heart, "you cut me to the quick. Do you think that I would ever be involved with anything that wasn't the highest quality?"

"So the great dope drought of 1969 is over? I haven't been able to score since last June," Reggie said.

"Oh, yeah, it's over. The dope is flowing freely again. Well, not freely. The dealers, I'm sure, created the drought to drive up prices. It's now $15 to $20 per lid. A rip off, but what are you going to do? Call the cops?" Trent explained with a carefree shrug and a smile.

"You know what's weird?" Reggie asked. "Nixon has just launched this thing called 'Operation Intercept,' an attempt to shut down marijuana shipments from Mexico. I find it strange that the dope starts flowing freely again at just the time they launch their big intercept effort. I bet, in the future, they'll take credit for the marijuana drought of '69, even though that happened in the summer before Operation Intercept. Bet they do. People will forget the dates. I bet this operation will have absolutely no affect on availability. But hey, light it up. Let's toke. I really need some right now."

Soon the joint had been lit and passed around among the three of them. By the time it got to roach status, Reggie was really beginning to feel a definitely strong buzz.

"Hey Trent, you ever heard of John Mayall? I just heard part of his new album and it's really great, even though there's no drummer."

"I've heard of John Mayall, but I haven't heard his new album yet.

But wait till you hear this," Trent said. "These guys were at Woodstock. They're really different, and they're really good." He put a record on the stereo and then handed the album cover to Reggie.

The cover was a big lion's head drawing in black and white. Not that spectacular. Then the music started. It was different, with a definite Latin flare. It put Reggie off a bit. He wasn't used to rock mixing with Latin rhythms. But there it was. Then the dope took hold. Looking at the album cover, he realized the lion's head was made up of many small human forms. There were faces and bodies to be found all within the head. And when "Evil Ways" kicked in, with the drums going from one speaker to the next and back to the first, Reggie was sold.

"They're called Santana, the name of their lead guitarist. They really knocked them dead at Woodstock. Do me a favor, will ya? When the first side's over, flip it. Sheila and I are going to my room, we'll hear it on the speakers I set up in there" Trent explained.

Reggie just nodded. The grass was really strong, and he was deeply into the music. It completely captivated him. What great music to fuck by. And sure enough, during the last cut of side one, he heard Sheila squealing. Then screaming. At least with a waterbed there'd be no pounding against the wall, but he did think he heard some heavy sloshing. Sheila kept screaming out about how she was cumming. Then she'd go quiet for a while. But soon, she'd start up again. Normally, Reggie might be interested in listening to their passion noises, though he heard nothing from Trent. Of course not, that would spoil his image. But he grew tired of it and it distracted from the music. He flipped the album over as asked then put on the headphones, making sure the speakers in Trent's room were still live. Then he sat, stoned to the bone, listening to Santana, and wishing he had someone to fuck.

Chapter Two

OCTOBER 1969: The Girls Next Door, the Ebony Attraction, and the Available Alternative.

Music albums making the charts:

The Band
The Beatles—Abbey Road
Johnny Cash
Marvin Gaye—Easy
Grand Funk Railroad—On Time
The Guess Who—Canned Wheat Packed by the Guess Who
The Isley Brothers—The Brothers Isley
Waylon Jennings—Country Folk
Jethro Tull—Stand Up
Janis Joplin—I Got Them Old Kozmic Blues Again Mama
The Temptations—Puzzle People
Stevie Wonder—My Cherie Amour

Reggie couldn't stand it any more.

"Hey Donnie," he asked. "Wanna come with me? I'm going to walk by that house over there and see what's up with those chicks. It's Friday night for Chrissake and no parties that I know of. Gotta do something. How 'bout it?"

His roommate stretched as he lay on the bed. "Naw, I don't think so," Donnie answered. "I'm going over to some friends' apartment. We're thinking of forming an anti-war group or maybe joining one that already exists. Why don't you come with me? We could use your political science knowledge."

Reggie sat on his bed and sighed. "What group would you join, the SDS?"

"Actually, there's a new group here not affiliated with SDS. They used to be, but SDS nationally is going through some kind of split. The main group here is the Radical Union. They're growing fast and even elected some of their leaders to important student government positions last spring for this school year. They also have members or sympathizers on the staff of the student newspaper El Gaucho and the student radio station, KCSB. Then there's also the Black Students Union and the United Mexican American Students, but I obviously won't be joining either of those."

"So the Students for a Democratic Society couldn't keep it together? Democracy is a dangerous thing. Why don't those groups all work together?"

"According to some of my friends, last year they were together as the United Front. But that fell apart," Donnie admitted.

"Shit. And let me guess. The blacks and Chicanos want programs that study blacks and Chicanos and they want more black and Chicano professors and more black and Chicano students."

"Well, yeah," Donnie answered. "Anything wrong with that?"

"I guess not," Reggie replied. "I just don't know what one could do with a degree in Black Studies except work in a college that teaches

Black Studies."

"Well, these groups are the only ones here openly opposed to the Vietnam War. They're taking the lead on that. And there're lots of local issues, too, like that freeway they want to build across the Goleta Slough, the help the university gives to the Isla Vista slum lords, and some other stuff I can't remember right now." Donnie trailed off, looking at the ceiling.

"I'm afraid I agree with Trent. I'm certainly not a crusader. And I don't trust radicals. They can tear down, but they can't build. You keep trying to suck me into the anti-war movement almost like you're an evangelical Christian trying to get a convert," Reggie noted.

"I just believe this is the most important thing happening right now, and we've got to stop it. People are dying. It'll affect you and Trent, too, just wait," Donnie answered.

"Well, you may be right. But right now, I need some recreation of some kind with the opposite sex. And although I probably would do one, I'm not really interested in unshaven hippy chicks on an anti-war kick."

Reggie went out the sliding door, across the deck, and stepped out onto the ground. He walked up to the edge of the cliff, looking across the deep blue water to the islands offshore, and looked down at the thin strip of beach. Then, his eyes followed the line of beach up the coast to the west, past the nearby headland opposite the oil rig.

Directions were confusing. Because of the way the coastline curved, facing the ocean in Isla Vista was actually facing south, not west. He then turned and looked down the cliff line to the east and the other house. The next door house, though, was quite a ways away. The sun was getting low on the horizon and people were gathering for the sunset. This seemed to be a daily ritual. The open area between Windward House and the girls' house would be speckled with people, most walking up close to the cliff, just to watch the sunset. And, usually, they would be rewarded with a great light show of intense colors of red and yellow and pink. Many, he supposed, had enhanced the experience with adequate amounts of cannabis.

He turned and walked down the cliff line toward their house. He didn't have a real plan. In a few minutes, he had drawn even with the house and was walking past in front, several yards from their balcony. On the other side of their house was another empty field, maybe a hundred yards or so, but then came an apartment building that stopped at the cliff edge with no room for anybody to walk by. In a moment, he would simply have to turn around and walk back as there would be nowhere else to go. However, standing out by the cliff was a girl. She had fiery red hair, extremely white skin, red freckles all over, and a substantial pair of tits. She wore a t-shirt and jeans, and smiled at Reggie. Everybody smiled at each other in I.V.

"Hi," she said happily.

"Hi," Reggie answered.

"Do you live in that house over there?"

"Sure do. You live here?" he asked, nodding at the house.

"Yeah, this is my place. Just mine and four roommates'," she chuckled.

"Well there're only three of us over there. One's out on a date, the other's going to visit some friends. I was going buggy on a Friday night," Reggie explained.

"Why don't you come in and have some beer, or wine, or," she switched to a whisper, "some grass?"

"Thank you very much, I believe I'll take you up on that. I'm Reggie."

They turned and walked toward a side door that faced Reggie's house.

"This door goes to the kitchen. Oh, I'm Maureen by the way. Glad to meet you Reggie."

"And I'm very glad to meet you," Reggie answered.

Maureen pushed open the sliding glass door and they went inside. The kitchen was off to the left, a dining table was right in front of them. Sitting around the table were three very pretty girls. One had long blonde hair, a nice bod, and a really neat smile. Another had long dark hair and a cover model face, but also a cigarette in her hand. The last one was a very cute Asian girl with a tightly compact body that had more cubic boob than one would expect. She, too, however was smoking a cigarette.

"Guys," Maureen began, "this is our neighbor, Reggie. His roommates aren't home right now so he was lonely and decided to come visit us."

"Awwww" the three girls said in unison, and then began laughing. Reggie felt a tinge of embarrassment. How he handled this would go a long way to determining what kind of relationship he would have with any of them.

"Oh, that didn't sound right," Maureen said, herself embarrassed a bit.

"No, actually, that's just about right," Reggie said, laughing and feigning nonchalance. "Mind if I sit down?"

"Please," Maureen answered. "Okay, that's Sandy," she pointed to the blonde, "that's Joyce," she pointed to the brunette, "and that's Janice," she pointed to the Asian.

"Isn't there one more?" he asked.

"Oh there's Mary, but she's out with her boyfriend. She's always with her boyfriend."

"Why aren't you with your girlfriend?" Sandy asked.

"Sandy!" Maureen exclaimed.

Reggie laughed again. "Well I guess because I'm over here with you guys. Or was that really a question as to whether or not I have a girlfriend?"

"Well," Joyce asked, "do you?"

"In the past, yes. But not at this time," Reggie answered. It was true enough. His last girlfriend had warned him that if he went to Santa Barbara, they'd be through. And so it was.

He sat around the table with them talking about various things, trying to get to know them a little. Joyce had a boyfriend, as did Sandy. But Maureen and Janice were currently unattached. None of the girls went to UCSB; they all went to Santa Barbara City College, yet they weren't from the Santa Barbara area. They were from Menlo Park and Atherton, a couple of towns near Palo Alto in the Bay Area on the peninsula between San Francisco and San Jose. They came all the way to Isla Vista to get away from their wealthy parents. But not too far away. As Reggie looked at the four girls, he felt he had struck the jackpot. This had to be the foxiest house in Isla Vista. Every one of the girls was absolutely pretty. Taking that walk had been a good move.

After a couple of beers they moved to the living room. It was impressive. You had to go up a couple of stairs from the kitchen area. There was a nice thick carpet and a couple of large, comfortable couches. It was much bigger than Windward House's living room, maybe twice the size. Then, of course, there was a huge sliding glass door that led out to the raised deck.

They sat on the couches and listened to music. Joyce had left to get with her boyfriend, and Sandy's boyfriend, a longhaired kid with a friendly smile named John, had come by. Maureen sat next to Reggie on the couch, Janice on the other side of him. A joint came out and was passed around.

"Okay," Reggie asked, "What's this we're listening to?"

"It's Sweetwater," Maureen answered. "We all saw them in a concert and liked them. So we bought their album when it finally came out. Pretty good, huh? They have lots of instruments, like a flute and a cello. The girl lead singer has a great voice, don't you think?"

Indeed she did. Reggie listened. The singer's voice showed its range and power on a neat version of "Motherless Child." Most of the rest of the songs on the album were not as interesting, though. Still, the instrumentation was good and the singer excellent.

Sweetwater was soon replaced by Crosby, Stills, and Nash. Reggie took the opportunity to listen carefully. The dope helped with that. He decided finally that he liked it, in spite of "Marakesh Express," which he still thought was silly. Next came It's a Beautiful Day. "White Bird" he had heard before. The vocal harmony between the male and female singers gave a unique sound that was perfectly complimented by the violin. He was surprised, though, to find other songs of interest. The haunting "Girl With No Eyes" and the pleasing "Hot Summer's Day" were well worth listening to. He liked their album cover, with the girl in the turn of the century style dress, complete with bonnet, standing on a hill in the breeze.

He was about ready to go, figuring he didn't want to wear out his welcome, when John, Sandy's boyfriend, passed around another joint.

"Wait, Reggie," John said, "you have time for one more album. Enough of that soft stuff. Let's go for Led Zeppelin."

"Okay," was all Reggie could muster. He looked over at Maureen, but she was too stoned to respond. Janice had stretched out on the couch and drifted off to sleep.

Then the first chords of "Good Times, Bad Times" hit. He was hooked. The sound was new and was not just crashing electric guitars. Following that was "Babe I'm Gonna Leave You," a very interesting tune in which Page went from acoustic to electric and back to acoustic. Plant's soaring vocals fit perfectly, creating a sound that was almost eerie, filling the room with a unique reverb effect. He would end up listening to this album many times in the months to come. From that night on, he would always associate Led Zeppelin with his year at Santa Barbara.

Despite all the good music and decent weed, Reggie didn't forget to keep his effort up in his classes. Vicky had taken to sitting next to him regularly in Gupta's class. She had continued to be friendly to him, and he began to think on how he should proceed. Should he ask her out? She continued, however, to meet up with the two black guys after every class, and it must have been obvious to her that Reggie made some effort at not appearing too interested in her by the time they exited the building.

Gupta was still unfathomable, but Vicky still seemed unconcerned. She even took notes. Reggie did, too, but they weren't very comforting. When the class was finished for the day, Reggie ended up walking next to the tall skinny kid again. He had this ridiculous smile on his face.

"What's up?" Reggie asked. The kid kept smiling.

"It didn't work."

"What didn't work?"

"I got stoned before class just to see if that would help. It didn't. But it made trying to follow him more fun."

Reggie laughed as the kid walked away to the elevator.

"What's that about?" Vicky asked, coming up from behind.

Reggie looked around to see who was within earshot.

"He got loaded before class to see if it would help him understand Gupta any better. It didn't," Reggie explained.

"Okay," she said, "that's pretty weird."

"I actually thought about it, but it breaks my third rule about college," Reggie said.

"You have a third rule? You only told me about the two. What's this third rule?"

"Never go to class drunk or stoned."

"Shouldn't that be obvious?"

"Apparently not," he answered. By that time they had reached the elevator. "Hey Vicky, I have to ask you. Who are those two guys you meet up with after every class?"

"Oh, one's just a friend; the other's my little brother. They're both sophomores."

"Kinda young then?" Reggie noted.

"Oh, you mean for me? He's just a friend." She playfully slapped his shoulder and leaned into him, her full breast pressing against his arm. She held it there just long enough for him to realize it was intentional.

Reggie just didn't know how to interpret her. He was strongly attracted, but scared to death of her as well. She was, he knew, part of the UCSB Black Students Union Donnie had talked about. A year earlier, they had taken over the administration building to demand a Black Studies program. He had experienced a constant vibration of hostility whenever he tried to interact with militant blacks at UCLA. He had eventually decided it best to steer clear of them.

Outside, she met up as usual with her brother and the friend and as they walked away he marveled at how round and firm her ass was inside her tight jeans. Reggie biked home, thoughts churning about the possibilities.

A few nights later, Reggie and Donnie stood on the beach near El Embarcadero, the road that connected the top of the loop to Del Playa. They passed a joint back and forth, the off shore breeze blowing the smell out to sea. Not that they needed to worry. The smell of marijuana was not an unusual occurrence in Isla Vista.

They had walked the mile from Windward House, gone out to the beach, gotten stoned, and now were ready for the show.

"C'mon, Donnie," Reggie said. "Let's go watch the people and get some food. I want to try that new crepe restaurant, should be interesting."

"Okay," was all Donnie could manage. The dope was pretty strong.

They walked the short distance from Del Playa to the loop. It was about eight at night, and the place had people walking all over. Reggie loved that. Everybody, literally everybody they passed said "hi." And smiled. There was a group of people standing around listening to some speaker in what was called Perfect Park, which was in actuality a large empty lot.

"Let's see who that is," Donnie managed. "Shit, I'm ripped! Reggie where'd you get that stuff? C'mon, let's go check it out."

"Uh, you sure? I got a bad feeling about them," Reggie hesitated.

But Donnie had continued walking toward the group. Reggie shook his head and followed. Donnie stopped just behind the small crowd and listened. As Reggie came up behind him, his fears were realized. Up on some raised stand, perhaps a literal soapbox, somebody was preaching. Haranguing was more like it. Jesus this and Jesus that. Don't you want to be saved? On and on he went, then stepped down and began to go through the crowd.

Donnie was hypnotized. He stood there listening, mouth open. Reggie grabbed his arm.

"C'mon let's split. I've heard all this shit before, many times."

Donnie snapped out of it for a second, and turned to follow Reggie. Just then the preacher accosted Reggie, apparently having heard Reggie's remark.

"I used to be like you, ya know," he began, blocking Reggie's path. "You know he's coming back. You can be saved, or you can stay lost. This material world will all go away, it really isn't real. The real life is the eternity to come in the presence of the Lord."

Reggie stared hard at the man.

"Really? He's coming back, huh? I want you to open that Bible, is that King James?"

"Yes, actually," the preacher answered.

"Okay, open it up to Matthew 16:28 and Matthew 24:34. Now, let me explain. In both, Jesus is explaining to his disciples what the second coming will be like, or what the signs for it will be like. Then, he says no one knows when this will happen, only the Father. But, in 16, he tells his disciples that some of them will not die before the second coming happens and in 24 he says this generation will not pass away before these things happen. Now, good sir, I submit to you, they've all died, and he hasn't come back, and it's been 2000 years, and you Christians are still waiting. When are you going to realize you've been scammed? And the sad thing is; you're scamming yourselves."

The preacher was caught trying to turn to the verses Reggie had cited, and was completely put back by Reggie's attack on what was the core belief of his very being. He was young, maybe only a couple of years older than Reggie, and probably not that experienced in dealing with unbelievers who knew the Bible. Reggie pushed past him, dragging Donnie by the arm.

"Shit, Reggie, what'd you do? That was weird; he didn't know how to answer you at all. You really put him down," Donnie observed.

"Yeah, well, I'm not proud of it. I didn't want to mess him up, but he started it. He's not that experienced. I've run into preachers that can go toe to toe with me, have an answer for everything. I just hate the fact that we live in a world where 90% of the population believes things that are just patently absurd."

"Whoa, are you an atheist?"

"What's this? Reproach from the campus radical?" Reggie joked.

"Man, I'm just too ripped," Donnie said. "I can't focus, or stay focused. It's like trying to listen to that new comedy album Firesign Theater when stoned. Hey, far out. We are stoned."

"Firesign Theater? What's that?" Reggie asked.

"Oh," Donnie struggled for words. "Shit, I'm ripped. They're a comedy group. I think there're four of them. They tell long, complicated stories. If you listen to them stoned, you get lost in the middle. Can't remember how you got there, no idea where they're going with it."

"One of the guys wouldn't be named Gupta, would he?" Reggie asked.

"Gupta, no, I don't think so," Donnie answered, missing the connection. "Hey, check out that chick!"

The dope was making Donnie switch concentration from one stimulus to another. They reached the crepe restaurant. There was a lot of variety. You could get sweet kinds, filled with fruit, or others designed more as a meal, filled with chicken or beef or something else. The crepes themselves were pretty good, nice and thin. Reggie helped Donnie choose and they ate what would count as their dinner.

They finished off the crepes, the taste enhanced quite a bit by the grass, and then they walked over to the donut shop. They splurged on jelly filled, and sat and devoured the sugary goo. Devoured the delicious dough balls with gusto. The shop's stereo was playing Dylan's "Nashville Skyline" album, keeping a mellow theme for the night intact. There were four other people in the shop sitting at another table and nursing their coffee. Three of them were smoking cigarettes and the smoke hung in the air of the donut shop like LA smog. That bothered Reggie a lot, since he didn't smoke tobacco. He encouraged Donnie to finish so they could leave and get out into fresher air.

They walked out of the shop and into the street. There were still lots of people out. The preacher's group had split up and his supporters were going around, trying to "witness" to the students. Reggie and Donnie headed for the music store. Some Janice Joplin album was playing. Reggie hadn't listened to her enough to make up his mind about her. She screamed too much, but when she wanted to, she could really put feeling into a song. He really liked her song about taking a piece of her heart. He didn't recognize any of the songs belting out of the music store. Must be a new album.

Reggie and Donnie walked around some more, said "hi" to more people, breathed the crisp but oily sea air, then went back to Del Playa and headed for home.

"Hey Donnie, congratulations," Reggie said.

"What? Why? What for?" He stumbled.

"You went one whole hour without talking about Vietnam."

Donnie stopped in the street and stared ahead. "No shit," he said.

"C'mon. I didn't mean to freak you out or anything. Sorry I brought it up. But I just wanted to make a point that there is life outside of the whole Vietnam War thing," Reggie explained.

"Yeah, I know. That's exactly the point. I loved what we just did. It's why life is so good. To be free and walk around and see people and eat good food. I really don't want to get drafted. We've got to stop the war. Kids are dying, Reggie. They're dying and will never be able to do what we just did."

Reggie sighed. His point had backfired. But, anyway, it had been a cheap show. Reggie would do that many more times, sometimes with Donnie, sometimes alone. Every once in a while he'd get the urge, get stoned, and then walk around the loop. He never grew tired of it.

About a week later, Reggie and Maureen sat on the couch at Windward House, listening to Judy Collins' "Who Knows Where the Time Goes," and Richie Havens' "Mixed Bag." It was older stuff but fit well with I.V. He had been spending lots of time at the girls' house, just relaxing and socializing. He'd heard Sweetwater many more times, and CSN and It's a Beautiful Day. But also Led Zeppelin. Occasionally they put on Neil Young's "Everyone Knows this is Nowhere," and he would enjoy the long cuts of "Down By the River" and "Cowgirl in the Sand." John, Sandy's boyfriend, really liked BB King. He had several albums of his that he kept there and played from time to time. Reggie really liked BB's clean blues, especially his impeccable guitar.

He had taken Maureen out a couple of times when he could afford it. Lack of funding was a definite drawback. But he had not made any moves on her. They seemed to get along well. In fact, he seemed to get along well with all the girls in the house.

He leaned over and kissed her. She returned his kiss, but not enthusiastically. Almost apologetically.

"Okay, where are we?" Reggie asked.

Maureen sighed. She pulled her knees up to her significant chest and wrapped her arms around her legs, bare feet on the couch as she dropped her sandals on the floor. Her red hair cascaded down, some of it across his arm.

"Reggie, I had a boyfriend last year. We broke up over the summer. It messed me up pretty bad because I really, really loved him. I promised to give myself some time. I was really afraid of ending up in something on a rebound that I would really regret. I'm just not ready yet to get involved with anybody."

Reggie listened to her explanation. He liked to accept people at face value, but it was hard to know when to believe and when to be skeptical. He thought about it, and wondered if he had wasted his time focusing on her. Janice had shown lots of interest in him as well. But Maureen was so sweet, had been so nice to him, and was such an absolute knockout.

"Okay," he responded at last. "I'll back off..."

Just then the front door opened and Trent came in.

"Hey Reg," he said, "what's up? Donnie around?"

"No, I haven't seen him since this morning when we he left for class."

Trent sat at the eating table, a sly smile on his face.

"Well," he said, "aren't you going to introduce me?"

"Oh, shit, I'm sorry," Reggie began. He then turned to look at Maureen, but she was looking at Trent. And the look on her face bothered Reggie. "This is," he continued, "Maureen from next door. Maureen, this is my roommate, Trent."

"Hi," she said, smiling that sweet smile of hers.

"Hi," Trent said, exuding some kind of magnetism. "Next door, you mean all the way across that field?"

"Yup, that's us," Maureen answered. "Why don't you come over and visit some time?" Something in her tone made Reggie a bit apprehensive.

"Maybe I'll do just that," he said.

"What do you want with Donnie?" Reggie asked, changing the subject.

"Oh, just some girl called earlier for him, something about some Vietnam moratorium meeting, I just wanted to tell him before I forget," Trent explained.

"Uh, gee Trent, they have these new things now called paper and pens. You could leave him a note," Reggie offered.

"Nah," Trent responded, "that would take effort. Hey," he continued. "I bought that Mayall album, it's right here," he took it out of a bag and held it out to Reggie.

"Far out," Reggie exclaimed.

"And," Trent continued, "I also bought this. These guys are new but have a really neat sound. It's Jethro Tull, the album is called "Stand Up." He handed it to Reggie. The album actually opened up and paper cut outs of the band members stood up, like in a little kid's book.

"Jethro Tull, is that a guy?"

"Hey," Trent smiled confidently, "I actually know this. Jethro Tull is a British historical figure, from the 1600s I think. Anyway he is credited with inventing the way of planting in rows instead of just scattering the seed. The leader of the band is the singer and flute player, Ian Anderson."

"Planting in rows?" Reggie asked. "And this is the guy they chose to name their band after?"

"It just sounds very renaissance: Jethro Tull. You can just see minstrels performing at a town marketplace. Let's put it on, then we'll listen to your Mayall."

The first two cuts were interesting. The band definitely had its own unique sound, and often that was what Reggie looked for. But as soon as he heard first notes of the third cut of the Jethro Tull album, Reggie sat up straight. He listened carefully for a few more bars.

"Wait a minute," he said, "that's Bach!" And so it was. The band's version of something called "Bouree." It was only an instrumental, and infused rock rhythms and Anderson's idiosyncratic flute playing into the delicate Bach counterpoint. He loved it. The rest of the album was great as well. Anderson's flute work was original, and his vocals helped paint the pictures the interesting lyrics were laying out. A definite find. "Nothing is Easy," "For a Thousand Mothers," all the cuts were different, yet tied together with an overall texture Reggie found fascinating. Then they listened to the Mayall album, and Reggie's original estimation of its value was confirmed.

He walked Maureen back to her house, hung around for a while talking with Sandy and Joyce, then came back home.

Unfortunately, life wasn't filled only with fun, music, and those beautiful girls living next door. Back in his comparative politics class, Reggie didn't know how much more he could take. Professor Baer droned on, in his noticeable German accent, talking about the books on his reading list. As usual. The class was supposed to be *Comparative Political Systems*, but it amounted to a three hour per week bibliography. All he did was talk about the books on his extensive reading list, and give them more books to add to it. They never actually discussed comparative politics. It really sucked. To top it off, the guy actually expected all the students to read all the books. Reggie leafed through the list. It was several pages. Must have been more than 50 books on it. He could never keep his rule #2 and that really bothered him.

One of the students raised his hand. "Sir, but how does the Soviet government and party structure differ from Yugoslavia's?"

"Oh, yes, well," Baer began, "you have to understand Tito to understand that, and there is a very good book about that very subject, well, part of it anyway. Let me see, oh yes it's called...." And on he went. Why couldn't they actually discuss the topic?

"Professor Baer?" Reggie raised his hand. "This reading list is the longest I've ever had in any course I've ever taken. And you keep adding to it. Do you really expect us to read all of these books? Because so far I've only managed to finish about four or five."

The professor looked at Reggie, a hurt expression on his face. "Well, I think perhaps you haven't read as much as others in this class."

He'd done it now. Why hadn't he kept his mouth shut? All Baer had to do was give him a "C" and his master's degree was down the drain unless he could pull an "A" somewhere else. He'd lied anyway, as it was only two books he had actually read. At the rate of 50 pages per hour, roughly, it took a lot of time to plow through these poli sci books.

Walking out of the class he was approached by a classmate, the kid who had tried to use grass to help him understand Dr. Gupta.

"Man, why did you tell him that?" he asked. "That's a mistake. He'll look at you suspiciously from now on. And I haven't read any of the books on his list."

The next weekend Trent stood in the middle of the living room, buttoning up his shirt.

"C'mon Reggie, you wimp. Let's go check out some parties. I bet you haven't been laid since you've been here. If the Mets can win the World Series, you can get laid. Forget about those chicks across the field, they won't put out for you," Trent bellowed.

"Oh and I suppose they'd put out for you?" Reggie asked, grabbing his jacket.

"Hey, Reg, you don't want me to go over there. You really don't," he added, giving Reggie a long look.

"Oh, I don't know. It might get interesting with you over there."

"Did Donnie go over to that anti-war chick's apartment?" Trent asked, changing the subject.

"Yeah, left about an hour ago. Think he's doing her?"

"I hope so. She ain't exactly a beauty, but she's got a pussy like they all do. More power to him if he's gettin' some."

More power indeed. Reggie had, in fact, not been laid since coming to I.V. He needed some, too, and the girls in the house next door, as foxy as they were, were not likely to provide him any anytime soon.

They locked up the house and started walking down Del Playa, past the girls' house and on toward campus. Quite a ways down, they heard the party sounds and went into a walled-in courtyard that surrounded a large house on the bluff. Reggie followed Trent, who appeared to be well known. Nobody challenged or questioned their presence. It was pretty crowded, with the ratio of about three guys for every girl. The music playing loudly on the stereo sounded like The

Band, but Reggie wasn't sure. He listened carefully and decided it was, indeed, Levon Helm's voice. But he was unfamiliar with the song.

It didn't take Trent long before he was standing next to and talking with one of the prettier girls there. How did he do it? Reggie just stood around, nursing a beer. He didn't know anybody. They all seemed like underclassmen.

He felt Trent grab him by the shoulder.

"Listen, I've got this girl who's ready to go with me, but she doesn't want to leave her roommate. Can you help me out here?"

"Sure, why not?" Reggie answered. Then, he wished he hadn't. While the girl Trent had picked up was very pretty with nice brown hair, a photogenic face, long legs, and not large but nicely shaped boobs, the roommate was another story. She was a drab, mousy looking girl with a pageboy hairstyle, glasses, and a total lack of confidence. She did seem to have a fairly decent bosom, but was at least a little hefty on the rear end.

The four of them left the party and stood out on Del Playa.

"So, shall we all go back to our place," Trent asked, "or is there somewhere else you'd like to go?"

"Yeah, sure, we can go to your place," the pretty one said, "what about you, Tammy?" she asked her roommate. Tammy? She sure didn't look like a Tammy.

"Actually, I think I just want to go back to our apartment," Tammy answered.

"If that's what you want, I'd be happy to walk you there. Where do you live?" Reggie asked.

"On Cordoba," Tammy responded.

The two couples parted company, Reggie walking with Tammy toward her apartment several blocks away. He tried small talk, but she seemed not too interested, or maybe intimidated, or he didn't know what her problem was. They reached her apartment door and she unlocked it, then turned and looked at him.

"Well, okay," he said, "you're here."

They both stood silently for a moment.

"Um," she began, eyes looking down "do you want to come in for a while?"

For what, he wondered. Was this opportunity? She surely wasn't the stuff of erotic fantasies, not like the neighbor girls, but she was here and this was now.

"Okay," he said. And they both went inside.

What followed was an awkward several minutes. They both sat on the couch, but neither said much. What was she thinking? What did she really want?

He suddenly leaned over and kissed her. She immediately relaxed, and kissed him back. It was nice, actually. At last someone who wanted his amorous attentions. They slid closer together on the couch and continued to make out. She parted her lips and he inserted his tongue, then she gave him tongue. He began to get hard as the possibility seemed at hand.

His next move would tell a lot. He slid his hand back and forth a bit along her side, stopping just short of her boob. Then, while they were still kissing, he moved his hand ever so slightly so that his thumb was touching the underside of her breast. After a few seconds with no protest from her, he began moving the thumb back and forth, stroking her there. With still no protest from her, he made the strong move, and cupped his whole hand around her breast. It was a little bigger than he thought. He squeezed it gently, and felt the nipple harden against his palm. He then began to play with the nipple, moving his thumb back and forth across it.

He stopped kissing her for a moment and looked in her eyes. They had been closed, but she opened them and looked up at him. His hand was still playing with her tit and she made no move to stop it. He kissed her again, then stopped what he was doing and reached his hand under the back of her t-shirt to unhook her bra. He accomplished this quickly, then took both his hands and reached into her two sleeves to grab the bra straps. He then pulled them out through the armholes and moved her hands so he could pull the straps off her arms. Then he reached under the back of her shirt again, grabbed the now unhooked back strap of the bra, and pulled the whole thing out. As he did this she sat up and looked at the bra in his hands, dumbfounded. She now was braless under her shirt.

"Wow," she exclaimed, a look of complete surprise on her face. "Nobody's done that to me before. I didn't even know it could be done."

"Well," he explained, "that's probably because you're not that interested in removing girls' bras."

He then kissed her again, and while doing so put his hand under her shirt to feel her naked breasts and erect nipples. She actually had a very full pair. Her skin was so soft and her breasts so full and surprisingly firm. He rubbed and squeezed them ever so gently as they continued to make out on the couch.

She began breathing hard. Then, she sat up and pulled off her shirt over her head. She threw the shirt on the floor next to the bra and began unbuttoning his shirt. That done, she pushed it off him, and then leaned in to hug him, her breasts pressing against his naked and hairy chest.

"You got a rubber?" she asked.

"Sure do," he answered.

"C'mon," she said. She then stood up, picked the shirts and bra off the floor, grabbed his hand, and led him into the bedroom. He then hugged her from behind, cupping her breasts with his hands while he gently rubbed his straining erection against her ass. He then reached down, undid the snap of her pants, pushed the zipper down, then pulled her pants down to her ankles. She stepped out of them, and he pulled her underwear off as well. Although her thighs and ass were full, they were not grossly fat. In fact, he kind of liked them. She turned to face him, totally naked. He unbuttoned his own pants as she watched, then pushed down his jeans and underwear at the same time. His erection popped up like a jack in the box. She stared at it. He pulled her to him, pressing against her, leaking on her skin. They kissed again. Reaching down, she pulled back the covers of her bed, and got in. He climbed in after her.

"Listen," he said, as his fingers played with her labia and clit, "don't hold back. I want you to let it go whenever you're ready. I'm the one who's got to wait."

She said nothing, but continued her hard breathing. He fingered her as he kissed and licked her breasts. He took his time, and her juices began to flow.

"Please," she pleaded, "put it in now. I want it now."

He deftly fit the rubber on, climbed up on her, and then moved his manhood back and forth along her slit. She moaned.

"Now, now, dammit, put it in!"

He obliged her, thrusting in to that wonderful place from which all ecstasy flows. It was tight and hot. She came almost immediately, digging her fingernails into his back and squealing like a scared rabbit. His duty done, he focused on his own orgasm, which arrived only a few seconds after hers. It wasn't that great, but it was okay. He at least felt a great sense of relief. He'd finally gotten laid in I.V.

Back in the high desert earlier that same evening, Charlie sat on his favorite chair in the living room of his Lancaster home reflecting on the realities of a very different world. Beer in hand, he stared angrily at the television. He had hoped to see some sports, or maybe a good movie. But he got caught up in watching the news.

"Look at those assholes!" he exclaimed. "Protesting the Vietnam War. Look at 'em. Long haired, America hating…" he trailed off. Words escaped him.

"Charlie," his wife called, "Joe's here."

Joe, Charlie's partner, walked into the living room and sat on the couch.

"What's up, Charlie?" he asked.

"Look at this shit. It's some goddamn moratorium protest against the war in Vietnam. Why do so many Americans hate America? There're thousands of them in cities all across the country."

"Because," Joe offered, "they don't understand that we're trying to protect the very freedom they have to protest."

"Look," Charlie continued, "I can understand someone disagreeing with the government. We're a democracy and we're free to do just that. And I can understand someone believing the Vietnam War was a mistake though I don't agree. But we're in it over there now, and we should pull together and support the troops. Like we did in World War II. Hell, we used to be the good guys, remember? WE put an end to the Nazis. WE stopped the Japanese militarists." He smacked his open hand against his chest, punctuating his comments.

The images on the small screen continued and the announcer attempted to describe the action.

"Look there," Charlie pointed at the screen. "See that, that's the North Vietnamese flag. Some of those people are actually carrying North Vietnamese flags. Do they want them to win? Do they want us to lose? Do they really want communism to take over there, and if they want it to take over there, do they want it here as well?"

"They surely wouldn't be able to demonstrate against government policy if they were in North Vietnam," Joe observed.

"If the damn politicians would let us fight the war properly. But no, we can bomb here, but we can't bomb there. Watch out or the Chinese will come in. Careful or the Russians will come in. How do they expect us to win a war when they won't let the military use the tactics and strategy that would actually win it?"

"I don't know, Charlie," Joe answered, "I just don't know."

On the beautiful bluffs where the Windward House perched, a much different life was taking shape. There, Reggie was musing, while sitting looking out at the ocean, about food, a common enough topic for a young man. Cooking was a problem for Reggie. Breakfast was okay, he'd just have a bowl of cereal, or maybe some toast. He could even fry himself an egg on occasion. He'd usually eat lunch on campus at the student center. They had some reasonable stuff there and he liked the feel of the place. Dinners were the real problem. Since the three of them each were on their own for cooking, he usually ended up with a toasted tuna and cheese sandwich.

Donnie, on the other hand, was a real cook. When he felt like it, he could make a knock out meal with salad, entrée, starch, vegetables, and desert. He'd often go to the supermarket, looking for the freshest produce and best cuts of meat. Eventually, Trent, who could cook but was usually too lazy, and Reggie would just give a few bucks to Donnie for ingredients and he would throw together a great meal for the three of them. Soon, it became a Sunday evening regular event. No matter what else was going on, Donnie would always fix a big dinner on Sunday night. He enjoyed doing it, actually. Most good cooks do.

Sex and food were important, but Reggie was here to go to school. And, finally, he found himself in a class he actually liked. It was taught by a visiting professor, a Dr. Chadderton from the United Kingdom, where he was a leading Conservative politician. He was noble class all the way, and his wardrobe was stylish and impeccable. Even when he tried to look casual, it was always very dapper. The class was a seminar in public law, and his specialty was morality and the law. The class was thus filled with good discussions of such things as pornography, prostitution, gambling, drugs, homosexuality, and abortion. There were only five students in the class. In this one, Reggie held his own, except when having to confront Mr. Pompous Asshole. Well, that was Reggie's name for him. He was probably a Ph.D.

candidate. He was a TA, and had his own office right down the hall from the class. And he was a jerk. Thing was, he and Reggie agreed on most issues. All the stuff should be legal. Professor Chadderton, a longtime Conservative in Britain, didn't quite see it that way. However, he was so reserved it was hard to tell when he was getting upset.

There were only five in the class and each took a topic to do a paper. Pompous Asshole took pornography, Reggie took illegal drugs. He felt confident that he might be able to squeeze an "A" out of this class, which would be really helpful if Baer dumped on him and gave him a "C."

Leaving campus on his bike, he decided to stop at the donut shop in I.V. He had a weakness for donuts. The texture and the sugar had him hooked. He walked in, purchased two glazed donuts, and sat at one of the tables. The shop had music on, and they were playing Donovan's "Greatest Hits." Reggie liked the album because Donovan had done brand new and quite different arrangements of both "Colors" and "Catch the Wind." And "Season of the Witch" was just a classic. The rest were light and airy hits that were actually quite enjoyable over all.

There were three kids in the shop sitting at another table. To Reggie, they looked more like street people than students. There were two guys and one really burned out looking chick. They kept looking at Reggie and talking in low tones. Finally, one of the guys stood up and walked over to Reggie. He was skinny, had rather long, scraggly hair, wore a tie die t-shirt and bell bottom jeans that should have been thrown away a year ago. On his belt, he carried a sheathed knife.

"Excuse me," he began, "you see our friend just got busted and we need money for his bail. I was wondering if you have any spare change."

Reggie set down his half eaten donut and looked up at the kid.

"Spare change? What's that? I don't know what you mean."

"You know, spare change, change you can spare. Change you don't need."

"Spare change?" Reggie sat there with concentration on his face. "Actually, I don't think I've ever had any spare change. Nope, I'm sure of it. Every last piece of change I've ever had, I ended up spending for something. Spare change? What an interesting concept. I'm sorry; I just can't relate to that."

The kid looked at him with an expression of disbelief and a bit of anger.

"Come on, man, you gotta have something you can spare," he tried again.

"Look, I'm a student. Believe me when I tell you this. I need every penny I have. This here," he held up the last bit of his remaining donut, "is lunch." He swallowed the rest of his last donut, wiped his hands and mouth on his napkin, then stood up and walked out of the donut shop.

Back at the girls' house later that evening, John was smiling, as usual, and quite excited. "Here it is," John announced happily. "The new Beatles album, 'Abbey Road'." He unveiled it proudly, took the vinyl carefully out of the cover, and set in on the turntable. Reggie sat next to Maureen and Janice. Sandy and Joyce sat on the floor.

"Wait," Reggie spoke. "I brought these to help us appreciate this a little better." He pulled out a joint. They began smoking as the music started. "Come Together" captivated them. The dope began to take hold, but he wasn't that pleased with the rest of side one. "Octopus' Garden" was catchy but was also Ringo at his most irrelevant. "Maxwell's Silver Hammer" he also thought was rather silly. Then, that one song just went on too long about being so heavy.

But side two was another story entirely. It was like the whole thing was a symphony, strung together purposely. It started with Harrison's "Here Comes the Sun," and eventually moved into a medley of short songs. They harmonized. Ringo had a drum solo. There were three guitar solos that turned out to be McCartney, Harrison, and Lennon in that order all together like it was one riff. And when McCartney hit "She Came in Through the Bathroom Window," Reggie was hooked for good. Side two of "Abbey Road" was the Beatles at their best. And it was only proper to listen to it all the way through.

Chapter Three

NOVEMBER 1969: Just Friends, Stone the Professor, and Stranded on Third Base

Music albums making the charts:

The James Gang—Yer' Album
Jefferson Airplane—Volunteers
The Kinks—Arthur or the Decline and Fall of the British Empire
Led Zeppelin II
The Monkees—The Monkees Present
Laura Nyro—New York Tendaberry
Buck Owens—Tall Dark Stranger
Charlie Pride—Best of Charlie Pride
Steppenwolf—Monster
The Turtles—Turtle Soup
Frank Zappa—Hot Rats

"Hi! This is Reggie from lacrosse. You signed up at the rec office that you might be interested in playing. Well, we just got some equipment in and they've found a place for us to practice and made us a goal, so we're going to start getting together. Our formal practices will start in January but we're going to see what we have by meeting once a week or so until then. We're going to try Thursday afternoons at 3pm at the field over by Devereux. Can you make it?"

A moment later, Reggie set down the phone and sighed.

"How many calls you made?" Donnie asked.

"God, I don't know. About 20, I guess," Reggie answered.

"Who are these guys who signed up?" Trent asked.

"Well," Reggie explained, "some of them are preppies from back east, played lacrosse in high school. The rest are just curious and want to learn a new sport."

"How many do you need for a viable team?" Trent asked.

"Probably a minimum of 16, Better to have around 20 though. Why don't you guys play? You can learn; I did. It's fun."

"I'm not athletic at all," Donnie said. "I almost flunked PE."

"And I don't want anywhere near those sticks," Trent explained. "I did my duty as a high school quarterback. I thought it helped me get girls, but now I think I could have gotten just as many without it. Games were okay, but I hated practice. Don't want that road again. You are dedicated though, I'll admit. 'Hi, I'm Reggie from lacrosse; Hi, I'm Reggie from lacrosse.' I woulda gone nuts saying that over and over."

Reggie shrugged, stood up from the floor where he'd made his calls, and stretched. It had already been a lot of work. Flyers had been made and posted around campus, articles submitted to El Gaucho, the student daily newspaper. He'd even carried a lacrosse stick to class, hoping someone would ask him about it. One did, but he'd already signed up to play.

"Hey Trent," Reggie asked. "I've been meaning to ask you. Who are those guys who hang out in the loop and wear knives on their belts? Are they students?"

"I'm not sure, but I don't think so. I never see them on campus. There seemed to be a group of street types hanging around the loop, especially near the donut shop since it's open all night. I haven't seen many of them this year, though. Why?"

"Oh, nothing. Just one hit me up for spare change the other day. I don't believe in the concept of 'spare' change. I would have made more of an issue about it, but he did have that knife and I felt a little threatened. I don't like that. I like donuts, but I don't know how often I'll be going in there now," Reggie explained.

"Yeah, they're kinda weird, I guess," Trent replied.

"Hey guys," Donnie interjected. "You should come with me to see Angela Davis, she's going to speak here."

"The communist black chick from UCLA?" Trent asked.

"And what's wrong if she's a communist?" Donnie asked.

"Nothing, really," Reggie put in. "There's no law against being a communist. As long as you work peacefully and democratically through the system, you can advocate communism."

"Did you take any classes from her at UCLA?" Donnie asked.

"No. Saw her on campus a couple of times. Looked good," Reggie noted.

"You can say that again. Don't want to listen to her speeches, but I'd sure like to fuck her," Trent observed.

"Can you imagine those black legs wrapped around your neck?" Reggie added.

"I don't believe you guys. She's a hero and well respected leader in the struggle and all you can think about is fucking her. Is sex all you guys focus on?"

Reggie and Trent looked at each other.

"Yeah," Trent said, "that's pretty much it."

"True, true. That's about it," Reggie agreed.

"You guys are hopeless," Donnie said, chuckling to himself in semi-frustration. He then got up, put on his jacket, and walked out the door. Trent and Reggie just laughed.

Reggie looked over his books and notebooks for school. He'd tried a couple more books from Baer's list, but he was still worried about the class. For Gupta, there was no paper due and the reading was manageable. He'd done most of it. The Brit's class actually had the most work. He'd spent quite a bit of time in the library researching drug laws. He had a lot of information, from Anslinger looking for something to do after prohibition of alcohol was lifted and an even earlier report that said marijuana was harmless. But he was having trouble putting it all together.

Then, he would have to type it up, leaving room for footnotes, and making sure the footnotes were in the proper format. Ibid, opcit, locit, and all that nonsense. This meant being sure to leave enough space at the bottom of the page to put in the damn footnotes, which in turn required one to figure out just how much space you would need. That would be his real headache. The content he was sure he could do a good job on. The formatting, however, could be his downfall.

The next morning, Reggie woke up and prepared for class. Donnie had already left. Trent didn't have any classes until the afternoon. It was a bright, sunny morning and Reggie enjoyed the view as he ate his meager breakfast. The ocean was so blue, and the islands offshore as clear as he'd ever seen them with morning shadows revealing hilly contours. As he left Windward House on his bike, he noticed Maureen on the girls' deck looking over at their house. She waved at him and he waved back. Reaching campus, he discovered class had been cancelled for the day as the professor was sick. Unprepared for the free time, Reggie went to the library.

After only a half hour, though, he got bored and decided to bike back home. He parked his bike and tried the door. It was locked, which was unusual because Trent should still be there. On a hunch, he decided to enter as quietly as possible, just in case Trent was fucking somebody. Once inside, he heard Santana on the stereo and noticed the door to Trent's sleeping and fucking room was closed. More clues. He decided to have a bowl of cereal and wait and see who came out of the bedroom. He didn't hear any passion noises, but then maybe this was someone quieter than Sheila.

He sat at the table, facing the little hallway between Trent's two rooms, eating his cereal. Eventually the door opened and out stepped —Maureen, completely naked. She saw Reggie and froze. He looked at her, spoon halfway to his mouth. She was beautiful. Her boobs were unrealistically firm and oh so round and full. Her beautiful red hair hung so seductively down her back, across her arms and around her boobs. She had those red freckles all over her body. These contrasted strongly with the whiteness of her skin. And there, staring him in the face, was a patch of genuinely red pubic hair. She had, of course, been fucking Trent.

"Reggie, I, I," she stopped, still naked and still facing him. Then she quickly turned and disappeared into the bathroom. The spoon was still halfway to Reggie's mouth.

Trent appeared, naked also, and looked at Reggie. His dick was still half hard, and Reggie noted it was rather significant. Why wouldn't it be? Trent shrugged, then turned and followed Maureen into the bathroom.

Reggie dropped the spoon into the bowl, stood up, put the bowl in the sink, grabbed his jacket, and went out the sliding door. He turned right toward Devereux, and walked along the cliff until he came to the horse corral. He then walked down into the so-called "Magic Forest," a stand of evergreens right next to the beach. Inside, the forest was peaceful and the forest floor was blanketed with pine needles. There was a stage in the middle for some kinds of events he guessed the school had from time to time. He walked on out to the beach. Here, sand dunes began and went at least a mile or two on up the coast. Not huge, but dunes nonetheless. He sat on one and stared at the waves and, of course, the oil platform that was just too hard to ignore. The wind was on shore, and it blew grains of sand at him, stinging his face and sometimes getting close to his eyes.

He had promised himself long ago that he would never let jealousy give him as much pain as it once had. He hated jealousy and fought it with all his might. She fucked Trent. She couldn't wait to fuck Trent. All that stuff about needing time was all bullshit. Sweet Maureen. Waited until he had left for class, figured she had three hours at least before he came back. Damn. He was fighting jealousy, but he was losing.

"Reggie," came her voice from behind him. "Can I talk to you please?"

He turned, looked at her, and shrugged. She came up slowly and sat down next to him on the dune. He said nothing and just kept looking out to sea.

"I really, really am sorry. I didn't want to hurt you."

"Then why were you so devious? Why did you lie to me about not wanting to get involved with anyone, and then wait till I left for class to go fuck him? That does kinda hurt. I mean, did you think I'd never know?" He threw a small rock out toward the ocean. It fell just short of the surf.

"I'm sorry," was all she could muster.

"Look, Maureen. I have no hold over you. We have no understanding about anything. We're not going together. You wanted me to back off and I did. If something was going to happen between us, it would've happened by now I suppose."

"You see, Reggie, I really do like you. Honestly. It's just that, well, I think of you more as a friend."

He stared at her in disbelief.

"Maureen, that's the meanest thing you could have said to me. Why not just call me a dork? Go on, call me a dork."

"What do you mean? Why are you mad? I want to be your friend. Can't you have girls that are friends?" She looked at him in total confusion.

"When you say that, you're telling me that I don't measure up, that I'm not sexually attractive, that I'm fine to talk to but never to have sex with. That I'm a dork. That's what a girl is really saying when she tells a guy she wants him to be just a friend."

"But that's not what I mean at all," she protested, a tinge of desperation in her voice.

"Think about it, Maureen. I'm not sexually attractive to you. That's what you're saying. Do you think I want to hear that? Do you think I don't want to be sexually attractive to you? Yes I know, Trent is the animal. Trent gets any girl he wants. And by the way, do you realize what you are to him, do you know?"

She fidgeted nervously on the dune. A tear was visible in the corner of her eye.

"No, what do you mean. What am I to Trent?"

"You're number 45."

"Number 45, what do you mean?"

"Think about it, Maureen. You're number 45. That's all. And when he's done with you, and mind you I actually like Trent, but when he's done with you, he'll move on to number 46."

She sat on the dune, mouth agape.

"That's really mean, Reggie. You've never been mean," she began to sob.

"Well maybe I should be. I mean what you girls don't understand is that it's the guys you classify as friends you should be making love to, not the studs like Trent. The heartless guys get more action, I guess."

Maureen was sobbing quietly. Now Reggie began to feel bad. He knew he'd be just like Trent if he had Trent's overpowering attraction. He put his arm around Maureen.

"Look, I'm sorry. But you hit me pretty hard in the gut. I've got to work it out, that's all. And you know, your hair is really pretty in this morning light. It's all glowing, like it has its own fire. And the way the wind is tossing it around, you are just such a fox."

She looked up at him, tears streaked on her face. "Thank you," she said softly.

"And," he continued, "as long as I'm trying to make lemonade having been given lemons, you know what the neatest thing about this whole experience for me today is?"

"What?" she asked.

"I saw you naked!" he exclaimed proudly.

"Reggie!" she said, giving him a slap on the shoulder.

"Well I did, and you can never take that away from me. I know exactly what you look like. And you are absolutely beautiful, from the top of your head to the bottom of your feet and everything, I mean everything in between. And every time I look at you, you'll be wondering if I'm thinking about what you look like without clothes."

She slapped him again. He stood up. "Come on, let's go back. I need to talk to Trent."

"Are you still mad at me?" she asked.

"More disappointed, I guess. But I'll live. You see, I hate jealousy. I'll do anything to drive it out of my being. I just refuse to let it interfere with my life."

Trent was sitting at the table when Reggie came in through the sliding door. Reggie took off his jacket, draped it over a chair, and sat down across the table from Trent. Trent shook his head.

"Hey, I'm sorry man. I mean, she came over here. And it became very obvious very quickly why. I didn't want to fuck her, but man, just can't turn something like that down. Not much gets in the way between me and pussy, especially some prime pussy like that. And I'm sorry to talk about her that way 'cause I know you like her, but what was I supposed to do?"

Reggie folded his arms across his chest and looked Trent in the eye.

"Never mind about it, Trent. She put me in the friend zone."

"Oh, shit, no. That's really cold. She actually did that?"

"Yup. The good ol' 'I like you but only as a friend,' bullshit. Wasted a lot of energy and time on her. I don't suppose you've ever been put in the friend zone?"

Trent sat, looking out at the sea and thinking.

"No, no I never have. Many of my friends have, and my brother. But no girl has ever said that to me."

"How do you do it? What do you have?" Reggie asked, frustration in his voice.

"Well, as long as I can remember, I've had 'it.' I don't know what 'it' is, and I sure wish I could bottle and sell 'it,' I'd make a fortune. But I have always, always been comfortable and confident when talking to girls. I just instinctively know exactly what to say. I was always big for my age, and I've always had this model/movie star face. Half the time the girls come to me. I fucked my first girl when I was 13. My parents were foolish enough leave to me with a 16-year-old babysitter for my younger brother. She was foxy, too. And it just got better from there."

"Well, I think you ought to know. I told her she was number 45. Sorry, but I was pissed, especially after she classified me as only friend material."

Trent shrugged.

"It's okay. I understand. And it doesn't matter. They all think they're going to be the last one on the list. I'll probably do her two or three more times, then she'll start pushing for some kind of commitment, and I'll bail."

"Must be nice," Reggie noted.

"Don't sell yourself short, Reg. You're actually a pretty good lookin' guy. Not in a homosexual way or anything, but a couple of the girls I've had over here asked me about you. You've been laid a few times I bet. Got laid a couple of weeks ago, didn't you?"

"I'm not anywhere near 45. That girl the other night was only number six. It's been a long, difficult struggle. And I usually end up with the Tammy's, not the Maureen's."

"Better than nothing. And I bet at least a couple were decent looking."

"Actually, Tammy would look a lot better if she carried herself differently and paid more attention to her hair style and clothes. She's actually got a good bod," Reggie said.

"Hey, I'd probably do her," Trent noted.

"But Trent, can you go on like this forever? Do you see yourself still balling random foxes when you're in your 30s or 40s or even your 50s? I mean, I'm not ready to settle down, but someday I hope to get married and raise a family. Is that in your plan?"

"Sure, but not for a good while yet. I figure I'll get married in my mid to late 20s, after I get my Ph.D. I want to be a college professor. Like you, I love college campuses."

Reggie began to laugh.

"Trent, you're too much. Everything planned out. Get laid whenever you want with the foxiest chicks around. And I suppose you're a straight 'A' student, in math no less. I don't get it."

"What can I say? I love numbers. Especially numbers 1 to 45."

They both laughed.

"Really Trent, you're too much. Studly and studious. Do you have a weakness?"

Trent shrugged his shoulders.

"So," Trent asked, "are we okay? Is today gonna be problem for us or can we move on?" His expression was serious, his tone sincere.

"Hey, it hurts, what can I say," Reggie explained. "But I'll get over it. In fact, I'm going right back to their house to hang out like I've been doing. There's other foxy chicks over there, and I like the atmosphere anyway."

At that very moment, far away from the drama at the Windward House, Charlie and Joe raced along the desert highway, lights flashing and siren screaming. Ahead of them was an old Lincoln doing about 70, but weaving back and forth across the road.

"We got to get ahead of him, push him off the shoulder before he gets too close to town. You ready?"

"Go ahead. We're not gonna get help for a few more miles at least," Joe answered tensely.

"Hang on!" Charlie warned.

He crept up to within a few feet of the speeding car. Suddenly, it weaved to the right and Charlie saw his chance. He gunned the motor and got alongside the car then just enough in front to cut it off. As he physically bumped the Lincoln's fender the driver jerked his car to the right, went off the road, and came to a dusty stop in deep soft shoulder. Charlie pulled the cruiser to a stop and both he and Joe jumped out.

The driver of the Lincoln opened his door and stepped out, brandishing a quart of scotch.

"Hey you fucking cops. Fucking pigs, look what, look what…." He staggered, looking for words. "Why did you mess up my car?"

"Sir, put the bottle down," Charlie ordered.

"You want, you want my bottle? I'll give you my bottle." He then proceeded to run shakily at Charlie. He was a big man, 6'4" at least and maybe 280. Charlie began to reach for his service revolver when Joe, with an amazing burst of speed, tackled the drunk from behind, knocking him down. Charlie immediately jumped into the fray, and in a matter of seconds the bottle was removed from his hand and he was cuffed. By this time more sirens could be heard as backup units were closing in. Even though cuffed, the behemoth shrugged off Charlie and Joe and began to run toward his car. Joe was on him in a flash, Charlie soon after and then the other police cars began to arrive. Soon the man was completely subdued, and Charlie and Joe were leaning against their cruiser, trying to catch their breath.

"How bad's our fender?" Joe asked.

"Dented and scratched, but it will live," Charlie answered.

"Whew," Joe exclaimed, and then chuckled. "What a rush!"

Charlie, still breathing heavily, looked sternly at Joe.

"Now listen up, Joe," he began. "Don't get hooked on the rush. That will take you down the absolute wrong path."

"Come on, Charlie, you got to get off on the adrenalin, too."

"We can't, and we better not. The rush you get from this should be because you probably saved some lives today. People are right this minute walking around, going about their business, oblivious to this excitement out here, because you and I stopped that drunk from killing them. Might have even saved his life, too. That's your biggest reward, Joe. That's what keeps me going."

Back at UCSB, Reggie slowly raised his hand.

"But Dr. Gupta," Reggie heard himself say, "just what does the 'it' in 'it's raining' stand for?"

"Now that is a very good point, a good question. Just what is the antecedent of 'it'? You see language determines a lot about the way we think, and for English and many languages to describe a simple thing like the weather…" And he was off. He went on talking about the topic for a good 20 minutes, looking at Reggie most of the time. Reggie couldn't believe his good fortune that an opening had occurred where he could slip that in. It didn't seem related to political inquiry, but after Gupta finished, it sure did.

Reggie congratulated himself. This would surely earn him some brownie points with Gupta. Vicky kicked him under the table, then smiled and shook her head.

In the hall after class, Vicky teased him.

"Way to go, brain child! And just what do you think that will get you?"

"It certainly won't hurt anything."

"Hey, Reggie, are you doin' anything right now? Why don't you come with me, there's some people I want you to meet."

"Oh, gee, I'd really love to, but I made an appointment to see the poli sci department chair and then I've got a lacrosse practice. Can we do it some other time, seriously I want to."

"I believe you," she said assuring him. "Yeah, we can make it some other time."

He left Vicky at the elevator and went down the hall to find the chair's office. He knocked and entered, sitting where indicated by the professor.

"I'm coming to talk to you, Dr. Edwards, because you're the department chair and I'm concerned about Dr. Baer."

Reggie was unsure if this was the right move, but he had to do something before grades came out next month.

"What seems to be the problem?" Edwards, a short, fat, frumpy looking professor, asked seriously.

"Well, to start with, he's not very good. We never discuss anything except the books on his reading list. Every time someone tries to start a discussion, he cuts them off and tells them what book to read that covers the topic. But the real problem is his reading list itself. It's unrealistic."

"In what way?" Edwards asked.

"Look at it," Reggie offered, handing him the five-page list. "It goes on forever. And he doesn't differentiate between required and recommended. And every class he adds at least two or three books to it."

Edwards took a moment to leaf through the list. He remained expressionless. At least Reggie couldn't read him.

"Well, yeah, this is quite a lot. But I don't know what you expect me to do. At least for this quarter. He's well within his purview to create whatever reading list he thinks is appropriate."

"Well," Reggie began, "I guess maybe he's a good researcher. But he can't teach. And you need to know that for whatever process you have to assure teaching takes place. I assume you have such processes. But my main concern is really my own grade. I made the mistake of challenging him on the reading list and admitting to only having read four or five of the books. I'm up to six now, by the way. However, his reaction was rather defensive and I'm afraid he might retaliate against me on my grade."

Edwards shrugged. "I still don't know what you think I can do."

"This is just for the record, in case he does give me a 'C.' I'm sure you'll be talking to him about this in one way or another. Just so you know, several other students in the class have come up to me and told me that they've read even less than I have."

"Okay, your concern is noted," he replied.

"Look, Dr. Edwards. I'm here for my master's degree. I want to earn it legitimately. I want to do all the work I'm supposed to do, and take and pass all the tests I need to. I'm not trying to skate. I'm not asking for a break. I actually want to learn something. But this reading list is too much. And I don't want to lose my master's because I hurt his feelings."

"As I said," Edwards said, "your concern is noted."

Reggie scribbled some notes in his memo book, making sure Edwards knew he was making a record of their meeting, and stood up. "Thank you for your time, Dr. Edwards," Reggie said as he turned and walked out the door.

He rode on his bike as fast as he dared, heading for Windward House. Had that been a good move? He didn't know. He reached home, went to his room, dropped his notebook, and picked up a big duffle bag. In it were lacrosse helmets, gloves, balls and smaller sticks.

He loaded everything into his Ford and headed over to the practice field.

He got there and saw about five people standing around. Two had their own sticks, but there were no balls.

"Okay, all of you come over here," Reggie began. "I'm Reggie, I've talked to most or all of you on the phone. This," he swiped his arm towards the field behind them, "will be our practice field. You see they made us a goal already."

"This place is a real pit," one of them interjected.

"Maybe, but it's our pit. Now our schedule doesn't begin until March, so we have lots of time to get ready. All I want to do until regular practice starts in January is just get together and work on stick work, picking up the ball, passing, playing catch, simple stuff. Any questions?"

"Yeah," asked one with his own stick. "Anybody else sign up?"

"Well, I've got a list of about 20. Maybe we'll pick up some more. I know some of you have experience playing in high school and some of you are brand new to lacrosse. So today, if you've never had a stick in your hand, the guys with experience will help you learn how to catch, throw, and cradle." He began handing out balls and middie sticks to those who didn't have any. "Oh, one more thing, I'm not the coach. I'm only the organizer. I'll be looking for a coach. Many of you probably know a lot more about lacrosse than I do. I only played one year, last year, at UCLA."

They paired off and began playing catch. Reggie walked over and examined the goal. They had done a good job of fabricating one by welding pipes together as per Reggie's instructions. There was a six by six foot goalmouth and then two pipes extending on the ground behind to hold it up. Then they had stretched a fishing net behind the goal mouth. The mesh was small enough so the ball wouldn't go through, but it sure didn't look good. He'd take it, however.

A few more players showed up, and soon there were about 10 of them throwing the ball around. After about an hour, Reggie called them together and began to collect the balls and sticks.

"Okay, not bad, not bad. I see at least a few of you have pretty good stick work. I think in time this will all come together. We'll do this again next week. Any questions?"

"Yeah," said one of the experienced players, "do we have a goalie?"

Reggie sighed.

"Not yet, but I'm working on it. I got a line on somebody who played hockey goalie before."

"Hockey goalie is different from lacrosse," the kid said.

"I know," Reggie answered. "But if you're a goalie, you got that goalie mentality. The proper mechanics can be learned, but the goalie mentality has to be there."

The next morning, Reggie stood on the deck, looking at the ocean. "Hey Trent, check this out. Are those waves ridable?"

Rather large rollers were coming in toward the beach, breaking a couple hundred yards out or so. He'd never seen it like that. Trent quickly appeared at his elbow.

"Hell yes! I heard there was an early winter storm out there, must have generated these. I don't have class till this afternoon. I'm gettin' my board." He turned to go back in the house.

"Won't the water be cold? It's a warm day, but it is November." Reggie noted. Indeed, it was a bright morning with the sun having come up from over the mountains to the east. The ocean had a bright blue sheen.

"Not enough to bother me. If this was February, yeah I'd put on my wet suit. But the fall has been pretty warm and the water should be okay."

Reggie sat on one of the deck chairs and watched the waves. Soon, he noticed two other surfers paddling out. Trent came out onto the deck, maneuvering his board through the sliding glass door.

"Somebody's beat you to it. Already a couple guys out," Reggie noted.

"Yeah, but there's plenty room. Look at those waves. It's rare you can surf off this beach." He hopped off the deck and strode over to the cement steps leading to the beach and disappeared from view. Reggie would have to leave soon, but he wanted to see Trent in action. Shortly, he saw Trent paddling out, almost exactly in front of Windward House.

Reggie watched as Trent positioned himself and paddled furiously to catch a nice one. Soon, he stood up on his board, made a left cut, and was zooming in toward the beach. Reggie thought he heard a whoop of joy from Trent. Effortlessly, he played the wave out as long as he could, then cut out and dropped off his board. Reggie stayed and watched him catch about three more waves, riding them perfectly. Of course. The water by this time was getting crowded as word had evidently spread. There would be many cut classes today. Reggie finally got up to leave, noting that Trent was no longer in his field of vision and had probably come on in. Just another great morning in Southern California.

Later, on campus, with his seminar meetings over for the day, Reggie stayed back, waiting for Dr. Chadderton to finish talking with Pompous Asshole. God but that guy could go on. Finally, when they were alone, Reggie approached his instructor.

"Dr. Chadderton, you know my paper is on drug laws especially related to marijuana, right? Well, I just wondered, and mind you this is a personal question so if you decide not to answer, I'll understand. Anyway, I wonder, have you ever tried marijuana?"

The classy Englishman was tall, maybe Trent's height, and looked down on Reggie with that constant reserved and controlled stare.

"If you must know, no, I've never taken any illegal drugs."

"Well, don't be offended, but I just want to ask you. Would you like to try marijuana, see what all the fuss is about? Many people think it should be legal. In many respects it's quite innocuous. It's not addictive. It's much less powerful in effect than alcohol, actually."

The prim man stood for a moment, looking up at the ceiling, lost in thought.

"Actually," he answered in his strong British accent, "that sounds rather interesting. Yes, I think I might like to try some. This will be discreet, of course."

Reggie was quite surprised. He'd fully expected Chadderton to turn him down especially since he was always so proper about things. For Reggie, the whole drug question was a simple equation. Drugs exist. Their use has some deleterious effects on society. The question becomes then what is the best way to mitigate those deleterious effects. There were two general paths for society to take. One was complete prohibition. Prevent people from taking and abusing the drugs in the first place.

For Reggie, the experience of the country with prohibition of alcohol in the 1920s showed the folly of that approach. It didn't stop people from drinking, but it did make a lot of criminals rich and suck up a lot of police and court and prison resources to try to enforce. Just like the current situation with marijuana and other drugs. The other option was to legalize drugs, especially marijuana, and sell them through tightly regulated and licensed stores, much like alcohol. The money saved from enforcement efforts and the taxes raised on the sale of legal drugs could be put toward treatment centers and other programs to help people stop abusing drugs. The one big difference between alcohol and marijuana, in addition to alcohol being much worse in all respects, was that a majority of Americans wanted to use alcohol. Those who wanted to use marijuana were probably never more than 20% of the entire population.

Reggie preferred marijuana to alcohol because the effects were much easier to control. Besides, it made everything more interesting, more intense. Music, food, and especially sex were immeasurably enhanced by the devil weed. How could that be bad? Why was it okay for his father to have a martini before dinner, but not okay for Reggie to have a joint before dinner? It was, in his final analysis, unfair.

Later that evening, Reggie sat at the table, joints rolled, waiting for Chadderton. Donnie was there with his girlfriend Rebecca, the anti-war chick he had met. She looked plain, but intense. Average face, average bod. Nothing spectacular about her, but if she liked Donnie that was fine with Reggie. He just hoped they could hold their rhetoric in check for the evening. All he needed was for them to start going on about the My Lai massacre again. That's all he'd heard about all week.

A knock came on the door. Reggie answered it and there, to his surprise, was little Janice with the good professor towering over her from behind.

"Hey Reggie, Professor Chad…um…"

"Chadderton," the Brit completed.

"Professor Chadderton showed up at our house by mistake. He said he was looking for you so I told him I would bring him over."

"Oh, well, great," Reggie said, "come on in, you, too, Janice."

Suddenly, he wanted Janice to come in real bad. She was looking incredibly desirable with that tiny, tight body, long dark hair, and delicate Asian features.

They gathered in the living room. Reggie made introductions and had Chadderton sit in the one easy chair. Trent was out on a date and wouldn't be back until late. Donnie and Rebecca sat at the table, Reggie and Janice on the couch.

"This is for you alone," Reggie said, handing his professor a joint. Go ahead, here's some matches, light it. Now the trick is to inhale slowly but deeply and hold it, keep it in your lungs."

Chadderton's first try had him in a coughing fit. But he soon got the hang of it and was smoking it down. The four of them shared a different joint.

"Am I not supposed to pass this around, too?" Chadderton asked.

"No, that's okay. That's just for you like I said. You want to take a lot your first time. It's often hard to tell the effect right away."

Reggie waited until Chadderton finished the joint. Then he put Richie Havens on the stereo and handed earphones to Chadderton. After two songs, Chadderton took off the earphones.

"Don't you have anything else? This man is so morose."

Reggie got up, took off the Havens, and put on the Santana. Chadderton re-adjusted his earphones and began listening to the seductive sounds of the new Latin-Rock genre. As the album went through cut after cut, the expression on his face was intense. He sat with his eyes closed and his fingers against his cheek, elbow resting on the arm of the chair. He listened to the full album, then took the headphones off and stood up.

"Thank you very much. I think I had better go now."

"Well, did you feel the effect of the marijuana?"

"I would certainly say so."

"Well, what do you think?"

Chadderton adjusted his tie, smoothed out his vest, put on his coat, and began walking to the door.

"I never realized rock music was so hedonistic," he said, then opened the door and left.

The four of them waited a bit and then they all started laughing.

"What's hedonistic mean?" Janice asked.

"Pleasure seeking. Mindless, down and dirty, pleasure seeking," Reggie explained. "Sex is usually involved," he continued.

"Like Trent," Janice said, catching Reggie by surprise. "Oh hey, speaking of pleasure, John's bringing the new Led Zeppelin album over to the house tonight. Sandy told me to tell you to come over, check it out. Wanna come? It's only 9 and he's probably gonna show up about 9:30."

"Sounds good to me. Donnie, you and Rebecca want to come?" Reggie asked.

"No," Donnie said. "I never really went over there. Anyway, Rebecca and I are going to stay here for a while."

"And Reggie," Rebecca said, a serious expression on her face. "Please don't come back too soon."

"Uhhh, okay, got it," Reggie answered. "Have fun. Be hedonistic."

Reggie and Janice walked over to the house. They got there just as John was showing up with the prized "Led Zeppelin II." Reggie had two joints remaining from what he had prepared earlier. Janice sat next to Reggie on one couch; Sandy and Joyce sat on the other. Maureen sat on the floor, occasionally looking at Reggie, who acted as best he could like everything was normal. They passed around the joints as well as beers and Janice even had a bourbon and ginger ale.

John started the album. It was a continuation of the sound from their first album, but ratcheted up a notch. "Whole Lotta Love" was a masterpiece. Plant's vocals were eerie as usual, Page used a bow on an electric guitar to great effect, Jones' bass lines were inventive, and Bonham's drumming tied it all together. When the song died down and before the next one started, Reggie spoke.

"'Gonna give you every inch of my love.' Boy that was sure subtle."

They all cracked up. Janice punched Reggie on the leg. She was beginning to act a little drunk.

They listened to the whole album and all decided it was as good, if not better, than the first. Led Zeppelin was here to stay, with a sound no one else could duplicate. That was always the key. Do you have your own sound and do you keep it pure and prevent it from being smoothed out, stripped of all originality, and turned into commercial pap?

Everybody left or went to bed. Only Reggie and Janice remained. She had continued drinking, and now kept leaning into Reggie.

"Tell me something, Janice," he asked, "what's a decent Asian girl like you doing hanging out with rich white girls?'

She giggled drunkenly.

"I thought I told you I was adopted. My parents are as white and as rich as any of them. My roommates, I mean. I'm actually Korean, but I don't know one word of Korean. I was a war orphan and I don't know my birth parents or my original name. I have always been Janice Stewart. Got that?" she finished, drunkenly poking his arm. "Wait right here a minute, I'll be right back. Don't go anywhere," She got up and staggered down the stairs to the hallway that led to the bedrooms.

He sat there alone in their living room. No music was playing, and only one lamp was on. He started thinking that he should go back. He wondered if Donnie and Rebecca had had enough time to do whatever they wanted to do. He sat there for what seemed an extra long time. Maybe Janice had passed out in her room. And just as he was preparing to get up and leave back to Windward House, she reappeared. She was wearing a full length, Asian style robe with slits up the sides that showed most of her legs.

He was admiring her appearance when she turned off the one light, leaving only a light on around the corner in the kitchen to provide illumination in the living room. She then walked over to him, sat right down on his lap, put her arms around him, and gave him a long, passionate kiss. She tasted a bit of bourbon and tobacco, but he didn't mind. It was a great kiss, and he was getting hard. Her sitting on it however was somewhat problematic. They continued to make out. He unbuttoned the top Asian-style buttons of her robe and stuck his hand in, going for her boob. To his surprise, she had no bra, and his hand was soon full of great, firm, Asian tit.

They continued to make out, and he continued to play with her tit. Then he took his hand out and rested it on her thigh. He moved it down to the slit and felt the soft skin of her leg. Moving it back and forth along her outer thigh, he eventually moved it in between her legs. She let him, and soon he was stroking naked inner thigh, moving closer and closer to her bush. They kept making out and she began breathing harder and harder as his hand neared the pleasure zone. The hedonistic zone. And soon it was there. She didn't have any panties on either. He felt her soft, straight pubic hairs and began stroking her outer lips.

Suddenly, she stopped kissing him and whispered in his ear.

"Do you have rubbers?" she asked.

"Uh, yeah, but back at the house. I don't have any with me." He kicked himself for not being prepared. He should have expected something, what with his lack of relationship with Maureen exposed and Janice acting friendlier and friendlier.

"I'm in the middle of my cycle, so I can't do anything. But I'd really appreciate it if you would finish me off with your finger."

"I'd be honored."

He proceeded to finger her. He played with her labia and clit, moving down to her opening to bring up lubricant, which she was producing in copious amounts. When he finally did put his finger into her, it was very tight, and it only was one finger. How would he ever get his member into her? He kept moving back and forth along her female parts, enjoying as much as he could the slippery softness. Eventually he began to feel her tense. She stopped kissing him, but was still sitting on his lap. With her eyes closed, she breathed heavily. He was hard, but his erection still was trapped under her bottom. She had to feel it. He looked at her with her closed eyes and her expression of approaching ecstasy. She was beautiful. No other way to describe her. He continued stroking her. She came, muffling back a groan and shaking all over. She kissed him again, with tongue, while grabbing his arm to hold his hand pressed against her mound. Her hips pounded up and down. After a few more convulsions, she relaxed and released his hand.

"Thank you, thank you," she panted. "Thank you."

He walked home, balls aching. He should have brought a rubber along. Or maybe he should have offered to go down on her so she would feel obligated to return the favor. Never mind. He'd bring rubbers next time and finish what she started.

Early the next afternoon, he went back to the house. Janice, however, was completely cold. She avoided him, staying for long periods of time in her room while he sat in the living room or at the eating table, talking with Joyce or Sandy or even Maureen.

It was Maureen, in fact, who took him out on the deck to talk.

"Did something happen between you and Janice last night?"

"Uh, well, why what do you mean?"

"She does this sometimes. She gets drunk then makes it with some guy she kinda likes, then when she sleeps it off and sobers up, she wishes it hadn't happened."

"Without admitting anything about what may or may not have happened last night, could you ask her to come out here and talk to me, tell me herself what the problem is? She owes me that."

"I'll try," Maureen answered.

After a few minutes, Janice appeared, reluctantly it seemed.

"Janice," Reggie asked, "are you mad at me for something?"

She sighed and leaned against the railing, looking out at the ocean. She had a lit cigarette in her hand.

"I'm not mad at you, I'm mad at myself, it isn't you, it's me," she answered with a sigh.

"Does this mean we're not going to continue where we left off last night?"

She shrugged. "I've just got conflicts. Yes, I'm attracted to you, but I can't explain. You just should forget about me."

"That would be hard to do. But if you want me to back off, I will. It just feels like déjà vu. What's with you girls in this house? Whatever you do, don't give me any bullshit about not wanting to get involved and don't tell me you want me just as a friend."

"Okay," she said.

"Looks like I'm 0 for 2 over here."

"No," she contradicted him. "With me, you at least hit a triple."

Chapter Four

DECEMBER 1969: The Draft, Race Relations 1A, and the Importance of Grades

Music albums making the charts:

The Byrds—The Ballad of Easy Rider
Creedence Clearwater Revival—Willy and the Poor Boys
Neil Diamond—Touching You, Touching Me
Fleetwood Mac—Then Play On
King Crimson—In the Court of the Crimson King
Smokey Robinson and the Miracles—Four in Blue
The Rolling Stones—Let It Bleed

"Donnie, wake up man. Come on, wake up." Reggie shook him on the shoulder.

"What's up?"

"The lottery was yesterday, man. And the results are in the paper today. I just went to the loop and bought a Santa Barbara paper. Isn't your birthday September 14?"

"Yeah, why?"

"Here," Reggie said with a sigh, "check it out." He handed him the paper.

Donnie sat up in his bed and took it from Reggie. He looked at what was at first a confusing table. But he finally found his month then traced his finger until it lined up with 14.

"Shit! Shit, shit, shit, shit, shit! This can't be. I'm fuckin' number one! Number one? It's not fair. I don't want to be drafted. I ain't going; that's all there is to it." He tossed the paper across the room. It fell apart mid-air, with different sections ending up in different parts of the room.

"Well now take it easy," Reggie said, sitting on his own bed and picking up some of the discombobulated paper. "You still have your II-S. You're only a freshman so it can keep you out until at least '73. By then, surely the war will be over. Don't panic yet. Unless you're blowing your grades. Are you blowing your grades?"

"Well…I'm not sure." Donnie said hesitatingly.

"Have you been going to all your classes and doing all your reading?"

"Not really," Donnie said, collapsing back onto his bed. "I've been really busy with the movement and all."

"Shit, Donnie. Take care of business first. What's more important?"

"Stopping the war! Nothing is as important as that," he said loudly, sitting back up and glaring at Reggie.

"Well, you can't stop the war if you're in it," Reggie said, exasperation in his voice. "But hell, I'm not your mother hen. You gotta do what you gotta do."

"I'll get an 'A' in anthro, I'm sure of that." Donnie said, half thinking out loud. "And my English will be a 'C,' I haven't missed many of those. But my philosophy class and my geography class, well, I don't go very often and I might flunk. What's your number, and Trent's?"

"I'm okay, over 300, just what I needed."

"And Trent?" Donnie asked.

"You won't believe it," Reggie said.

"Don't tell me he got number 365?" Donnie asked incredulously.

"Well, no, he didn't get 365. But the numbers actually go up to 366 because of leap year."

"And?"

"Trent was born on June 8. He ended up with 366."

"What? Something stinks!" Donnie shouted. "How can two guys living in the same house get both the lowest and highest draft lottery numbers? That's impossible. Really, what are the odds?"

"I don't know, but Trent could probably figure it out for you. He's good at math, you know."

A few days later, Reggie sat at the table with Baer's final test and a blue book in front of him. He looked over the questions. They were reasonable enough, at least if Baer had bothered to talk about the material at all. But Reggie still had some tricks up his sleeve. He had prepared well and at least two of the questions fit into his plans. Luckily, he only had to choose two. He organized his thoughts and began writing. And as he wrote his essay, at appropriate places, he would cite one of the books on Baer's list. He managed to mention five different books on each question, and he knew he had cited them correctly. That should go a long way to assuring his needed "B."

He left the test drained, but satisfied. He couldn't have done any better given all the circumstances. He was surprised to see Vicky in the hall waiting for him. She wasn't in Baer's class.

"Think you can come with me now?" She asked bluntly.

"Yeah, sure, okay. That was my last final, and I turned in my paper for Chadderton. Hey, I'm done for the quarter!" He reached out, put his arm around her shoulder, and gave her a quick hug.

"Did you hear what happened in Chicago?" She asked, ignoring his attempt at minimal affection.

"Uh, no, what?"

"Two Black Panther Party members were shot dead in their sleep by the Chicago police. Shot dead while sleeping," she said, anger barely concealed.

"Oh, yeah. I heard about that. Did you know them?"

"Personally, no. But I have friends in the Panthers."

"Is that where you're taking me now, because maybe it's a bad time."

"No," she said, "It's precisely the right time. And these aren't Panthers, but they may join now."

"Why, what point are you trying to make to me, Vicky?"

"You'll have to come with me to find out. The eventual reward, if things go right, will be worth it, I think."

They walked together in the early afternoon of an Isla Vista winter. It would get dark soon, about 5:00 or so. There was a chill in the air, but nothing like the blizzards back east. They reached an apartment building and walked up the stairs. Vicky simply opened one of the doors and walked in, Reggie following. Inside were five black guys sitting in the living room. Their eyes all went to him.

"Guys," Vicky said, "this is my friend Reggie. Reggie, this is…" and she proceeded to give all their names which he would never remember. Her brother was Sam, he got that, then there was a Lionel and a Jeffrey and then he lost track. They all had big afros, like Vicky. Nobody asked him to sit, and there were no open chairs anyway.

"So," one of the older ones, maybe Lionel, began, "do you feel uncomfortable here with all us blacks?"

"Uh," Reggie began. "No, not at all," he lied. "I mean, I'm not prejudiced or anything."

"Oh," Sam said. "Thank goodness. He's not prejudiced. Did you hear that? He's not prejudiced. What a relief!"

"Yeah," one of the others said, "I was really worried he might be prejudiced."

"So you're not prejudiced like the Chicago police. Murdering brothers in their sleep?"

"I heard about that," Reggie spoke, trying to find a way to connect, "I'm really sorry. I know how you must feel."

"What?" one asked, standing up and glaring at Reggie. "How can you know how we feel?"

Reggie felt a growing sense of panic. He looked over at Vicky, but she had an expression that told him he was on his own.

"Have you ever been pulled over by the cops because you were white and driving in a black neighborhood? Have you ever driven through a black neighborhood?"

"Well, no, you got me there. I don't usually go to that side of town. Venice is the closest I get to driving in a black neighborhood."

"When you've been pulled over by a cop simply because you

have the wrong color, then come talk to me about how you know how I feel." He folded his arms across his chest and continued staring at Reggie.

"When you wake up in the morning, do you think about being white? And as you go through your day, are you constantly reminded that you're white? Because when I wake up, the first thing I think of is that I'm black. When I walk down the street and I see the fear on people's faces I'm reminded that I'm black. When I see a cop car, I'm reminded that I'm black. When I try to apply for a job, I'm reminded that I'm black. It's with me all the time, all of my life. When that happens to you, when you're constantly reminded that you're white, then come talk to me about knowing how I feel," Lionel said, walking up close to Reggie's face.

"But remember, it's okay because he's not prejudiced," another one said.

"Okay," Reggie began, "I don't know what this is about. Vicky asked me here for some reason. No, it's true I don't have much experience with blacks or black culture, except a lot of the music. But do you just want to fuck with me, make me nervous and freaked out, even beat the shit out of me, or do you want to educate me, and maybe I'll understand something that I didn't before, because there's something here I'm really missing."

The five of them looked at each other, then at Vicky. The tension in the room seemed to ease exponentially.

"All right, all right," said Lionel, "we can help you understand."

"You say you're not prejudiced, but you don't realize that you really are," another said. "Now I bet you liked Martin Luther King's speech and supported the Civil Rights Movement and you probably really dislike overt white racists like the KKK. I'm sure of that. But you ever gone to a black doctor?"

"There aren't very many black doctors," Reggie said.

"No shit," Sam said.

"But as a matter of fact," Reggie continued, "I did have a black doctor once at this clinic I was using."

"And what did you notice when you first saw him?" Lionel asked.

"That he was black, and a doctor."

"What you mean is, he was a doctor in spite of being black. That's what you were really thinking," Lionel pointed out.

Reggie looked at him, considering the implications. "I guess you're right. That is what I thought. I was a little amazed. See, when I grew up, all blacks on TV did was shine shoes, scrub floors, dig ditches, or wait on people."

"Ding, ding, ding! He gets it, I think he gets it," another said.

Lionel nodded his head. "Congratulations. Now you understand how you're actually prejudiced, even though you don't want to be."

"What can I do about it?" Reggie asked. He had prided himself on his attitude toward race. He really didn't want to be prejudiced.

"Just be aware, man, just be aware," Lionel said. "Now, don't make the mistake of thinking everything's okay. You're still white. You better go now because we have some things to decide, and, quite frankly, white people aren't welcome right now."

Outside he and Vicky headed toward Windward House. Reggie was walking his bike. Vicky's apartment would be reached soon.

"Why did you do that to me?" Reggie asked. "Are you trying to convince me of something?"

"Hey, you did okay. I thought you would. I think you found out a little about yourself, and I think you'll be better for it. You just need to know, my experience as a black, a black woman at that, is like nothing you can even imagine."

"And why do I need to know that?"

"Maybe someday you'll understand."

"You know," he began "I'm reminded of something Jefferson once wrote."

"Thomas Jefferson, the slave owner?" Vicky asked.

"And slave fucker, from what I understand. Yes that very one. Must have been a conflicted man."

"Well what did this great white founding father write that you're reminded of?"

Reggie, one hand in his pocket, the other on the bike handlebars, looked ahead and tried to remember. "He said something to the effect that if the slaves were ever freed, they would all have to be sent back to Africa, they could never stay in America. He said the whites would never accept them as equals and would always treat them poorly, and the blacks would always be bitter about the treatment they had received as slaves and would actually continue to receive as free people. I think he said he believed it would lead to race war."

"Score one for the dead white man. That was pretty perceptive considering the history of blacks in America since Jefferson," Vicky noted.

"Do you think," Reggie asked, "that blacks and whites in America will ever be able to treat each other normally, with no one being constantly reminded of their skin color?"

"Maybe we can change things, one person at a time." She leaned over and kissed him on the cheek. "This is my apartment. I'll see you later."

Back near Lancaster, Charlie and Joe pulled their police cruiser up alongside the road, stopping right in front of two hitchhikers. The boy had hair almost as long as the girl, their clothes were dirty, and they had backpacks each decorated with a big peace symbol.

"Okay, Joe, let's see what we got here," Charlie said.

The two officers exited their cruiser and slowly walked up to the couple. It was then that Charlie noticed how young they were.

"Anything wrong, officer?" The boy asked. The girl stood next to him, clutching his arm. A look of fear was obvious on her face.

"May we see some identification, please?" Charlie asked.

The boy slowly reached for his back pocket as he eyed Charlie's hand resting on his service revolver. He pulled out a wallet and fished out a driver's license and handed it to Charlie.

"What about her?" Charlie asked. Joe, meanwhile, was looking more closely at their backpacks lying on the ground.

The girl reached in her pocket and pulled out a piece of paper. It was a birth certificate.

"This isn't a legitimate ID," Charlie explained. "This could be anybody's birth certificate."

"She doesn't drive. She doesn't have any photo ID," the boy explained.

Charlie looked hard at the kid. "Can she speak for herself?"

"I," she said quickly and nervously, "don't drive and don't have a photo ID."

"Hey," Joe called, "tell me, what do these symbols mean?"

The boy looked over at Charlie's partner. "Um, they're just peace symbols," he said.

Joe stood up and walked over to get right in front of the boy. "Peace symbols? Peace symbols? Don't you realize the peace movement is giving hope to the North Vietnamese and causing the war to go on longer than it should? Don't you realize we might have won the war by now except for the anti-war movement? Think of how many more of our boys have died because this thing has been dragged out by the anti-war types."

"Where are you going?" Charlie asked, ignoring Joe's mini-tirade.

"LA, actually Culver City. My parents are there."

Charlie studied the ID. It did, in fact, have a Culver City address.

"And you came from where?" Charlie asked, still keeping his official composure.

"We left Lone Pine this morning," he answered.

"Lone Pine," Joe asked, "what the hell were you two doing in Lone Pine?"

"Visiting friends. I've got friends in Lone Pine."

Charlie looked at the ID and the birth certificate, and then looked at the two. They were so young. He was only 18, and if her birth certificate was legit, so was she.

"Do you have any illegal drugs or weapons on you?"

"No sir, no, no, no. I don't want trouble," the kid answered sincerely.

"Okay," Charlie began, handing back the ID and the birth certificate. "Young lady, you should get a California ID card even if you don't drive. You can get them from the DMV. And you two be careful. There are lots of nasty people who could pick you up and give you a really bad time. And it's already kinda cool right now, but will get pretty uncomfortable at night. You don't want to be out in the open in this high desert at night."

He turned and walked back to the cruiser, Joe following, a slight look of disappointment on his face.

"Why don't we run them in?" He asked quietly as they entered the car.

"Nah, not worth it. They're just young and stupid. No law against that. And we got no probable cause," Charlie answered.

"We could think of something," Joe answered. "I bet they're holding some grass at least."

"Maybe, but never mind. Why ruin their day? It won't stop the anti-war movement."

Later that evening back at the Windward House, Reggie, Trent, Donnie, Rebecca, and Maureen sat on the deck, watching the sunset. It was glorious. There were pastels of red, orange, and yellow streaked with green. It filled almost half the sky. The empty field next to Windward House soon filled with people, all watching nature's show. They wished it would last forever. Soon, however, it began to fade, and eventually was replaced by the gray of dusk. The crowd dispersed, and the five moved inside to the living room.

"So you're not going home for the holidays?" asked Trent, sitting on the couch next to Maureen.

"No," Donnie answered, sitting at the table with Rebecca. "My parents are going on a Christmas cruise in the Caribbean, and my uncle, who lives about a mile away, is going to watch the house. And Rebecca is not going home either since she lives all the way back east in Delaware. She and I can watch the house while you and Reggie go home."

"Well, great," Trent said. "I was worried about leaving my record collection and stereo. And some other stuff I wouldn't want to get ripped off."

"Yeah," Donnie said, "we'll hang around. I want to see Tom Hayden. He's going to speak here."

"Hayden," Reggie said, "isn't he on trial in Chicago?"

"Yeah, but there's a recess for a few days and he's flying in to speak. It's just so cool."

"Why are we getting so many radical speakers? First Davis, now one of the Chicago 8." Reggie asked.

"I told you last spring several radicals got elected to student government positions. They've been bringing these speakers in. I hope they get more. The Chicago 8 trial is just so wrong. Some of those guys never met each other before they got arrested. It wasn't them who disrupted the Democratic Convention, it was the Chicago police." Donnie explained.

"Right," Reggie said, unimpressed.

"But anyway, as I said, I'm staying here for the holidays. And I'm going to celebrate because I got my grades in."

"Well, that sounds good," Reggie said, sitting on the floor next to the fireplace. They had splurged on wood, and now logs were crackling away, flames were dancing, and the room was getting nice and warm. "What'dja get?"

"Like I told you, I got an 'A' in anthro. What's screwed is that they're firing the teacher, won't give him tenure. He's got long hair, a beard, and is against the war."

"That Atkins guy?"

"Yeah. Anyway I got my 'C' in English. But I got two 'D's' in philosophy and geography. Still, I didn't flunk them, and that comes out to a 2.0 overall! Woo-hoo! Far out! Far fucking out!" he threw his arms in the air. "My II-S is safe." He leaned over and gave Rebecca a kiss. "What about your grades, Trent?"

"Don't know, haven't checked. But I'm sure they're all 'A's', they always are."

Maureen gave him a disapproving nudge.

Reggie looked at the two of them sitting on the couch. They had already lasted longer than he expected.

"How about you, Reg?" Donnie asked.

"Got a 'B' from Gupta," he said, using a poker to play with the fire, "but I only got a "B" from Chadderton, that asshole. After we got him good and stoned. My big fear, though, was Baer. He gave me a 'B-.' Now, mind you, minuses and pluses don't count, they don't go on the transcript. A 'B-' is as good as a 'B+.' He only gave me the minus to send me a message. He wanted to give me a 'C,' he really wanted to."

"So why didn't he?" Trent asked.

"Either because I complained to Edwards or because I worked information from some of his assigned books into my final answers. He couldn't accuse me of not reading the material because I used a lot of it on the test. Or maybe because they don't want to flunk anybody out once they've been admitted. I don't know, but I don't care. I've got a 3.0 and that's all I need. And I'll never have to worry about Baer again."

"Hey Reg," Trent called, "you got any stash left?"

"Nope, all out."

"Donnie?"

"Sorry, did the last one last night. And lo, it was good," he said, looking slyly at Rebecca. She gave him a shove softly on the shoulder, feigning anger.

"Well," Trent said, "I guess we'll just have to listen to this sober." He reached down and pulled up an album from under the couch. It was the Stones' 'Let It Bleed'."

"Hey, far out, you got it!" Reggie exclaimed. "You're good for something after all."

"Didn't Brian Jones die?" asked Maureen.

"Yup," Reggie said, "but he had quit the group first, or they forced him out. Pretty sad, really. He was their best musician. Wonder what they'll sound like without him?"

"Actually," Trent said as he put the record on the turntable, "they have replaced him with a good guitar player, Mick Taylor."

"We'll see," Reggie said. "Jones started that band and he was very creative playing lots of different instruments on different songs. I'm dubious. And that name: 'Let It Bleed,' is an obvious swipe at the Beatles' single 'Let It Be.' I think the Stones have been slipping."

"Well, let's check it out." Trent said, and started the record.

From the first notes of the guitar intro to "Gimme Shelter,"

Reggie was ecstatic. "Gimme Shelter" was the kind of earthy rocker that had attracted him to the Stones in the first place back in high school. "Country Tonk" was an interesting remake of the original; the title cut was another good rocker. On the second side, "Midnight Rambler" was powerful though disturbing, "Monkey Man" was just as powerful, and "You Can't Always Get What You Want" was almost symphonic, the perfect way to end the album. He couldn't believe it. Overall, it sounded like a mature version of their earlier work. The Stones had done it. They'd returned to the pinnacle of rock's pantheon. They were, without a doubt, the best rock and roll band ever.

Chapter Five

JANUARY 1970: The Monkey's Reign of Terror, a Disappointing Class, and Anthropology Made Easy

Music albums making the charts:

The Allman Brothers Band
Grateful Dead—Live/Dead
Moody Blues—To Our Children's Children's Children
Roberta Flack—First Take
Pink Floyd—Ummaguma
Merle Haggard and the Strangers—Okie From Muskogee
John Lennon/Plastic Ono Band—Live Peace in Toronto 1969
Traffic—Best of Traffic

"Hold on a minute, Reg, you can't come in yet. Just hold on, give me a minute, I'll explain," Donnie spoke from behind the front door.

Reggie dropped his bag and stood, confused, in front of the entrance. Christmas vacation was over and he had made good time since leaving LA. He was anxious to get inside since he had to take a piss real bad. So it was with some consternation that he was made to wait. What was going on? Were Donnie and Rebecca running around naked in the house? He heard strange sounds from inside, as if Donnie was chasing something around.

Finally, the door opened, and Donnie stood there beckoning Reggie to come inside. In the crook of his arm he held a small monkey. Reggie looked at it, mouth agape.

"Donnie, what the fuck is that?"

"That would be a monkey, Reggie."

Reggie came inside, eyes glued to the primate. The monkey looked back at him, and he couldn't help but feel the look was at least slightly hostile. Reggie shook his head, went to his bedroom to drop his bag, went to the bathroom to get that wonderful relief and then returned to the living room to find out what was going on. Donnie was sitting on the couch with Rebecca. Trent was on the chair. The monkey was on Donnie's shoulder, using his hands to look through Donnie's thick hair. It watched Reggie come in and made a cooing sound.

"All right, Donnie, please start explaining," Reggie asked.

"Well," he began as the monkey continued to look through his hair, occasionally making little squeaks or coos, "Rebecca and I were drunk and stoned and listening to 'Let It Bleed.' The song 'Monkey Man' came on. I said 'gee, wouldn't it be neat to actually have a monkey?' and Rebecca said 'Hey, I know a pet shop in Goleta that has monkeys.' So the next day we went and bought this little rhesus monkey. Her name is Heather."

Reggie just sat there, stunned.

"Are you fucking out of your fucking mind?" he asked, rather loudly. He looked at Trent, but all Trent did was shake his head.

"It's just a little monkey," Rebecca said. "Donnie and I will take care of it."

"Well, with all due respect, Rebecca, you don't live here. And Donnie sometimes is not around very much. I'm not taking care of it. Trent?"

Trent said nothing, but continued to shake his head.

"Look," Donnie said, "she has a cage. We put it in this closet we never use. When we're not around, just leave her in there. Her food is in there in this bag. We just feed her these monkey pellets."

Reggie just sat and, like Trent, kept shaking his head.

"Donnie, didn't you read the part of our lease that said 'no pets'?"

"They'll never know. It's just a monkey. What damage can it do?" Donnie mused.

"How much did you guys pay for her and the cage?"

"Only $75," Donnie answered.

"Shit Donnie. Do you know how many albums I could buy with $75?"

The monkey suddenly left Donnie's shoulder and scrambled very quickly across the floor and up onto the table. Her movements were incredibly quick. She looked at Reggie a moment, then climbed up on his shoulder and started going through his hair. Reggie didn't know what to make of it. Her efforts at finding lice would go unrewarded, of course, but the feel of her looking through his hair was not unpleasant.

The next morning, Reggie was jerked out of sleep by a racket that was completely unfamiliar. As the fog cleared and he groped his way into consciousness, he realized he was listening to monkey screeches accompanied by tremendous banging noises.

"Donnie!" he called. "Donnie!" he said again and looked over only to discover Donnie's bed empty and still made. "Shit," he said as the commotion continued.

He got up and stumbled out into the living room. There a sleepy Trent was standing at an open closet door, looking at the monkey cage.

"Where's Donnie?" he asked, obviously pissed.

"The jerk must have spent the night at Rebecca's. Buys a monkey then leaves us alone with it. Shit!"

The monkey was still upset, screeching and rocking against the cage so that it crashed against the back of the closet.

"What does she want?" Trent asked.

"Probably hungry," Reggie said. He reached into a bag in the closet and pulled out a handful of monkey food. This consisted of inch-long pellets, which he immediately dropped into her food bowl. She grabbed for it and began stuffing the pellets into her mouth. Soon, her cheeks were bulging.

"Check it out, she's trying to eat everything at once," Trent observed.

"I think that's for survival. When they get food, they eat it quickly, or at least put it in their mouths quickly. See there, she's pushing it out of her cheek pouches so she can swallow it."

They closed the closet door and both went back to bed. About ten minutes of silence went by, then she began screeching and rattling her cage again. More minutes went by and the racket didn't let up. Soon, Trent and Reggie were standing in front of the open closet door again.

"She wants to come out," Reggie guessed.

"You want to take her out?" Trent asked.

"Not really," Reggie answered. "Where's that leash? Look, she's got that harness on so we attach the leash to her and put her out on the deck. She'll like climbing around on those beams."

"Okay. You take her out and put her on the deck. I'm going to call Donnie, have him get his ass over here and take care of his monkey."

Later, Reggie left campus on his bike, riding through I.V. He was smiling. All his classes were on Tuesdays and Thursdays. Every week he'd have a four day weekend, and Wednesdays off to boot. It was going to be a good quarter. He was looking forward to *American Constitutional Law*. The professor was well renowned and had written several very successful law books. Then, he had a class in Chinese politics taught by, of all things, a Chinese professor. From Taiwan, no doubt. Finally, he had a class in international organizations. Wasn't looking forward to that one so much, but maybe it would be okay.

He reached Windward House and went inside. He noticed activity on the deck so he walked up to the sliding door to check it out. Donnie and Trent were out there, trying to untangle Heather's leash. The monkey was stuck up on a beam, the leash wrapped around several different beams leaving her unable to move anywhere. She was screeching in anger while straining against her restraint as Donnie stood on a chair and tried to free her. Trent saw Reggie standing at the door.

"I guess leaving her out here is not such a good idea either," Trent said.

"Donnie," Reggie asked, "what is that little thing sticking out on her ass?"

"Um," Donnie said, still working on the leash, "that's just a little piece of shit that doesn't quite fall out."

"Great," Reggie said, then walked across the field over to the girls' house.

"You guys bought a monkey? Really?" Sandy asked after hearing about the simian.

"No, not us guys. Just Donnie and his freaky girlfriend. The thing makes me nervous. I got a real bad feeling about it."

"What's its name? Is it a male or female?"

"Heather, it's a girl rhesus monkey. But really nervous."

Maureen walked in and sat at the table with Sandy and Reggie.

"Hi Maureen," Reggie said.

"Hi," Maureen said, and let out a little sigh, then went silent.

Reggie knew something was wrong. Trent had been back a week and hadn't called her. He knew Maureen wanted to ask him about Trent, but was too proud. Reggie resisted, nobly he thought, the urge to start a conversation about it that would enable him to say "I told you so." So he just looked at her and smiled sympathetically.

"I got to get going. Got a lacrosse practice," Reggie explained.

There was a good crowd at the practice field when Reggie pulled up. They would start full contact practices and try to at least get in shape. He counted 17 bodies, including himself, and was pleased.

Reggie hated the drills of practice. They were designed to push athletes to their extreme and beyond. But they needed it. He made them, he included, do a two on one ground ball drill for half an hour. They did wind sprints across the field. Then they played half-field scrimmage for almost an hour. They finished it up with more wind sprints.

Reggie was totally wiped out. He was not in shape at all. He was sweating and his sweat was dripping into his eyes and stinging. His shirt was soaked. His side ached. He bent over, hands on knees, and tried to catch his breath. Why was he putting himself through this again? Oh yes. To have fun.

"Okay," he began as they gathered around, most just as exhausted as Reggie, "good start. We need to get in shape. Next month, we'll have some practice games against some local prep schools that have teams. Our league schedule starts in March. We'll practice three times a week, on Monday, Wednesday, and Saturday. Those of you who can't make Monday and Wednesday afternoon, at least make Saturday."

"What if we can't make Saturday?" one of the players asked.

"Well, all the games are on Saturday or Sunday. If you can't make a Saturday practice, how can you make a Saturday game? I know everybody has different schedules, but this is what we have. Okay, please give me all your equipment."

"So," asked another, "is Russ here going to be our goalie?"

"Unless someone else challenges him for it. Anybody else want to be goalie? Russ's been in a hockey goal. He knows what it takes to be a goalie."

Indeed, he had made several good saves during the scrimmage, but he didn't know what to do after getting the ball.

"How about a coach?" the same player asked.

"Still looking. I'll try to run practices until we find one. Unless somebody here wants to take responsibility for running practice. Anyone?"

Nobody answered, not even the ex-preppies who had played a lot more lacrosse than Reggie.

"Okay, I'll still do it. My main concern now, besides getting in shape, is learning how to clear. That takes a team effort and a lot of work. This field is not the greatest for that. But if you can't clear, you can't go on offense, and your defense will get worn out as your attacks get bored. And your opponent will score a lot. So we'll start working on that next time."

Reggie got back to the house, put the equipment away, and took a long shower. He had bumps and bruises all over, but it felt good in a way. After showering, he had that peaceful, relaxed feeling one gets after a good workout. Walking into the main room, he saw Trent at the table and Donnie on the couch. Trent was trying to eat an apple, but Heather was on his chest. Every time he took a bite of the apple, the monkey would try to pry his mouth open and reach in to take the pieces of apple out.

"Donnie, get this monkey off me!" Trent ordered.

Donnie got up, walked over to the table, and picked up the monkey. She immediately protested with screeches of indignation.

"No, Heather," Donnie said in a firm voice. But this only made her angrier and her screeches increased in volume and pitch as she struggled to get free of Donnie and continue her quest for the apple in Trent's mouth. Donnie held on to the struggling monkey and managed to put her back in her cage. He then got an apple from the refrigerator and gave it to her. She quieted down and worked on the apple.

"Donnie, that cage stinks. You need to change the papers," Trent noted.

On campus, Reggie tried to concentrate and pay attention to Palmer's very dry seminar. The law class had turned out to be a disappointment. Palmer's approach was rather bland and matter-of-fact. He made no effort to be interesting. This was such a departure from Reggie's constitutional law classes at UCLA. His teacher had been dynamic and made him interested in a subject he thought was going to be boring. Now he loved constitutional law, and Palmer was a recognized expert. But his class was disappointing. He brought no life, no humor, and no controversy into the discussion. It was all cut and dried, even in all its complexity. In a word, Palmer was boring. But maybe that was just because it was the first day. Reggie hung back after the class.

"Dr. Palmer, I'm Reggie Blake. I'm really looking forward to this class."

"Thank you," Palmer said, a slight smile on his face.

"You know, I didn't think I'd like law, but I had a really good prof at UCLA. Maybe you've heard of him, Dr. Dobbs?"

Palmer's smile never changed. He shook his head. "No, I don't know him."

"Well, okay, anyway, I'll see you next class," Reggie said.

He left there a bit befuddled. He thought Dr. Dobbs was well known, too. Why hadn't Palmer heard of him? And would all his classes be that boring?

In the elevator, he ran into Vicky coming from another class.

"Long time, no see," she said disapprovingly.

"Same to you," he replied. "How are your classes this semester?"

"Pretty good, I think. You got a 'B' from Gupta, right?"

"Yeah, and Baer begrudgingly gave me a 'B-'."

"So you're still sitting on a three point?"

"Yup, so far, so good. I just don't think I'll like Palmer's class as much as I thought I would."

"I've never had him so I don't know," she said.

They reached the bottom floor and went outside. Nobody was waiting for her and they continued to walk together.

"Your friends and your brother—did they join the Panthers? Is there a Black Panther organization here at UCSB?"

"Some of them joined. They liked your courage and your attitude, but whites can't do anything for us now. We have to do it ourselves."

"Do you think militancy is the way to go? Martin Luther King wouldn't agree."

"Yeah, and he's dead. Killed by a racist. You want that for the rest of us?"

"Well, Vicky, all I know is he accomplished a lot by not fighting back. He exposed segregation for what it was, and exposed the south for what it was. The Civil Rights Act and the Voting Rights Act were a direct result of his efforts."

"Actually, I think they had more to do with LBJ's landslide '64 election and the huge Democratic Party gains in both houses of Congress at the same time. But even so, things haven't changed much. We have a right to defend ourselves."

"Vicky, do you want me to ask you out? Because I'm really confused. Your attitude towards me, well, I can't put my finger on it. I don't know what to do with you."

"Don't expect me to tell you what to do. You'll have to ask me out and see."

"Well, just understand. I'm pretty broke. Whatever we do, if we go out, it won't cost much. That hinders me a lot."

"Your choice. You didn't have to live in that beach house."

"Maybe. But I'm glad I do."

Meanwhile, in the Antelope Valley, Charlie and Joe were on patrol driving around some of the new Lancaster neighborhoods.

"Look at that car," Joe pointed out. "What do we have here?"

"Hmmm," Charlie agreed. "A car full of Neg…blacks."

Joe smiled. "Kinda the wrong neighborhood for these guys, isn't it?"

"Well, yes. But let's just follow them for a bit. No need to create an incident," Charlie answered. "Okay, the driver just checked his mirror, they see us."

They followed the big Buick for several blocks until it found a freeway onramp. The car quickly ascended it and disappeared.

"Shouldn't we have pulled them over? Maybe they were scouting for houses to break into. They may now just go ruin someone else's day," Joe said, a hint of disappointment in his voice.

"Well now Joe, we got nothing on them. They were doing nothing wrong. Got to be careful these days. Any unnecessary confrontation could lead to another Watts riot."

"Gosh I hope this doesn't mean more of them will move up here. It's kinda nice without them," Joe noted.

"So you're prejudiced against blacks?" Charlie asked.

"I know, I know. It's wrong. I've taken the racial sensitivity classes. But I just don't like being around them. When I was a kid in junior high, my school went from 75% white to 85% black in just a few years. I used to get hassled all the time. They would steal my lunch money and there was nothing I could do. I got to hate them."

"What about black deputies? You get along with them?"

"Well, there're not too many. And like the cliché goes, one on one they're good people, but in a group, they scare the shit out of me. Blacks I mean, not black deputies. Just wish they'd stay down in LA," Joe said.

"Joe I know how you feel. But you need to fight that feeling. It will only get you in trouble," Charlie explained.

"I know, I know. But I can't help how I feel," Joe explained.

Back in Isla Vista, at lacrosse practice, Reggie's mind wasn't focused on race relations or anything with philosophical or political overtones. No, for a graduate student in poli sci, he was in a zone that was primal, physical, and simple. He took a pass during scrimmage, faked out his defender, and broke for the goal. Just before he was to take a shot, however, he ran into a wall. The wall was Dan, the 6'4" ex-medic and Vietnam vet whom Reggie had playing crease defense. Reggie saw stars. He heard a muffled thump that turned out to be his own body hitting the ground. The ball rolled free as he gasped for breath. Ryan got the loose ball and passed it out. Reggie was slow to get up.

"Sorry Reg," he heard Dan say. "Are you okay?"

"No, but don't be sorry," Reggie said, sitting up on the grass. "That's exactly what you're supposed to do." He used his stick to help him get up and they continued the scrimmage. Reggie began to realize that they might not score much, but other teams were going to pay heavily for their goals. If there was one thing the Gauchos could do, it was hit.

Back at the house, he found the monkey's cage in his bedroom.

The monkey was unhappy, making noise and shaking the cage. The cage was slowly working its way across the floor. Reggie ignored it for the moment and took his shower.

"Donnie!" Reggie called, walking out of the bedroom. "Where the fuck are you?"

"He ain't here," Trent answered, sitting on the couch and none too happy.

"So who put the cage in my room?"

"I did!" Trent bellowed. "I was trying to do some math work and the damn thing was screeching and banging the damn cage. Shit, it's right next to my working room. I couldn't concentrate. So I put the cage in your room and shut the door. It helped. I couldn't hear her as much."

"Well," Reggie began, "she sure the hell isn't going to stay in my room."

"Your roommate bought her. Work it out with him."

Just then there was a crash coming from Reggie's bedroom. Reggie and Trent walked in and were hit by the overpowering smell of English Leather. The cage was right next to the dresser, and Heather had knocked an almost full bottle off and onto the floor where it broke. Pieces of glass were everywhere, and the liquid was spreading out over the floor.

"I ain't cleaning that up," Reggie said. "I'll make Donnie do it."

"Hey, it's your room," Trent pointed out.

Disgusted, Reggie went to his hamper and took out a towel destined for the laundry. He put it on the floor over the cologne and then went for a walk. He decided to head out past Devereux to the

Magic Forest and the dunes. He liked the beach at winter time. It was usually empty. He hadn't smoked anything and his head was clear. He needed to think about Vicky.

He walked through the cool forest, the pine needles softening his footfalls and the sea breeze whispering through the branches, and then out to the beach. He looked west down the beach where the dunes stretched out a good mile. The beach was deserted. Behind the dunes was another slough, like the one on the other side of campus, and no development had taken place. This was just a wild, lonely stretch of California beach.

He walked about halfway down then stopped. Looking around, he felt good. He picked out a dune, walked up its sandy slope, and sat down. He felt like a king surveying his realm. God but he wanted to fuck Vicky. But at the same time, he was scared shitless of her. How could he deal with the black militant thing? And where could he take her? Out to eat? McDonald's maybe. To a movie? Then what? McDonald's? His budget was stretched to the breaking point, and he had to break down and borrow money from his parents. His work-study hours would be exhausted before the lacrosse season even started. As long as he didn't waste money on incidental things, even with the money from his parents he had enough to pay his fees, buy his books, pay his rent and utilities, do his laundry, and buy some food. But nothing else. Well, maybe some dope.

After almost an hour, he stood up and began walking back to the house. He reached it, came inside the sliding door, and saw Trent on the couch with a pretty brown skinned girl.

"Donnie back yet?" Reggie asked.

"Nope, and it still stinks in there," Trent said. "By the way, Reggie, this is Juanita. I met her at that Mexican restaurant I like in Santa Barbara. She works there."

"Hi Juanita," Reggie said, "I'm Reggie."

"Hi," was all she said, smiling shyly. Was she used to gringo college kids? Reggie assumed she would soon become number 46.

Just then the front door opened and Donnie came in. He stopped and stood for a moment outside the door of his and Reggie's shared bedroom.

"Jeez," he said, "smells like a French whore's been in here."

"C'mere Donnie," Reggie said. "There's a mess I need you to clean up." He opened the door to the room. Heather had been reasonably quiet but upon seeing Donnie she began screeching and rattling the cage. It seemed stuck, wedged between the dresser and the wall.

"Why is the cage in here?" Donnie asked.

Reggie went through the long explanation and then left Donnie to clean it up as he went back to the living room. He was a bit worried that Juanita would think the "French whore" remark had something to do with her, but Trent and Juanita had already disappeared into Trent's fucking room and the Mayall album was on the stereo. Why not Santana, Reggie thought. Should have been perfect.

A couple of weeks later, everybody was in the living room. Donnie and Rebecca were at the table, Trent on the chair, Reggie on the couch. Trent was eating a peanut butter sandwich. Heather was loose, and soon had climbed up on Trent's lap trying to grab the sandwich. Trent held the sandwich out of the monkey's reach, and

Heather proceeded to again try to open Trent's mouth to extract the food he was chewing.

"Donnie, goddamit, will you do something?" Trent pleaded strongly.

"No, Heather, no!" Donnie said forcefully.

That only made the monkey furious. It began screeching then suddenly grabbed Trent's arm and bit it, sinking her razor sharp incisors into his flesh and shaking her head back and forth to inflict maximum damage.

"Shit!" Trent screamed as he slapped the monkey hard enough to make it fly halfway across the room. "Will you look at this? Look at the blood. Damn it hurts!"

"Damn, Trent," Rebecca said, "don't kill her!"

"What the hell? Look what she did to my arm!"

He got up and went over to them. Donnie had collected the dazed Heather and was cuddling her in his arms. Trent held out his arm revealing a bloody wound a good inch in diameter. He then moved it in front of the animal's nose.

"See, bitch, see what you did!"

The monkey, still subdued by Trent's slap, didn't respond.

Back in class, though, Reggie was frustrated. No doubt about it, Palmer was boring. Reggie felt the biggest letdown as class after class went by and nothing got any better. He was not systematic, did not take them through case by case as the law developed, the way Dobbs had at UCLA. Reggie knew all this stuff anyway, all the cases about the first amendment and other constitutional issues. Schenk vs. US and Abington vs. Schemp and all those cases of Jehova's Witnesses blasting anti-Catholic propaganda in Catholic neighborhoods. He knew the cases, he knew the decisions, he knew the arguments, and he knew the precedents set. What more was he learning now? He couldn't tell.

The bike ride through I.V. was pleasant as usual, though it had rained a little earlier in the day. He passed an apartment out of which blared the "Led Zeppelin II" album with Plant singing about every inch of his love. He'd sure like to give Vicky every inch of his love. But would it measure up? He assumed she would be used to black guys. How could he have enough to satisfy her?

He reached home and went to the kitchen to figure out what to eat. He decided on just bread and butter and sat down at the table. Donnie was on the couch with the monkey. Seeing Reggie, the monkey broke away from Donnie and ran up onto the table right next to Reggie. She proceeded to go for the bread.

"Donnie, will you get this monkey, please?"

Just then Trent appeared. Suddenly he belted out in as loud a voice as he could muster: "No, Heather, no!"

Before Reggie could react, Heather screeched at Trent, then grabbed Reggie's hand and bit down, shaking her head. In less than a second, Reggie's right hand was bleeding profusely.

"Fuck!" Reggie screamed as he threw the monkey off the table. "What the hell did you do that for, Trent?"

Trent, by this time, was cracking up. Reggie didn't appreciate that. He went back to his bathroom and cleaned off the wound. It was on his right hand, no less. The cutting surface of the monkey's incisors was curved, not straight like a human's. It thus left a round wound on the top of his hand.

Two days later Reggie got his revenge. Donnie had the monkey out, and he and Trent were on the couch. Trent was reading a magazine and not paying much attention. The monkey was between the two of them.

"No Heather, no!" Reggie yelled out. "No, no!"

The animal cooed angrily at Reggie, then turned and bit Trent on the leg. Trent screamed, stood up, and kicked the animal away from him.

"Fuck you, Reggie!" he said, leg bleeding.

"No, we're even now. No more."

Later, Donnie and Rebecca were in a friend's apartment with several other like-minded students. Donnie felt the thrill of working for a cause.

"Okay," one of the leaders said, "there's going to be a demonstration on behalf of Dr. Atkins. As you know, the university did not grant him tenure. In effect, they're firing him. Here are some copies of a petition. We're not demanding that he be rehired, we're only asking for an open hearing. We think we're on strong ground here. So take some petitions and we need them back by next week."

Donnie took a few copies of the petition.

"Can we stay a little while, talk with these people?" Rebecca asked.

"Well, you can if you want to. But I better get back. Don't know what Heather may be doing. I think they want me to get rid of her. Best not to leave her alone too long."

"Yeah, I think you're right, let's go," she agreed. They left the apartment and walked in the cool night air over to Del Playa and back down to Windward House. As they entered the door, they heard Trent and Reggie laughing hysterically.

Reggie had the monkey on his lap. Its cheek pouches were full of food. Trent was looking angrily at it.

"No, Heather, no!" Trent yelled.

The monkey was furious, but could not bite because her mouth was full of food. Reggie and Trent were both cracking up.

"You guys!" Rebecca said. "No wonder this monkey is freaking out. You're tormenting her."

Trent and Reggie sat for a moment, thinking about her remark.

"Yup, that's what we're doing," Trent said.

"We are, that's true, we're tormenting her," Reggie agreed.

Rebecca grabbed the simian from Reggie and sat down at the table. Heather swallowed her food and began grooming through Rebecca's long, black hair.

"Hey guys," Donnie said. "Will you sign this petition? It's to ask for an open hearing on the firing of Dr. Atkins."

"Wasn't he your anthro teacher?" Reggie asked.

"Yes, he saved my ass with that 'A'."

"But Donnie, didn't you tell me the class was a complete mick? I mean, he gave everybody 'A's', didn't he?"

"Yeah, he did; everybody got an 'A'."

"And he never really talked much about anthropology, did he?" Reggie continued.

Donnie sat at the table and took off his coat. "Well, no, maybe a couple of times."

"So what did he talk about during class?" Reggie asked.

"Usually the war and the establishment and the university administration. Stuff like that. Sometimes even rock lyrics."

"Okay Donnie, look I love you man and I'm really glad that 'A' helped you keep a 2.0, but I have a real problem with Atkins."

"Why?" Donnie asked, confused.

"Because he didn't do the job he was hired to do. He wasn't hired to teach about the war in Vietnam or the university administration. He was hired to teach anthropology, and from what you and a couple other guys I know who took his class have told me, he didn't do that."

"Oh come on, Reg. The war trumps everything. If we had more professors like Atkins, we might end the war quicker," Donnie pleaded.

"I doubt that, I really do," Reggie said. "I had a teacher almost as bad as him at UCLA. In fact, it was *Comparative Politics*, just like with Baer. I've really had bad luck with that topic. Anyway, he had a beard, long hair, and was a darling of the activists. But all he did in class was talk about logic, quote from Bob Dylan, and refer to Arlo Guthrie's 'Alice's Restaurant.' He wasted half the quarter that way, then finally got around to talking about what he was supposed to, constructing a framework for comparing political systems. He was a really popular teacher, too, but I couldn't stand him. What bothers me is that you're just giving Atkins a pass because he's got long hair, a beard, and is against the war. You're doing what the establishment does in reverse. I'm sorry, but he deserves to be fired."

"Man, Reggie, you just don't get it. Trent, how about you?"

"Hey Donnie, I got to agree with Reggie. What if every professor did what Atkins did? Nothing would get taught. As it is, Atkins' students will have to learn that stuff someplace else, and if they're anthro majors, they've been screwed."

"Well there's a bunch of anthro grad students who support him and have signed the petition. The administration is questioning his publication and research, but he has published and he's got funding for some field work next summer. And all his classes are always full, sometimes he takes in over the limit," Donnie explained.

"Full, yeah, full of kids who want an easy 'A'," Reggie noted.

"You guys don't care anymore because you both have high draft numbers, especially you, Mr. 366."

"Donnie," Trent answered, "this is wrong. I've got a real bad feeling about this. When students support an incompetent professor simply because he looks like them and says things they want to hear, your anti-war movement is in big trouble. I've got a bad feeling about this."

"Hey Rebecca," Reggie asked, "at your anti-war and/or pro-Atkins meetings, are there a lot of girls?"

"Some," she said, "but not a lot."

"Who makes the coffee and fixes the sandwiches?" he asked.

"We do, the girls I mean," she answered.

"And who are the leaders, do all the talking, and make the decisions?"

"Well, some of the guys I guess..." she trailed off, deep in thought.

"What's your point, Reggie?" Donnie asked.

Reggie didn't answer, but just smiled wryly. Rebecca was still staring off in space, thinking.

"And Donnie, the monkey has got to go," Reggie noted.

"Oh come on Reggie, at least leave me the monkey."

"No, Heather, no!" Reggie quickly yelled. And before Rebecca could react, the monkey had sunk her teeth into Rebecca's bare shoulder. Rebecca screamed and jumped up, blood streaking down her arm. The next day, the monkey was gone.

A few days later, Donnie and Rebecca sat on the hard concrete of the open space in front of the administration building. Monkey or no, Donnie was filled with a kind of exhilaration that he had never known before. At least a thousand other students were there as well. They had been there most of the day, listening to speaker after speaker condemn the firing of Dr. Atkins and the university's complicity in the Vietnam War. Atkins himself had been there, long hair blowing out in the breeze, beard untrimmed. He could have easily passed for one of the backpacking hippies hitchhiking at the stoplights in Santa Barbara. He had given an impassioned, rambling speech. Donnie loved it. They were doing something; finally doing something that just may have some effect. Almost 8,000 signatures had been collected on the petition. If everybody could just stay strong together surely the administration could not ignore them. They would have to grant the hearing.

The sense of camaraderie with the other students there that he felt was quite empowering. His heart felt light, his stomach was giddy. Power to the people seemed an achievable goal. The day wore on and the students waited for the administration's reaction. Their determination never wavered. The elements seemed to agree as the day was cool but not cold and there was no rain in sight.

Finally, something started to happen. A cordon of police escorted a university dean as he worked his way to the front of the demonstrators. He held up a bullhorn. The students waited expectantly, assuming that a hearing for Atkins would be announced. The dean finally spoke after the bullhorn squealed a bit with feedback.

"This gathering," he stated, "is in violation of university regulations. You all need to disperse or you will be arrested."

There was a disapproving murmur that turned into a roar from the crowd. Donnie saw a student jump up in front of the dean and shout something at him. He couldn't quite hear, but it sounded like the student demonstrator had called the dean a pig. The dean then swung the bullhorn at the student, hitting him in the face. Then all hell broke loose. Suddenly there were police streaming out of the admin building, swinging their batons. Students were screaming, many were panicking and trying to get away.

Donnie was furious. How dare they? He stood up, ready to rush in and do battle with the police, as small as he was.

"Donnie, no! C'mon let's get out of here," Rebecca pleaded, tugging on his arm.

"I have to help; we have to stand together," Donnie protested.

"No, no. Let's get out of here. I don't want to get arrested. I don't want cops groping me. I can't go through all that!"

Sensing the absolute fear in Rebecca's voice, Donnie reluctantly turned and pulled her away from the melee. Hundreds of other students, surprised by the ferocity of the police attack, were streaming away from the area, most headed for Isla Vista. The police were busy with the demonstrators who had been closest to where the dean was, and ignored the fleeing masses except for those they could catch right away. But soon many of the fleeing students stopped, re-grouped, and once again headed for the admin building and the campus police who were busy with the demonstrators they had apprehended.

"Look Rebecca, they're going back. Come on, let's go back."

"No, Donnie, please. Let's go. I don't like dealing with cops."

Soon Donnie and Rebecca, out of breath and with weak knees, were walking calmly down Del Playa, headed for Windward House which was, of course, as far away from the police as Donnie could take Rebecca. Their adrenalin rush was over and their legs and arms felt like rubber. Their stomachs were quivering.

Donnie turned and looked back toward the campus even though he couldn't see it.

"You've done it now," he said out loud to himself.

"What do you mean? Who are you talking to?" Rebecca asked.

"The administration, the establishment. They've done it now. Things will only get worse from here on out."

Chapter Six

FEBRUARY 1970: An Unappreciated Career Prediction, a Black Experience, and the Bank of America Conflagration.

Music albums making the charts:

Johnny Cash—Hello, I'm Johnny Cash
Chicago II
Aretha Franklin—This Girl's In Love With You
The Guess Who—American Woman
Simon and Garfunkle—Bridge Over Troubled Water

"I missed The Band concert. Just couldn't afford it. Heard it was good, though. Heard also there were some issues with police after it. Did you go?" Reggie asked.

"No, I was too focused on the Atkins situation. Didn't really think about going. They're a good group, though. It's nice to have concerts right on campus. Were you at any of the demonstrations by the admin building? I didn't see you there," said Donnie.

"I stayed completely away from the Atkins demonstrations. Remember, I only have classes on Tuesday and Thursday, and I just ride my bike to class and come home when they're done. I didn't see the demonstrators or the cops," Reggie explained. "Was there any more violence after that first day?"

"Not really. The cops would move toward us and we'd disperse and then reform somewhere else. But Reggie, they brought in outside police. They brought in pigs from Ventura and San Luis Obispo counties. And the Ventura sheriffs, they put tape over their badge numbers. Now why'd they do that?"

"So how many demonstrators?"

"I don't know, it varied from a couple of hundred to almost a thousand. It kept changing."

"And how many days did it last?"

"A whole week, I think. But what really sucks is that they arrested 19 students after the first day. They got bailed out right away, but they had to then stay away from the demonstrations or risk suspension or even expulsion from school. And the 19 were all the leaders, including the radicals from student government." Donnie said, lying back on his bed and looking at the ceiling. "If you don't need more proof than that that democracy is dead and our freedoms are in trouble, I don't know what would convince you."

Reggie let out a big sigh. He sat up in his bed. It was Tuesday and he'd have to leave soon for class.

"Okay, Donnie, how about this. Now mind you, I've studied this shit. I know all the Supreme Court cases on freedom of assembly. The Constitution says very clearly that people have the right to peaceably, I repeat, peaceably assemble. If your demonstration is hampering or preventing normal operations of the university, if the clerks can't do their jobs and people can't access the admin services because demonstrators have effectively shut everything down, that is not constitutionally protected assembly. It actually falls outside the realm of peaceable assembly. It amounts to using force to try to get your way."

"So, you're taking the side of the administration and the cops. Did they have a right to beat people? A lot of kids got hurt, you know."

"Excessive force, now that's a separate issue. Legally, cops can only use the force necessary to make an arrest and subdue a suspect. And no more. But in the heat of something like what happened on campus the other day, I wouldn't doubt that some, or maybe many, or maybe most of the cops got carried away. That, I don't support."

Donnie laughed. "You don't get it; you just don't get it."

"Well, Donnie, I'd love to continue this conversation. Maybe you can convince me. But I got to get ready to go to class. No matter what, I will take care of business first."

"Yeah, yeah, go to class, get that degree. Then what, Reg? What's a master's in political science going to do for you? Are you going to get hired by some think tank? Or are you going to teach?"

"Teach? Shit no. I don't want to teach. Teaching is helping other people prepare for their lives. I want to have one of my own. No, I'll just get hired by some company as a junior executive and work my way up from there."

"No you won't," Donnie contradicted him. "People with humanities type degrees are a dime a dozen now. You won't find anything. You'll end up teaching."

Reggie left for class, riding extra fast on his bike. Teach? Was that all that awaited him after all his schooling? Surely he was destined for bigger and better things.

The international organizations class was pretty good, better than he expected. They ended up in a really good discussion of the League of Nations. He actually learned several interesting aspects of that organization that he hadn't realized before. He was fascinated with the mandated territories system that the League had set up. The idea that countries would manage former colonies with the purpose of preparing them for independence was actually the first crack in the justification of European colonialism. Woodrow Wilson had accomplished something worthwhile after all.

He had an hour break that he spent in the library and then went to his Chinese politics class. It wasn't too interesting that day. The professor was okay but obviously had a Taiwanese bias against communist China. The Great Cultural Revolution, at least, was waning. That was enough to make the world breath easier. The sight of millions of Chinese young people all dressed alike in Mao jackets and holding up Mao's little red book, tears of adulation streaming down their faces as the great Chairman waves at them from a balcony overlooking Tiananmen Square, was enough to send a chill down the spine of the most committed American radical. Reggie guessed it was just the Chinese version of the 60s which, for better or worse, were now over for both countries.

Mao's little red book, however, did have some interesting things in it. He said that a revolution was not a dinner party. Meaning, Reggie supposed, that people get hurt in revolutions. He also said that politics grows out of the barrel of a gun. How true. With enough guns you can control the politics. Considering the events surrounding the firing of

Atkins, these things made Reggie nervous.

Reggie had little use for communism. But he did agree with Marx that religion was the opiate of the masses. This Reggie agreed with whole-heartedly. Drugs make people feel good. Religion makes people feel good. Drugs create an alternate reality. Religion creates an alternate reality. Drugs are addictive. And religion, well once a person has made a leap of faith, he or she is pretty much trapped for life.

Later, Reggie stood on the sidelines of the lacrosse game, watching the action. He watched Perry, one of their experienced preppies, take a pass, weave his way through the defense, and fire a rocket at the ground in front of the goal. The ball skidded just under the goalie's stick and into the net. Yet there wasn't much of a cheer or any celebration from Reggie's teammates. They were still losing 7-2 against a high school team.

Game over, they all gathered around Reggie, out of breath and sweating.

"Don't worry about this," Reggie began. "We're a bunch of out of shape college kids. Our practices haven't been consistent, and we still don't have a coach. We'll get better."

"I certainly hope so," Perry said, a hint of disgust in his voice.

"It's okay, Reg," Dan said. "I held back today. I didn't want to hit some high school kid and hurt him. They had one kid who scored most of their goals. There were a couple of times I think I could've leveled him, but shit, it's only a game."

"Well Dan, that's a tough call. But you better not hold back when league starts or we will get absolutely killed," Reggie explained.

"We're gonna get killed anyway," Ryan observed.

"There're some teams we can compete against," Reggie said. "Our first game will be against Claremont. We might be able to do well against them. And a couple of the club teams we play are not that strong, particularly the San Fernando Valley club team. And Russ, you made some good saves today but stop dropping the ball off to the side of the crease. This isn't hockey. You keep that ball and pass it out to someone to start the clear. If you can't find anybody open then get out of the crease, you've got three seconds, and pass it to someone when they get open."

"Okay," Russ said, smiling.

"Are you the coach?" came a voice from behind. It was the private high school coach.

"Not really," Reggie said. "We don't actually have a coach. I'm the organizer, that's all."

"Well, I just wanted to tell you that you guys are really out of shape. You need to work on that. And now I know you don't really have a coach, well, that's another thing you need to work on. Get a coach. You should not have lost to us. You've got some big boys on defense and some good stick handlers on attack. You're just unorganized and out of shape."

"Thanks coach, and thanks for the game. We kinda knew that but now it's pretty clear," Reggie explained.

The players gave all their equipment to Reggie and headed for their cars. Maureen, Sandy, and Janice, who had watched the game, came up to Reggie.

"Good game, Reg," Sandy said.

"You're not a good liar, Sandy. But thanks for coming to watch. I wish now I hadn't invited you guys."

"Why?" Janice asked.

"It's just so embarrassing," Reggie explained, "losing to a high school team."

"Oh," Maureen said, "I think you'll get better. Come by the house later. We don't see as much of you since your lacrosse practice started up."

Reggie smiled. Maureen was looking for information. Donnie and Rebecca, too, had come to watch the game and walked up to Reggie.

"Sorry man," Donnie said. "I know you put a lot of energy into this. Hope things get better."

"Thanks, Don," Reggie answered. "See you guys back at the house."

Reggie got home, showered, and came out into the living room. Trent and Juanita were there, but Donnie hadn't gotten back yet.

"Okay, what's this?" Reggie asked, listening to some strong guitar blues coming from the stereo.

"Another Brit group called Fleetwood Mac. Very bluesy." Trent answered.

Reggie fixed himself a sandwich while listening to the album. Soon, Trent and Juanita disappeared into the fucking room. The album played on; in fact the name of it was "Then Play On." Reggie took the liberty of flipping it when the first side was finished. He sat there, listening to the record. It was good, solid blues. But not outstanding. Nothing he wanted to spend his limited money on.

Trent emerged from his room to get something from the kitchen.

"So what do you think of these guys?" he asked.

"Solid, but not spectacular. Nothing to distinguish them from a hundred other groups. There's one kinda long song that's pretty good, but I think after another album or two they'll disappear. Doubt if five or six years from now we'll even remember Fleetwood Mac."

The sun had set and darkness fell pretty quickly. Reggie left and walked over to the girls' house. They had the Band's first album "Music from Big Pink" on the stereo. There was definitely a country feel to the group's sound.

"You don't have their new album? I know they have another one out," Reggie asked.

"No," Joyce said disappointedly, "haven't been able to get it. Too many albums, not enough money."

"Tell me about it," Reggie said.

A joint appeared and was passed around. "Led Zeppelin II" was put on the stereo and then the second side of "Abbey Road." Another joint came around. Maureen stood up and came and sat next to Reggie.

"Can we go out on the deck and talk?" She asked.

"Kinda cool out there this time of night," he said.

"I'll be okay; can we talk, please?"

They stood up and walked out to the deck. The sky was ink black with stars making scattered points of light. The oil platform was lit up and indeed looked like a fairy castle. The ocean was completely black, with no indication that it was even there save the noise of the surf crashing on the beach. And it was chilly.

"What's Trent doing? Is he with someone else?"

"Well, gee Maureen, I kinda like to mind my own business. I

don't think it's appropriate for me to divulge anything I might know about Trent's extra curricular activities. And I promised myself I wouldn't get into a conversation with you where I end up saying 'I told you so'."

Maureen sighed and leaned her back against the railing, staring up over the roof of the house into the sky.

"But you did tell me," she said softly.

"Well, yeah, I guess I did."

"And you hate me too. I bet if I wanted to make love to you now, you'd turn me down."

"Good grief Maureen, I don't hate you, not at all. But if you wanted to do something, well, you see, I think of you more as a friend..."

Maureen screeched and pulled back her hand as if to hit him.

"Just kidding!" Reggie said quickly. "But here's the sad truth. If you grabbed my hand right now and wanted to take me into your bedroom and fuck my brains out, I'd go. In a heartbeat. But you know what else is sad?"

"No, what?"

"If Trent called you up right now and asked you to come over for a romp on the waterbed, you'd go."

"Hell if I would!"

"Maureen..." Reggie said, drawing her name out and looking at her sternly.

She hung her head. "Yeah, I'd go," she finally answered.

A few days later, he and Vicky were in his Ford, heading for a theater in Goleta. He couldn't believe it. He had asked Vicky out and she accepted. The drama between Maureen and Trent was a million miles away.

"This movie is some kind of Korean War movie about medics and doctors. It sounds weird, but it's supposed to be really funny. How war can be funny, I don't know," Reggie explained.

"What's it called again, 'Mash'?" Vicky asked.

"Yeah, I think, 'MASH,' with all capitals. According to this guy on the lacrosse team it stands for mobile army surgical hospital. They're supposed to provide quick surgery close to the front."

"And how could that be funny?"

"I don't know, but Trent saw it and said it is a must-see, an absolute must-see."

And indeed, the movie turned out to be hilarious. The theater was filled and the audience laughed uproariously at the appropriate parts of the movie. Reggie had never seen a film like "MASH." It seemed to be like organized chaos, often with many actors talking at once. Yet it was put together masterfully, with just enough blood and guts to balance the humor. When they snuck a microphone into the room where Sally Kellerman and Robert Duvall were making love; when they figured out a way to find out if Kellerman was a natural blonde; when they showed the commanding officer in bed with a pretty nurse; and at many other parts of the movie, the audience howled. Vicky was cracking up, too, continually leaning against him with her ample breast frequently pressing against his arm. Donald Sutherland and Elliot Gould, Reggie decided, were destined for long careers.

After the movie, and a quick stop at McDonald's, Reggie and Vicky stood outside her apartment in Isla Vista.

"I had a good time and I hope you did. Did you?"

"Well I don't know, Reggie, what do you think?"

"Why do you play with me like this?"

She laughed. He stood there, considering his next move. Shaking his head, he put his arms around her, pulled her to him, and kissed her on the lips. Right on her big, full lips. Her body felt so good against his; he wanted to stand there and kiss her forever. He moved out his tongue and she opened her mouth to admit it, then she returned with tongue in his mouth. Then he stopped, dropped his arms, and stepped back.

"Well, goodnight," he said.

"Goodnight," she said, a slight look of puzzlement on her face.

Reggie went home, showered, and went to bed. Donnie was not there as he usually spent the weekends at Rebecca's. Reggie didn't know why he hadn't pushed it with Vicky. Something just wasn't right, or maybe he was still afraid of her blackness, of the cultural divide between them.

At about two in the morning, there was a furious pounding on the Windward House door. Reggie sat up, listened, and heard it again. He stumbled out of his room, wearing only his boxer shorts, and opened the door. There stood Vicky, a look of anger on her face.

"I want to talk to you," she said, pushing her way inside. "Where can we talk?"

"Uh, in here, my roommate's not here," Reggie said.

The two walked into Reggie's huge bedroom. There was no place to sit except on one of the two beds, so Vicky just stood there.

"Reggie," she began, "I'm a little tired of this game we're playing.

Why don't you come out and tell me exactly what you want? What are you waiting for? You must know I like you. Don't you like me? Tell me what you want, what do you expect? Tell me, dammit, and tell me right now. I ain't wasting any more time on you."

Reggie stood by his bed, a little stunned by her tirade. He looked at her and put his hands on his hips.

"Well, okay, what do I want? I'll tell you. I want you, naked, in my bed. I want to make love to you, for hours. I want to make love to you with me on top, I want to make love to you with you on top, and I want to make love to you doggy style. I want to bury my face between your legs and make you helpless with pleasure, and I want to watch my manhood disappear between your fantastic lips into your mouth. Okay? Is that clear enough?"

Vicky stood there, taking it all in. Then, slowly, she dropped her purse off her shoulder onto the floor. Then she took off her coat and let it drop to the floor. She pulled off her sweater, revealing that she wore no bra. He was amazed. Her breasts were so full and firm and her nipples so black. She then pushed down her pants and underwear and stood in front of him, naked, legs long and powerful. Finally, she climbed into his bed and lay there, naked, staring up at him.

"Well come on then," she said, "you got some work to do."

He pushed off his boxers and climbed in next to her. He was hard already, and one of her hands wrapped itself around his erection, squeezing gently. His hand rubbed her body. First, he felt along the curve of her breasts, briefly, then across her abdomen, and down to the increasing dampness hiding there in between her legs. His desire surging inside of him, Reggie started kissing and licking all over her body. It felt so good against his. Her black skin was such a contrast to his pasty whiteness. He loved that. He was amazed. After all this time they were actually going to make love.

"Are you on the pill?" he asked breathlessly.

"Nice of you to ask, but it's a little late, isn't it? You'd better not stop anything you're doing right now. And, yes, I'm on the pill."

With that, he moved on top of her and thrust inside, into a vice tight, slippery hot heaven. He moved in and out, trying to hold back. He felt her tense beneath him. She wrapped her long, powerful black legs around his back and rubbed them up and down along his side. After what seemed to him a long time, at least 15 or 20 minutes, she arched her back and let out a scream.

"Oh, yes, yes!" she yelled. Reggie was afraid Trent would wake up. "Yes, yes!" Reggie kept humping, thrusting in and out. Finally, he felt his own orgasm, which he'd managed to fight back several times, building. She was whimpering beneath him as he continued to make love to her. She squeezed her legs around him. He felt it rise up to that wonderful split second of absolute bliss, of knowing the orgasm was inevitable, and then he exploded. The relief was overwhelming, and he shot spurt after spurt into her as waves of pleasure coursed through him.

He rolled off her and caught his breath. She snuggled up to him, nestling her face against his neck. He was ready for sleep, but he knew there would be more to come. Sure enough, after several minutes, her hand reached for his now limp member. She began to stroke it tenderly while kissing his neck and nibbling on his ear. He turned and began kissing her. God but she was a good kisser. Her lips were fantastic, so thick and full. Soon, he was hard again. After a few more minutes, she climbed up on top of him, moved his dick against her clit for a few seconds, and then impaled herself, sliding all the way down until she rested on his abdomen. She then lied down on his chest and began humping him. This was what life was all about—to be making love to a beautiful woman. Her efforts became stronger and stronger. She sat up, her hands on his chest, and kept pushing herself up and down. The physical sensation of being inside her was intensely pleasurable. He fondled her breasts. And they were great. Round and firm and full. Suddenly, she began screaming again.

"Oh! I'm cumming again, Reggie, yes, yes; you made me cum again!" she shouted happily. She threw her arms up into the air in celebration.

"Okay," she said, lying back down on his chest. "Your turn. If I cum, you gotta cum. That's the rule."

"Whose rule?" Reggie asked. "Girls can cum more than guys. If I make you cum ten times but only cum twice myself, what's wrong with that?"

"My rule. I don't want to owe you any orgasms."

Reggie smiled. He wished Janice had felt that way.

So he made love to her from underneath. He hugged her down to him, feeling the fullness of her breasts against his chest, and thrust upward. After a long time, he felt another orgasm building. She kissed him to encourage it, and as her tongue swirled around inside his mouth, he exploded yet again.

They rested some more. They even dozed off to sleep. Dawn was breaking when he woke up and noticed her hand pulling on his hard-again dick. She was lying on her stomach and had pulled her knees up under her, sticking her butt up in the air. It was a black butt, much rounder and fuller than most white girls' butts. He climbed in behind her and inserted yet again. He was ecstatic at the view. As the gray light of early morning filled the room he looked down on her beautiful black body. He watched himself disappear into her, and saw her labia stretch along with him on the out strokes. He held on to her beautiful, black butt cheeks.

Could he cum again? He thought so. He increased his rhythm and she began to mumble and groan. He increased his forcefulness and she began to shake. Suddenly, she started screaming again, shaking her butt all over and making it hard for him to stay inside her. But he did, and soon after she came, he did, pouring himself once more into her.

They got up and showered. Reggie was exhausted. They enjoyed themselves in the shower, soaping up each other's bodies and rubbing against each other. By the end of the shower, he was hard again. She took him by the hand and back to the bed. He lied down and she smiled at him. Then, before he realized it, she swung her leg over his head and was straddling him with her head down at his crotch. They were in a perfect 69 position.

He loved oral sex, both receiving, obviously, but also giving. He loved the texture of a woman's soft, fleshy parts. He loved having his tongue inside a woman, tasting her essence, feeling her hot wet softness. Complete abandon of all restraints. It was exhilarating. Meanwhile, he felt her tongue and lips at work on him. She sucked gently, then licked the underside, then finally swallowed up his whole member down to the root. Her mouth was so hot and wet and soft, and his dick was in it. Soon, she tensed and came on his face, bumping her ass up and down on him, while at the same time, he filled her mouth with his fourth ejaculation of the day, something he didn't believe possible.

She moved off him, but continued to suck. He finally got to watch her work. It amazed him to see his pale white dick disappear into her black face. He wanted to lie there and watch it forever. But soon he softened and she came up next to him, head on his shoulder, arm across his chest. She was so black and his skin so white. He just stared at her skin against his and wondered how he had managed to get so lucky.

Later, back in Lancaster, Charlie was arriving home from his shift. "Tommy and that Jones kid had a fight today, right in our backyard," Susie announced as Charlie was changing his clothes.

"A fight, good grief Stevie is only seven, what could have possessed Tommy to want to fight him? Were either hurt?"

"No, but Stevie ran home crying and I had a long phone call with his mother. Seems Tommy has been picking on him more and more. You need to talk to him."

Charlie sighed. "Okay, okay, give me a minute. Where is he?"

"In his room. I sent him there to wait for you."

Charlie finished putting on a t-shirt then walked down the hall to Tommy's room. Their five year old daughter, Sally, was standing outside the door. When she saw her father, she began teasing Tommy through the closed door. "You're in trouble! You're in trouble!" she sang.

"Sally, stop that. Go to your room, or go outside and play,"

Charlie ordered sternly. The young girl obeyed leaving Charlie alone in the hallway. He knocked twice on the door and then opened it. Tommy was sitting on his bed, looking down at his feet.

"Okay, partner. What got into you today? Why are you picking on Stevie? There're hardly any other kids for you to play with in this neighborhood. Wanna tell me what happened?"

Tommy sat silently for a few minutes and just shrugged his shoulders.

"Not good enough, kid. Why did you fight with Stevie? C'mon, out with it."

Tommy blurted out defiantly. "Oh Dad, he's just such a wimp and a sissy I don't really like playing with him. He takes everything too seriously. I tease or scare him just a little bit and he starts cryin' and running home to his mama."

"Tommy," Charlie began, searching for words. "He's only seven years old. Why are you teasing or scaring him at all? Why do you torment him?"

"He's a wimp!"

"Do you enjoy scaring him; do you enjoy making him cry?"

Tommy sat silently for a moment, and then shrugged his shoulders.

"Well, kid," Charlie said, "looks like you're well on your way to becoming a bully. At least if the kid is younger and smaller than you. Is that what you want? Look at me!" He barked a command. Tommy was startled, but then looked up and into his dad's eyes. "Do not become a bully. You want to know something? Nobody likes a bully. Nobody! Are you picking on Stevie because Dustin teases you? Is this your way of getting even, to pass it along to someone helpless? Do you know anybody who really likes Dustin? All the kids who hang out with him are actually afraid of him, you told me that yourself. Do you want to be like Dustin?"

Tommy's lip began to quiver. He was still looking up into his father's stern face. Suddenly he broke, and the tears began to flow, accompanied by heavy sobs. Charlie reached out his arms and drew the crying boy to his chest. He just sat there as Tommy cried, holding him, rocking back and forth.

"It's okay now; it's okay," Charlie said softly. "You're not going to become a bully. You don't want to be a bully. Nobody likes a bully. Nobody."

Back in Isla Vista, Donnie and Rebecca sat in the football stadium and waited. Donnie was filled with excitement again. There must have been 2000 people, students mostly, there to hear a speech by William Kunstler, the attorney for the Chicago Eight. A few early speakers prepped the crowd, resorting to tried and true anti-establishment rhetoric. Donnie liked it. He had a sense that, by working together, the right people could bring the war to an end and re-structure society to make life fair and enjoyable for all. He truly believed in the possibility. Finally, Kunstler was introduced and the crowd roared. For Donnie, the Chicago Eight trial was just more proof of the bankrupt nature of the American political system. Eight people were charged with conspiring to disrupt the 1968 Democratic National Convention, yet some of them had never even met each other before the trial. Of course, the jury had found the Chicago Seven not guilty (one had his trial separated out). So the system worked at least somewhat. But not enough for Donnie.

Kunstler fed the crowd what they wanted. The war was wrong, the society corrupt, the system rigged. And the anti-war and counter-culture movements had been targeted by the establishment for elimination.

"The idea of this prosecution was to chill all of us…to set an example to show you what could happen if you became involved in any social movement—to put fear where fervor was and destroy fervor, to destroy involvement. No trial should take place in the United States that embodies a threat to the soul of mankind," Kunstler said in his speech.

Charged up and feeling righteous in their cause, Donnie and Rebecca filed out of the stadium with the crowd and walked on into Isla Vista. It was late afternoon and the sun would be setting soon. They felt happy and hopeful and the cool sea air was refreshing. But as they approached the loop area, they noticed a commotion on the street. Several cop cars were there, and a crowd had gathered across the street to watch.

"Let's go see what's happening," Donnie said.

They walked over and stood with the crowd, which grew larger and larger. The police were struggling with someone. All Donnie could tell was that the person was black, and the police were roughing him up quite a bit in front of all the other students and others watching. Soon they bundled him up and got him into the police cruiser and left. The crowd was not happy.

More and more people came out into the loop area. Little groups of ten and twenty huddled together, talking about the arrest. Donnie and Rebecca stood with one group, discussing their anger and possible options to respond. Suddenly they heard shouting and cheering and saw some smoke. Running toward the noise, they saw a cop car flipped over and in flames with people standing around throwing rocks at it.

Impulsively, Donnie picked up a rock and threw it at a passing police cruiser. He saw it strike the windshield causing an immediate spider web pattern of cracks. The cop in the car flinched as it struck, and looked right at Donnie in surprise and anger. Several other people soon joined Donnie throwing rocks at the same car, and the officer stepped on the gas and zoomed away. Soon, every police car in Isla Vista, and there were several after Kunstler's speech, was under attack. Rocks and bottles rained on them until they all left. Hundreds of people were in the streets and the parks of the loop area by that time.

Donnie was excited beyond belief. His adrenalin was pumping through his veins.

"Donnie, what are you doing?" Rebecca asked. "I'm afraid; I don't want to be here. The cops will come back and they'll be really pissed."

"Then we'll chase them away again," Donnie replied.

She tugged at his arm. "Let's go. This is going to get bad here."

Donnie turned at looked at her. "Rebecca, I really care for you, but this is where I was meant to be. This is what I have to do. Go on back to your apartment; I'll see you later." He turned and walked away towards a group brandishing trashcan lids and big sticks.

"Donnie!" she called. But he just kept walking, acknowledging her with a wave.

As Donnie approached the group they headed for a real estate office. One threw a rock and it broke the window. Others kicked at the door, trying to get inside. Donnie held back, watching the action. Just then another group approached, angry at Donnie's group.

"What are you guys doing?" one of them demanded. "Don't mess with the office, it's private property, you got no call to break their windows. You think if you trash their office you won't have to pay your rent?" There were five or six of them, and they were all pretty big and had just come from a frat house. Donnie's group backed off, not sure how to respond.

Just then came more shouts from down the street.

"The bank," someone shouted, "let's get the bank!" Indeed, there was a stream of figures heading towards the Isla Vista branch of the Bank of America located on Embarcadero del Norte. The group Donnie had followed quickly broke off their assault on the real estate office and followed the movement toward the bank. People were already attacking the front door, trying to break it and get inside. Other groups continued to attack the different real estate offices as there weren't enough jocks to defend them all.

"What's that?" Donnie heard someone ask.

A large bus had pulled into the loop area over on Embarcadero del Mar down a bit from the park. Out of it very quickly came cops armed with batons and shields. There must have been as many as 50 of them. They quickly formed up and began walking toward the park next to the bank where a large group of students was gathered. As the cops approached, the group in the park began to retreat. But then another large crowd, coming from near the Magic Lantern Theater across

Embarcadero del Norte, charged the cops' flank.

The first group then stopped their retreat and began charging as well. Everybody was yelling and screaming and rocks were flying. The cops were facing as many as 300 rioters who had just performed a classic pincer movement against them with no military training and no real leaders and no planning. Rocks continued to rain down as now it was the cops' turn to retreat. The cops held up their plastic shields but there were just too many demonstrators and too many rocks. Donnie joined in with glee. This is what he wanted, to attack the police, to attack the brute force minions of the establishment.

He threw a rock. It glanced off one officer's shield but Donnie saw another rock, thrown by someone else, strike the cop in the face by coming in under his raised shield. Donnie saw the man's face erupt in bleeding. Momentarily, Donnie felt a twinge of regret. He'd helped hurt someone. The cop dropped to one knee and was immediately picked up by another. With the rocks and bottles raining down on them from hundreds of students and street people, the police retreated. They made it back to their bus, boarded it quickly, and the bus left Isla Vista. The students had driven away the cops. Isla Vista, thought Donnie, was free.

Meanwhile, Rebecca pounded furiously on the Windward House door. Trent opened it and looked at her in confusion.

"Trent, help me get Donnie. It's real crazy down there at the loop. They're burning cop cars and throwing rocks at cops. Something bad is going to happen to him, I know it."

Trent stood there, taking it all in.

"Reggie's next door. Let me get my jacket and let's check him first."

They walked along the street until they reached the girls' house. Rebecca knocked on the door as Trent waited out by the street. He didn't want a scene with Maureen.

Sandy opened the door and soon got Reggie.

"Reggie, please help me get Donnie. He's down at the loop and things are crazy there. The cops, they've been chased out, but I know they'll be back," Rebecca pleaded.

"What the hell?" Reggie asked. "Okay, yeah, I'll go check it out. Hey John," he called to Sandy's boyfriend, "do you wanna go to the loop and check out the action?"

"Okay," John answered, still smiling as usual.

"Reggie," Trent spoke as they joined him outside, "I'm going back to the house. I really don't want to get involved in that mess. That's not why I'm here. I'll go if you ask me, but Donnie doesn't listen to me."

Reggie thought at minute. "Me either, but really that's okay; go on home. John and I will be okay. Rebecca, do you want to go wait with Trent or wait here, or go back to your apartment?"

"I'll go back to my apartment. Call me when you get Donnie home," she demanded.

Reggie and John began the long walk down Del Playa. The night was cool and the walk actually refreshing. It took them about 15 minutes to reach the loop. What they saw was total chaos. People were everywhere. Dumpsters were on fire in the middle of various roads around the loop. Reggie had no idea how he would be able to find Donnie in this crowd. The park was full of revelers. Music was blaring from the speakers of the music store. It was the Rolling Stones' "Street Fighting Man." A particularly large group seemed to be gathered around the bank. Reggie and John walked on over towards it, stepping over rocks that were scattered on the roadway. Everybody seemed so ridiculously happy.

"Reggie, hey Reggie," Donnie called from the sidewalk across the street from the bank.

Reggie and John picked their way through the crowd until they stood in front of Donnie.

"What are you doing, man? Rebecca's freaked. Come on, let's go home," Reggie said.

"No, Reg, I'm staying. This is just so great I can't believe it. I'll be home later."

"Man, she's really freaked. I've never seen her like this. It would be better if you left here with us," Reggie countered.

Donnie sighed and shook his head. "I'm not missing this. I'm staying right here, soaking up the pleasure of freeing Isla Vista from the pigs. Savoring the victory. I'll go to her apartment later, when I'm ready."

"In the long run," Reggie said, "nothing will change. You're foolish if you think it will. You realize that the cops will come back and you might get hurt."

"Fortunes of war," Donnie said.

Reggie shook his head and turned away. He looked around at all the people. Who were they? Who were these people trashing real estate offices and the bank? He didn't recognize anybody. He saw no one from the lacrosse team. He saw no one from his classes. Were these people real students? Were they just street people hanging out in a college community? No, most of them had to be students. Most of Isla Vista was populated by students. But UCSB was a party school, not a haven for activists. It wasn't Berkeley.

He and John crossed the street. The front door to the bank had been broken open.

"Let's go check it out," Reggie said.

They walked up to the front and on into the bank. Inside was chaos as well. Students were sitting at the desks and playing with the telephones. He saw some girls chasing each other around, throwing papers into the air. The vault, of course, was secure, but every other part of the bank had been violated. Forms were scattered all over the floor. In the very middle of the bank a protestor was trying to light a fire using a pile of bank forms. A huge 6'8" jock walked up to him and stomped on the barely lit papers.

"What are you doing? Get out of here, go home," he shouted. The would-be arsonist looked up at the huge form towering over him and backed away.

Reggie felt weird. Here he was inside a bank that was supposed to be closed. He was probably violating federal law and could easily end up a target of the FBI. He felt a strong urge to remove himself from the premises and not be associated with the bank break-in. He tugged at John on the arm and they went out the back door of the bank and into the park.

Suddenly, several large sedans roared through the loop. Reggie heard a popping sound and saw clouds of gas billowing up from canisters dropped in four corners of the loop area.

"Tear gas," said John.

"I see it," Reggie said. Immediately, even though they weren't in the cloud, Reggie's eyes began to hurt. In a moment, he was tearing up, his nose was running, and he was in total agony.

"Let's get the fuck outa here!" he said.

"Okay," John said. "Let's walk quickly, but don't run. Don't rub your eyes, just keep blinking. Let your tear ducts work it out. And when we get home, don't put water on it, just keep blinking. I've experienced this stuff in the army. I think they're using pepper gas."

Reggie was grateful for the advice of an expert. He was still suffering, but resisted the temptation to rub his eyes and continued to let the tears roll out. They made it out of the top of the loop and headed quickly for Del Playa. Soon they were well on their way down the street, leaving the chaos of the first Isla Vista riot behind.

They reached the girls' house and went inside. By this time Reggie was feeling much better. He called Rebecca and told her Donnie wouldn't leave. She wasn't happy, but Reggie did his best to calm her down. It took a while. Then the girls, John, and Reggie sat around trying to understand what was going on.

Back at the bank, the tear gas had had limited effect. It chased away the curious onlookers, like Reggie and John, and probably convinced most of the frat rats and jocks to give up trying to prevent damage and go home. But hundreds remained steadfast in the loop and the police didn't have the manpower to challenge them.

Donnie had watched two separate struggles going on. One between the rioters and the police, and one between the rioters and students trying to stop them. A flaming trash bin had been rolled up and into the bank, but the jocks and frat rats had put out the flames with fire extinguishers. There seemed to be an uneasy truce between them and the rioters, as if the rioters didn't want to turn on fellow students. But eventually, shortly after the tear gas attack, the fraternity members, athletes, and others opposed to the riot had given up and gone home. There were just too many who wanted to riot. A flaming trash bin sat outside the bank and some students were roasting marshmallows over the fire.

A small group of students disappeared into the bank carrying gas cans. They set a fire on the steps in front and moved it inside. They piled up furniture and doused the piles with gasoline. Soon, the entire bank was going up in flames. Donnie watched in amazement. He couldn't believe what they'd managed to do. Beat the police. And soon, with the bank in flames, he felt a peaceful, relaxed feeling. Hundreds stood around and watched the bank go up. The sparks flew upward into the black sky and the heat of the fire drove the rioters farther and farther back. They had destroyed a symbol of all that was wrong with America.

Back at the girls' house Reggie, John and the girls sat in the living room. No music at all was on the stereo. No booze was being consumed, no joints being smoked. They talked, in low tones, about what was going on.

"Hey guys, look at this," Janice called. They all went over to the window and looked. Off in the distance toward the loop an orange glow lit up the sky.

"What the hell is that?" Sandy asked.

"The bank," John said, "they're burning the bank."

"Good grief," Reggie said.

"Unreal," Maureen added.

"They're burning the bank," John repeated.

Reggie noticed he was no longer smiling.

Chapter Seven

MARCH 1970: A Lacrosse Almost, a Revolution Discourse, and Race Relations 1B

Music albums making the charts:

Badfinger—Magic Christian Music
Joan Baez—One Day at a Time
The Doors—Morrison Hotel
Van Morrison—Moondance
Mountain—Climbing
James Taylor—Sweet Baby James
Frank Zappa—Burnt Weenie Sandwich

Reggie saw the ball coming and managed to time it just right, slamming into the Claremont player just as the ball hit his stick. The kid let out a grunt and hit the ground, the ball rolling free. Reggie scooped it up and began running down field. An opposing midfielder challenged him but Reggie quickly passed the ball up to Ben, who settled it down into an offensive set. Ben fed the ball to Dominic who used a pick by Joey to get open and fire a shot at the goal. It went in, and to Reggie's delight the game was tied 3-3 in the fourth quarter.

The day was gloomy and it had rained off and on, leaving the field wet and slippery. The two teams played on. There were many slips and falls, and lots of good hits by Reggie's team. They did like to hit.

Claremont's best player was one of their attacks. With time running down, he took a pass from a teammate and began working against Ryan. Reggie, on the sidelines having subbed out, felt confident because Ryan was their best and most experienced defenseman. The attack began to work his way around from behind the goal. Reggie knew he was going to try a shot as soon as he had a halfway decent angle. Reggie saw Joey's opposing midfielder pull him away from the play. He yelled at Joey to ignore his man and back up Ryan. But it was too late. The attack saw his opening and fired at the goal. It went in right over Russ's shoulder. Ryan slammed his stick on the ground in disgust. The first ever UCSB men's lacrosse game ended as a 4-3 loss.

Reggie shook his head as the players gathered around. Yet, still, the game had been close. Maybe they could play in this league.

"Good game, guys. Don't worry about it, Ryan, shake it off. We just made too many mistakes in the end. Joey, don't let your man pull you away so far from the action, he was almost out of bounds and you were still with him. Now hey, we got UCLA in the stadium next Saturday. We can give them a good game. We're gonna win some games this year, I can feel it. Practice on Monday and Wednesday. And hey, this was a good game for us. A good start."

At Windward House, the three roommates sat in their living room.

"Okay, explain to me, Donnie. What exactly was accomplished

by burning down the bank? What's the point?"

It was another gloomy day as the foggy Santa Barbara winter had yet to yield to a brighter, more hopeful spring. They had been listening to music all morning: Mayall, Jethro Tull, Jefferson Airplane's "Surrealistic Pillow" album from 1967, the Stones "Let It Bleed," and Simon and Garfunkle's latest album, "A Bridge Over Troubled Water." It would turn out to be their last as a duo, but it had a pleasing quality that set a comfortable mood. They all felt like talking, so when the Simon and Garfunkle album finished, no one got up to put on another.

"Okay guys, try this," Donnie began to explain. "First, the Bank of America is the only U.S. bank to have a branch in Vietnam. It also is in bed with the growers against the United Farm Workers. It has defense contractors on its Board of Directors. The list goes on, but that's all I can remember now. Besides, it's the perfect symbol of the imperialist, capitalist system that has been and continues to be raping the world."

"Look, Donnie, I know you want to see an end to the war, but do you really want to tear down the whole government, economy, and social structure of the country?" Reggie asked.

"Yes, that's exactly what I want. We need a government that responds to the needs of the people and not one that just serves the interests of the wealthy corporations. We need a foreign policy that doesn't impose our will on other countries just because we have the strongest military in the world. We need to tear down the whole system…"

"And replace it with what?" Reggie demanded. "Communism? Look at the communist countries of the world. They're just as corrupt.

They've created their own elites, the party members, who get better treatment than everybody else. There's not one communist country in the world I'd choose to live in over the US. And I don't think there's any government system out there that I'd trade ours for. Who's gonna lead this new system you want? Kunstler? Angela Davis? The Chicago Eight or Seven or however many there are? Because if that's so, no thank you."

Donnie stood up and went to the sliding door.

"Look, see that?" he pointed to the oil platform offshore. "That's what's wrong with America. The oil industry is the worst polluter, like up here last summer with that big spill, and just has the whole country by the throat. Los Angeles used to have a very efficient public transit system, the Red Car Line. These were electric trains that radiated out from downtown. Standard Oil, Firestone Tires, and General Motors colluded to buy up the transit system and change everything to gasoline powered busses. Now LA has one of the worst mass transit systems in the country, and instead relies on the freeways. Meaning people buying more cars and more tires and more gasoline. And you know what? Those freeways follow along the same routes as the old Red Car Lines. And those three companies were actually convicted of breaking the law. You know what happened to them? They paid a $5000 fine. Five thousand. That's nothing for those companies. Big punishment."

"Well Donnie," Trent said, "I guess you're gonna have to stop listening to my albums."

"What do you mean?" Donnie asked.

"My father works for an oil company. In fact, if I'm not mistaken his company owns that platform out there. All the money I have comes from oil. You have a car and you drive it, I have a car and I drive it, Reggie has a car and he drives it. What would we do without oil? Now I'm not saying the oil companies are angels, I know they're not. But you want to tear down our whole society? I don't see how that will improve anything. What does your father do? You're still living off his money right now."

"As a matter of fact, he works for an insurance company..." Donnie began.

"Ah-ha," Reggie interrupted him, "insurance companies are another part of the mix. You can't get more capitalist than that. They offer protection to the corporations, allowing them to carry out their nefarious deeds. And you are benefiting from that. Could you live without your father's support? Could you pay the rent here?"

"No," Donnie replied honestly, then threw his hands in the air in frustration. "Not the way things are now. Can't you guys see we need to change things?"

"I'm not opposed to reform, to tweaking things. For example, I think we need to get rid of the Electoral College System. It never functioned as it was intended and it doesn't serve our needs today. You can lose the popular vote but still be elected president. It's happened before and will again, I'm sure. And I think 18 year olds should be allowed to vote. And drugs, especially marijuana, should be legal. But I don't want to tear everything down," Reggie said.

Donnie sat silently, his head in his hands. "You guys just don't see. I don't like to keep using this, but I think your high lottery numbers have left you too secure."

"Okay, Donnie, fair point," Reggie said. "But you know what the worst thing could be for the anti-establishment movement you're espousing here? The worst thing would be if the war ends. Or, even if the war continues but the draft ends. They end the draft, and go to an all volunteer army, and this whole movement you're swept up in will dissolve, leaving only a very few committed radicals whom nobody will listen to."

"The establishment is not going away, Donnie." Trent added. "We may be able to change it a little, but a complete revolution—not gonna happen. As long as the middle class is reasonably comfortable, and like Reggie said they will be as soon as the draft ends, you just won't have enough people behind your movement. Now you may be right or wrong about the need for change. But the truth is that doesn't matter. The establishment will outlast the counter-culture movement. Things are just not gonna change to the extent that you want, even if you're right that they should."

Donnie sat, head down. "Jeese that's a depressing thought."

Trent shrugged. Reggie just sat on the couch, looking at Donnie.

"Dylan said," Reggie began, "'money doesn't talk, it screams—obscenities.' Money will always control things. Money is like water, it will always go where it can go, it will always mean power. If you're rich, you're gonna be more powerful than someone who's poor. Or even middle class. And I'll tell you this…" Reggie stopped for effect.

"What?" Donnie asked.

"They'll just rebuild that bank. Probably out of solid brick, steel, and asbestos. And I hope the burning didn't hurt the people who have accounts there. I hope the bank has duplicate records or maybe has everything recorded on a computer somewhere. I know people who use that bank for their checking accounts. What if their cancelled checks were burned up and now they can't prove that they made certain payments? Do you think your bank-burning friends thought about the little people who use the bank? I know students who worked there, and I know the bank was very helpful to students wanting to open checking accounts with minimal amounts."

"Oh the bank will take care of everybody who deposited there, you can be sure of that," Donnie replied.

"Really? So now the bank is magnanimous? Just a few minutes ago you were talking about how exploitative the bank was," Reggie countered.

The three fell silent again. The only noise was the humming of the refrigerator and the surf outside.

"So, you guys don't want me to fix dinner tonight?" Donnie finally asked.

"Hell yes, we do!" Trent exclaimed.

"You're not getting out of that this easily, you commie pinko freak. You better fix dinner," Reggie added, throwing a small pillow at Donnie for effect.

"Okay," Donnie said, ducking the pillow. "I'll need to go to the store. Give me some of that oil money."

A few days later, Reggie and Vicky sat at a table in the Wooden Horse Restaurant, a small atmosphere rich café located on the loop but spared by the rioters. Huge cable spools, thickly laminated, served as tables. Big candles were everywhere and incense filled the air. The menu included exotic coffees and hot chocolates as well as unique sandwiches with lots of avocado and artichoke hearts. The music leaking softly out of the café's stereo was Spanish classical guitar, probably Segovia.

"So, is this the kind of place for aspiring hippies?" Vicky asked.

"Well, now, maybe not. Hippies don't waste money on created atmosphere."

"So you think this is phony?"

"Well, now, maybe not. I think they're trying to create an atmosphere that will appeal to at least some of the people who live in I.V. But I'd be surprised if they last very long," Reggie explained.

Vicky just stirred her coffee and looked at him. He wanted her again. They hadn't been together since their lovemaking, and he wanted some more of that. She looked good, as usual, though her wardrobe was always similar. Baggy sweatshirt, tight jeans. He never paid attention to fashion. It was what she looked like without clothes that interested him.

"You like this music?" she asked.

"Yeah, it's okay for here. Better than Muzak. Do you like it?"

"Not bad. But I prefer soul music. What about you, what do you listen to?"

"Some soul. I like most of the Motown groups: Supremes, Temptations, Smokey Robinson, Four Tops, Stevie Wonder. I also like Ray Charles, BB King, and even some James Brown. But not exclusively. I like a lot of rock. There's so much good stuff out now. How about you? Do you only like soul music?"

"Pretty much. I can't take that hard, acid rock stuff. Led Zeppelin and all that."

"What about Hendrix?"

"He's black but he plays for a white audience. Blacks don't listen to him," Vicky explained.

They went silent for a moment. Listening to any one kind of music exclusively was not Reggie's style. He liked to mix his music with a variety of genres.

"So, Reggie, where do we go from here?" she asked.

"Donnie's staying at my house, so we can't go there. I was hoping we might be able to use your apartment this time."

Vicky laughed. "I was talking long term, not just tonight. You are a horny honky, aren't you?"

"Well, yeah, I am." Reggie answered honestly.

"My roommate is there so I'm afraid my apartment is out anyway. But to my original question. Where do we go from here?"

Reggie fidgeted in his chair. "I hadn't really thought about it. I'm just happy to have made some connection with you; to have made love to you. I don't know what the future holds."

Vicky stopped smiling and sighed.

"Reggie, would you take me home to meet your parents?"

Reggie sat silently for a moment, considering her question.

"I hadn't thought about it. If we got real serious about each other, I guess I would have to. It would be…strained. They're not KKK type bigots, mind you, but they would worry about what kind of life their mixed race grandchildren would have. That's how they would frame their reluctance to have me get serious with someone not white. But, is that where you see us going?"

"Well, what do you want? Just to fuck me a few times and then move on?"

"Like I said, I hadn't really thought about it."

"And that's the problem. Let me ask you this. Could you come home with me, stay in Watts at my parents' house, hang out with me there? Would you feel comfortable with Sam and his friends? Could you listen to nothing but soul music all day long? That's part of my world, you know. I'm not going to abandon it."

"Look, Vicky, I like you. I like you a lot. We made love once, but I don't remember making any promises to you. Why are you pushing this so quickly?"

"Because I either push it now or push it after we've screwed a few more times, either way the question will still be there."

Reggie got a puzzled look on his face.

"Are you," he paused, "dumping me?"

"Yes, I guess so," she answered quietly. "I, like most women, need commitment."

"But you didn't need commitment the other night when you pounded on my door. Why did you come to me, what did you want?" he asked.

"Actually, you never asked me what I wanted. I asked you what you wanted, and you told me. At the time, that's what I wanted, too. So I took off my clothes and climbed into your bed."

"Now I'm confused. You want commitment, but the other night you only wanted sex. You're not making sense."

"Reggie, when do people's love relationships ever make sense? My hormones were raging, just like yours. I wanted to try a white guy and I've had a crush on you since I first saw you. It was a little bit of excitement, something exotic. And I enjoyed it. But we're not going to stay together. You'll fuck me a few more times and then go back to Santa Monica. Then, I needed sex. Now, I need more. Apparently, you can't give that."

"I can't promise anything, that's true. Wow, one great night of carnal pleasure, and you dump me. Unreal."

"Isn't that what you guys do all the time?"

Early during the second game of the lacrosse season, the action was a harbinger of what was to come in future games. Ben was loose for a fast break, sprinting from the centerline with nobody ahead of him. The UCLA goalie knew what he had to do. He came out of the goal straight at Ben, trying to give him no angle for a shot into a now open net. The distance between them closed quickly. Ben tried to shoot, the ball bounced off the goalie's chest, and the goalie slammed into Ben all at the same time. The ball rolled free and was scooped up by a Bruin. The scoring opportunity was lost. They would not get as good a one as that for the rest of the game.

Ben came out of the game, limping. He refused to go back in. Reggie called a time out.

"Lance, you gotta play attack for Ben. Ryan, grab a middie stick and replace Lance. Where's the new guy?" Reggie asked.

"Over here, name's Ted." Someone answered.

"Okay, Ted, you play defense. You'll get a lot of playing time today." With substitutions made, they just had enough for two lines of midfielders. They would have to sub each other out frequently to keep from getting worn out. The attacks and defensemen would get no rest.

When he was in the game, all Reggie could think of was hitting people. These were his former teammates, he knew all but the new players. And every chance he got he leveled somebody. He, himself, was hit hard a couple of times. But he played with an intensity he never knew he had. He fought tenaciously for every ground ball, challenged every pass, blew through every screen. By the end of the game, the Bruins were avoiding him, as he had laid out at least four of five with good, clean, solid, legal hits. The kind he loved. But they lost 11-0. They were shut out. Shut outs in lacrosse never occur unless one team is way overmatched.

"Shit, Reggie," one of the UCLA players said after the game, "you were possessed or something. My ribs hurt, man, I've never seen you play like that."

Reggie smiled and shook his hand. "What else could we do? You were killing us in the score. Might as well make you pay."

The next week they had their first road game down in the LA area. This was a concern for Reggie. How many would make the effort to drive down there? He didn't want to forfeit. But they had a full team show up, and got beat anyway by the San Marino Lacrosse Club, only scoring a couple of goals.

The following Monday Reggie dropped off the game details at El Gaucho, the student newspaper and went to check the recreation office.

"Did you get your note?" the recreation director asked. Reggie walked on in to his office and sat down.

"Yeah, here it is. Oh, great, a new player. All-American no less. This should…" Just then a burly man with a thick beard came strolling into the office and plopped down into the other chair next to Reggie.

A recreation staffer had tried to stop him.

"Sir, sir, he's with someone right now."

"He'll see me. He'd better see me." With what to Reggie was an obnoxious pushiness, he stared right at the director. "You've been advertising a concert with The Strawberry Alarm Clock. Well, I'm the manager of the real Strawberry Alarm Clock and you have no deal with me. Now it's my guess the guys you've been dealing with are former members of the band but they do not have rights to the name. You need to cease and desist all advertising and immediately cancel the concert. Or face action in court."

Reggie looked at the director. He stood up, raised his hands to shoulder level with his palms out, and then turned and left the office. The Strawberry Alarm Clock issue would be far more important to the director to handle than anything dealing with lacrosse. Reggie had seen the flyers and posters for the concert as they were all over the campus. He didn't think much of Strawberry Alarm Clock though. They were a one-hit wonder. Was there anything besides "Incense and Peppermints?" He thought he remembered them having at least one more Top 40 hit, but he couldn't recall it. If he couldn't afford to see The Band, he was damn sure he wouldn't waste his money on The Strawberry Alarm Clock. He couldn't name one member of the group and he couldn't fathom how there could be a phony Strawberry Alarm Clock trying to pass themselves off as the real band to the point of doing a concert, unless there was a fight as to which group was the real band. Musically, it was much ado about not very much.

He walked out of the building and looked again at the note. Somebody named Jack Tyler wanted to sign up for lacrosse. He claimed to be an All-American from Maryland and offered his services to play and coach. Reggie was ecstatic. This could be their missing piece.

He rushed over to the fraternity house where Tyler was supposed to be staying. Walking in the front door he approached the first guy he saw.

"Is there a Jack Tyler staying here, from Maryland?"

The frat brother scratched his head. "Well, there's a John Taylor here from Maryland, if that's who you mean."

"Uh, maybe. Where is he?"

"Upstairs, third door on the left," he replied.

Reggie stood in front of the door and knocked. It wasn't closed well, and the pressure of his knock forced it open. A guy was sitting on a chair, reading a paper.

"Jack Tyler, or Taylor?"

The guy stood up. "Yeah, Tyler. What can I do for you?"

"I'm Reggie, from lacrosse. I got a note that you can play and coach and want to join the team."

"Yeah, that's right."

"Well, you're certainly welcome. We need players and we haven't had a real coach. You're an All-American, is that right?"

"Yeah," Jack answered. "But I used up my eligibility."

"We're only a club team, not varsity. Eligibility is not an issue as long as you're associated with the university as a student, faculty, or staff. Even part-time counts, I think. What position do you play?"

"Attack," he replied. Reggie had been hoping for another midfielder.

"Well," Reggie began, "here's our situation. We've got about 16 players if everybody shows up. We lost our first game to Claremont but it was close, 4-3. They scored in the last two minutes to win it. Then we got shut out by UCLA 11-0, and the other day we dropped one to San Marino Lacrosse Club 8-2."

"Shut out?" Jack asked.

"Yeah, shut out," Reggie answered. "I know, that doesn't look good. But we've got some decent players. There's two good attacks, three big and pretty good defensemen, a couple of decent midfielders, and a goalie who makes lots of saves but doesn't know what to do with the ball after he makes a save. And that's what we got. I tried to get some football players to join since it's their off season but they're afraid of the sticks. Now I'm just the organizer. I'd like you to be coach, and play, too, of course. We could sure use you. We've got next week off then we go to play the Los Angeles Lacrosse Club, probably the strongest team in the league. How about it?"

"Sure, I'm in. I'll guarantee this, there'll be no more shut outs."

Back in Lancaster, Charlie and Joe drove their cruiser along the Sierra Highway in the afternoon during the middle of their shift. Nights were still pretty cool but the days were getting warmer. They were between Palmdale and Lancaster, and looked out over the expanse of desert with the signature Joshua trees dotting the landscape.

"Charlie wouldn't you like more action than here? There so little happening out here, don't you get bored?"

"Joe, how old are you?"

"Twenty-one, why?

"Well, I'm 35. And as a cop with 15 years on the force, I'll tell you this: I like boring. Boring means nobody shooting at you; nobody trying to stab you; no domestic squabble with some spouse trying to brain you with an iron skillet. And that's just fine with me."

"Just the same, a little action would be nice," Joe said.

"Well, just wait a few years. When they finish the freeway, when 14 goes non-stop from here to LA, things will change," Charlie said.

"How so?" Joe asked.

"When that freeway gets finished, after a few years people will start moving up here from LA to live, but they'll commute back down to LA."

"No way!" Joe disagreed. "Even with the freeway it will still take an hour, an hour and 15 to get just to the San Fernando Valley. Much longer if they want to go downtown."

Charlie laughed. "Doesn't matter, they'll come. This place will grow like you wouldn't believe. Then we'll start seeing some action. Hope I'm retired by then."

They drove on silently for a few minutes.

"Can you believe that shit up in Santa Barbara?" Joe asked.

"Pretty extreme. Never thought I'd see a bank burned in America," Charlie answered. "And the crazy thing is, these kids' parents are still supporting them, sending them to college to learn. Instead, they smoke dope and burn down banks. Using their parents' money. Wonderful. You know, if something like that happens again and the Santa Barbara units can't handle it, we may be called up to the tactical force we trained for last year."

"Hey Charlie look, do you see what I see," Joe said, interrupting. "Aren't those the kids we checked out a couple of months ago?"

Charlie looked. Sure enough, standing on the side of the road holding up a sign that said "Culver City", were the kid and his girlfriend they had almost arrested previously.

"I gotta ask that kid something," Charlie said.

They pulled off the road and stopped right next to the couple. Charlie and Joe slowly got out of the car and walked up to them. As before, the girl stood close to the boy, holding on to his arm. They looked unkempt and disheveled, and looked to be wearing the same dirty clothes they had on months ago. Their hair was long and dirty looking.

"Well hello again," Charlie said. Joe just stood silently and watched. "Coming from Lone Pine?"

"Yes sir," the kid answered.

"Tell me something," Charlie began, "are you an anti-war demonstrator? I mean, do you go to anti-war marches and things? After all, you have those peace symbols on your back packs."

The kid looked nervously at Charlie. "I'm for peace. Peace is better than war."

"Really?" Charlie asked. "Well, what about World War Two? Was that wrong? Was it wrong for us to defeat the Japanese and the Nazis?"

"Well," the kid began, his nervousness increasing, "that time we were attacked. The Japanese attacked us. North Vietnam didn't attack us."

"I have to admit that's true," Charlie said. "But do we have to wait until we're actually attacked before we defend ourselves?"

"Um, I don't know. Maybe sometimes I guess," he answered.

"You think the war in Vietnam is wrong, right. You think it's immoral, right?" Charlie asked.

"Yeah, I guess," the kid answered.

"Well tell me this. Why is it wrong, why is it immoral to help people who ask for our help? Why is it bad to help them defend themselves from being taken over by force of arms and forced into a political system they don't want? What's wrong with that? Why is it wrong to try and stop the spread of a system that destroys democracy, that doesn't allow free speech, that doesn't allow anti-government demonstrations? Especially if the people ask us. Why is that wrong? Why is that bad?"

By now the kid was backing off. Charlie knew he just wanted the cops to go away. He didn't answer Charlie's question but just stood there, looking helpless and scared.

Charlie smiled and then turned to go back to the car, Joe following. They got in and took off, going on down the Sierra Highway, leaving the kids with more reasons not to get stuck hitching in the Antelope Valley.

"That was pretty weird, Charlie," Joe pointed out.

"You know," Charlie replied. "I was really hoping he'd be able to answer my questions, because I really don't get it. I don't understand why stopping communist aggression is a bad thing. Hey Joe, you're not much older than him. You're the same age as most of the war protestors. Can you explain?"

"Don't lump me in with them. It's true they're in my generation, but I'm completely alienated from all hippy types. I don't even like the music. Ever heard Janis Joplin? All she does is scream. And Jimi Hendrix? He makes electronic distortions and convinces people it's music. I listen to country: Merle Haggard, Buck Owens, Sonny James, Loretta Lynn, Tammy Wynette. Now that's real American music. And if I want to listen to a "soul brother," I just put on some Charlie Pride. And I much prefer Hee Haw to Laugh-In or those pinko Smothers Brothers. In high school, all my friends were pro-America and conservative and liked country music. I'm not like those kids out there at all."

"Can't argue with you about the music, that's for sure. I like guys who can sing; who have a real voice. Sinatra, Crosby, Como, Williams, Bennet, Cole, Mathis. Those guys belong on recordings. And I like the big bands and Broadway musicals. Now that's music. I just don't get rock and roll at all. Why do kids go for it so much? Like you say, screaming voices and screaming guitars. Doesn't make sense to me."

"What about Elvis?"

"Well, yeah, I must admit he can sing. But I don't think of him as a rocker, at least not these days. Now I don't care too much for that country stuff you like either. Too many empty beer cans on the table as some guy sings about his lost love with as much twang as he can muster."

"Hey, hey," Joe said, chuckling, "don't put down my music now. And I still don't get what you were doing with those kids back there."

"Well," Charlie continued, "I still wish he'd answered my questions about Vietnam and the anti-war movement, because I really want to know."

Meanwhile, back in Isla Vista, Reggie was working the phones. "Hi, this is Reggie. Just wanted to remind you that we have practice coming up on Monday and Wednesday. Finals are over so I expect everybody to show. We have a coach who also plays attack now, so things are looking up. Please try to make it, okay? See ya later." Reggie hung up the phone. It was now part of his ritual.

"There you go again, 'Reggie from lacrosse, Reggie from lacrosse'." Trent mimicked him.

"I don't have to say I'm from lacrosse anymore because they all know me now. And I'll keep calling everybody until the season is over. I lost a chance at a summer league flag football championship in high school once because I didn't work the phones before a game. We played short handed and lost. Some of these guys might not show up to a game or practice, but it won't be because they don't have the details."

"How much do you think you've called? Shit, Reg, you've been doing it since November at least."

"I don't know. A lot."

Just then the front door opened and Donnie came in, followed by Rebecca. He walked into the living room, stood in the middle of the floor, and raised his hands in triumph.

"I'm here to announce my grades are okay. They're all in and I have, get this, a 3.0 for the quarter," he proclaimed.

"Way to go, Don," Reggie said, "howdja do it?"

"Well I…went to class more and I…turned in all my work and I…did the reading and I…studied for tests. Just like you told me to."

"And what about the movement, the war and all that?" Trent asked.

"Oh, I still was involved, you know that from the night of the bank burning. But you see, I'm actually kinda smart. I got pretty good grades in high school. And with my wonderful draft lottery number, I just can't take a chance of probation and dismissal. Don't even want to think about it. So I refocused a little and made better use of my time."

"Whatever it takes. Now you'll be around to help your friends stop the war," Reggie said.

"Yeah, far out," Donnie said. "What about you, Reg, whadja get?"

"Three more 'B's" he answered. "I'm not exactly knockin' em dead but I'm hangin' in there. Still have my 3.0, still eligible for oral exams."

"Don't you have to do a thesis for a master's?" Trent asked.

"No, they explained they didn't want students spending years trying to finish a thesis to get the master's. They'd rather have them get the master's quickly then spend the time on a Ph.D. dissertation. Fine with me. This next quarter will be my last for at least a good while. No Ph.D. for me," Reggie explained.

"That's good, I guess. I still have my 4.0, but I did get an A- in one class," Trent said.

They all looked at him in disgust.

"Hey Trent," Reggie said rather loudly. "What's the album of the month? Come on, Mr. 4.0 Oil Magnate, lay it on us. What have you bought lately?"

"Well, gee Reg. Donnie cooks and I buy albums for us to listen to. What are you good for?"

"Keeping everybody sane and on track. It's just a gift I have," Reggie said in all seriousness. "Like, if I'da been here, they never would have bought the monkey."

At that, Trent, Donnie, and Rebecca all cracked up.

"You worthless piece of shit, Reg," Trent said, "you provide bullshit, and that's all."

"Somebody has to. Come on, Trent, stop screwing around and enlighten us with some great new sound. I'll even provide this," he held up a joint.

"Now you're talking. Light that up and I will give you a treat for your ears." He disappeared into his room and soon emerged with a new album still in the shrink rap. "This," he said proudly, "is a brand new Van Morrison album called 'Moondance'."

"Van Morrison," Reggie said, thinking, "wasn't he the lead singer of Them and didn't he do 'Brown Eyed Girl' a few years ago?"

"Yup," Trent answered as he fit the album on the turntable," that's him."

The joint went around and the music started. It was a great album. The title cut was nicely long and painted such a great image of dancing in the moonlight. "Into the Mystic" took them someplace, but Reggie wasn't sure where. "These Dreams of You" had a wonderful feel to it. He fell in love with Morrison's voice. He had smoothed it out considerably since "Gloria" with Them but the raspy quality was still there when he needed it.

"Van Morrison," Reggie said, "not to be confused with Jim."

"No, but hey," Trent said, "they're both pretty good."

Chapter Eight

APRIL 1970: The Mysterious Player-Coach, Helpless in I.V., and Rioting Again.

Music albums making the charts:
Sonny James—It's Just a Matter of Time
Crosby, Stills, Nash, and Young—Déjà Vu
Isaac Hayes—The Isaac Hayes Movement
Joni Mitchell—Ladies of the Canyon

One more quarter to go in his academic career. Enough was enough. Reggie realized now they were going to give him all 'B's.' That's okay. His last three classes should be interesting enough. *International Relations*, *International Politics*, and *National Security Policy* were the three last seminar classes leading up to his final exams. This should be right up his alley. He'd gotten a fuckin' 'B' in law from Palmer. That shouldn't have happened. Why had law been so easy at UCLA and difficult here? Oh well.

His teachers, except for the one on security policy, were somewhat nondescript. Edwards taught one of the classes. He was oaky but nothing with lightning bolts of inspiration or insight. He kept forgetting the name of the other professor. But a special guest instructor named Harrison from an LA think tank was there for the security policy class. That was enjoyable. The obvious topic, of course, was Vietnam. It was enough to make up for Vicky being in the class. She had been cordial to him, but not warm. He still wanted to fuck her again.

"It's very easy to construct all kinds of arguments based on history or economics or perceived morality or even ethnicity to justify or condemn the war in Vietnam. Believe me, you can do either one. But the most important issue, and the only issue the United States government should consider, indeed is obligated to consider above and before all others, is the effect the war has on national security. Are we improving national security by being in Vietnam, or are we weakening it? In terms of the duty of the President and Congress, nothing else matters. Mind you, we have to take in consideration all the effects on surrounding countries, our allies in Europe, other communist countries, other liberation movements, and our reputation if we abandon a perceived beneficiary of our obligations," Harrison said.

Vicky raised her hand. "Does security policy," she asked, "take into account domestic fallout from the war? What if it is so disruptive of society that society breaks apart? Doesn't that affect national security?"

"Indeed it does, that's all part of the mix, but only a part. The government must decide which is more of a threat to the nation: continuing the policy that's causing social unrest, or ending it and dealing with all the consequences from that."

"It's the LSD war," Reggie chimed in and then wished he hadn't.

Vicky's question had been so good he had to jump in with something.

"Excuse me, what do you mean, LSD war?" Harrison asked.

"Well, LSD is a lot about colors. And in Vietnam it seems like we got black and brown people going over to fight yellow people to help the white people defend the land they stole from the red people." There were a few chuckles from the students. Vicky just looked at him and shook her head.

"That's very interesting, Mr. Blake. I'm not sure what it has to do with the point we were discussing, but interesting."

Reggie wanted to crawl into a hole. How long would it take him to repair the damage he had just done? And he really liked the class.

In their next game, the Los Angeles Lacrosse Club went easy on them. They only won 17-0. Another shut out. Tyler was pissed. He threw his stick down and glared at Reggie.

"I've never been shut out in my life," he said angrily.

Reggie shrugged. "We just played the best team in the league. We can improve; I know it."

Two of the LA players walked up to them. "Where's the Maryland guy, Tyler?" one asked.

"That's me," Tyler said. He shook hands with the two guys and smiled. They began to talk about players for Maryland, Hopkins, and other eastern college teams looking, Reggie assumed, for mutual friends. He moved away and began bagging up the equipment to load in the Ford and head back to Santa Barbara. As he was loading up, one of the LA players walked up to him.

"Hey, man, good game. You'll get better."

"Yeah, thanks. I was hoping with Tyler's help—we just got him you know—we would be more competitive," Reggie said.

The LA player stood there for a minute, a conflicted expression on his face.

"Something wrong?" Reggie asked.

"Well, I'm not sure," the LA player answered. "The guy you call Tyler, well he's decent enough with the stick, but he's not the Jack Tyler I played against in college. I'm pretty sure of that. Just be careful."

"Okay, thanks," Reggie said, wondering what it all meant.

The following Monday, Tyler sent everybody home from practice except Russ, the goalie. He spent a full hour working with him, shooting high, shooting low, moving back and forth across the crease. Shot after shot. Then, he made Russ come out of the goal and look to make a pass. Reggie checked on them a couple of times and they were still at it, then he waited until they finally finished.

Tyler came up to him. "Okay, we got a goalie now. He'll be okay. On Wednesday, I'll work with the attacks. We're gonna have an extra man play, we need one."

"What about everybody else?" Reggie asked.

"I can only do so much," Jack answered, "but I'll need them anyway. We'll scrimmage some. Who's our next game?"

"Temple City here this week, then we're at UCLA next week."

"Unh," he grunted and then walked away.

Reggie was becoming more and more uncomfortable with Tyler. He seemed never satisfied, never happy. He wondered what was churning in him.

At the girls' house, Joyce was animated.

"Have you heard?" She said excitedly. "The Beatles broke up. Paul says he's leaving the group. Can you believe it? The most successful band in history and they're throwing it all away."

Reggie sat at the dining area table with Joyce, Sandy, and John. Joyce had a cigarette in her hand, as usual. John was smiling again.

"What do you expect?" Reggie said. "They've got too much talent. I'm surprised they stayed together as long as they did. They always disagreed on what to do, how to arrange tunes, all that good stuff. Then you add Yoko Ono to the mix, and, well, you see what happens."

"It's still sad," Sandy offered. "I hope they get back together. Maybe they will, I mean, maybe they'll each make some solo albums then get back together every five years or so to make a Beatles album. That would be cool, actually."

"I don't know," Reggie said, "there's a lot of bitterness between them. They weren't getting along at all lately, according to what I heard. It'll take them a while to feel like working together again."

"And to think," John added, "they recorded 'Abbey Road' during all this strife."

"Yeah," Reggie agreed. "That is pretty amazing."

The front door opened and Maureen and Janice came in.

"Hey guys, we got the new CSNY album," Janice announced.

"'Y'?" Reggie asked. "Who's 'Y'?"

"Neil Young. He joined them you know," Janice answered.

"Yeah, that makes sense. He and Stills were in the Buffalo Springfield together. I guess they're still buddies," Reggie reasoned.

They all moved up to the living room and the album, "Déjà Vu", was quickly put on the stereo. The songs flowed from the album, with clean guitar work, both acoustic and electric, and wonderful harmonies. Neil Young seemed to flesh out their vocals more and his writing definitely added to the richness of the album. Nash's "Teach Your Children" was wonderful and more than made up for "Marakesh Express." It seemed so appropriate to the current turmoil in the country. Reggie thought about his own parents and how much they helped him, loved him, and were always there for him. He was also particularly taken with Young's song "Helpless." The images reached down into his soul.

Rather than a town in north Ontario, it could be a student ghetto in southern California. In fact, he knew it really was that; it was really Isla Vista. And all his feelings for the place and the people and the events of that school year seemed to be reflected in the images of that song. Indeed, when thinking about the year, he was left helpless.

They listened to more albums and talked some more until one by one the girls began drifting off to bed except for Joyce, who left to see her boyfriend down the block. Soon, only Janice and Reggie were in the living room. Reggie noticed that Janice was drinking hard liquor again. Rum and cokes this time. She was more than a little woozy, sitting next to him on the couch and getting very friendly. She was also wearing that Asian robe again. He wondered what, if anything, she had on underneath. From the way her boobs were jiggling with every slight movement, he figured at least she wasn't wearing a bra.

"So," she asked suddenly, "how's your love life?"

Reggie looked at her with mild surprise.

"Oh, hit and miss, I suppose. Mostly miss. How about you?"

As if to answer, she leaned over and kissed him. Reggie returned the kiss and they began to make out. He tasted the rum, which was nice. But also the tobacco, which was not. But he very quickly got hard and began fondling her breasts. They continued to make out, tongues fencing with each other, taking turns in each other's mouths. This time, he had a rubber. This time, they would finish what she started. This time, he would become her lover. He knew it. He had it right in his hand.

Things were getting pretty hot and heavy. Janice was yielding to his every move. Then, they heard the front door start to come open and they stopped. In came Joyce who ignored them and began to head down the hall toward the room she shared with Janice.

"Hey Joyce," Janice called, "could you please put that cat box outside. I really can't stand the smell."

Joyce stopped and came back to look up into the living room.

"You don't like my cat?" she said with some anger.

"C'mon Joyce, it's just the smell of the litter. All her piss and shit and everything. It makes me sick, hard to sleep."

"Okay," Joyce said curtly and then turned to go. She stomped off and went into their room, slamming the door.

"Shit!" Janice said, leaning forward on the couch and putting her hands under her chin. The whole mood had been broken. She looked at Reggie and shook her head.

"Sorry Reg," she said sadly, "I've got to go make peace with Joyce. I just can't stand that cat smell. She shouldn't have a cat anyway; we're not supposed to have pets."

"At least it's not a monkey," Reggie said. "But hey, Donnie's at

Rebecca's tonight. Want to come over to my place? We can continue this absolutely undisturbed."

She sighed and slumped her shoulders. "No, I have to settle this. I have to make peace with her or it just won't work." She turned back to look at him. God but she was beautiful. He loved Asians. She kissed him again. "You better go now. I've got to take care of this."

Once again, he'd been shut out.

A couple of days later, Trent entered the front door of Windward House in somewhat of a hurry.

"Hey Reg, where's Donnie?"

"Uh, I don't know. Haven't seen him, why?"

Trent came in and plopped down on the couch, looking straight at Reggie.

"I think the shit's gonna hit the fan again down at the loop," he said with a considerable amount of resignation.

"Why?" Reggie asked, "what's the problem this time?"

"Oh, some bullshit about the university not allowing some Chicago Eight or Seven guy to speak at the football stadium."

"Yeah, that's right. Jerry Rubin was supposed to speak. What, the admin cancelled it?"

"Guess so. Anyway people are gathering in the loop again, looking at the new temporary bank building they put up. Rumor is the cops are going to enforce a curfew," Trent explained.

"Like they did last time? Good luck," Reggie said. "They should not fool around and just bring in the National Guard right away this time before things get burned, not like February when they waited until the bank was a cinder before sending in the troops."

"Point is," Trent continued, "you know Donnie's gonna be right down there in it."

"And what can we do about that? I tried pulling him out last time, didn't work."

"Do you have stash in your bedroom?" Trent asked, seemingly changing the subject.

"Well, yeah, a little, why?" Reggie asked.

"So do I. But if Donnie gets arrested, they may come down here and question us. They may search this house even. We could get royally fucked over," Trent explained.

Reggie sat for a moment, thinking about the implications.

"I, I never thought about that. I don't think arresting Donnie in and of itself would give them probable cause to search his house. Not unless he runs in here and they follow him and arrest him in the bedroom. Then they could search the bedroom, but not your rooms because he didn't go in there. The rules on searches are pretty strict."

"You think the cops will worry about that? Even if they're wrong and we get everything thrown out, it will still ruin a considerable number of our days," Trent said.

"Point taken," Reggie said.

The two sat silently for several moments.

"So, what should we do?" Reggie asked.

"We have three choices," Trent said. "Flush everything now—get rid of it all. Or take it outside and bury it. Or not worry about it and hope the cops don't come here."

Meanwhile, down at the loop, Donnie and a group of students stood in front of the new bank building, a temporary structure that was more secure than the previous building. Up on the steps of bank was another group of students: jocks, Greeks, and others opposed to the violence.

"No more!" one of them shouted at Donnie's group. "Enough! We're not gonna let you burn this bank again. We won't let it happen."

"Why are you so quick to be tools of the establishment?" one of Donnie's companions asked.

Around the loop area, as night finally fell, the scene was repeated over and over. Groups of students attacked the real estate offices and the bank, other groups of students tried to stop them. The dynamic was, to say the least, interesting.

There were hundreds in the loop again, trying to recapture the initiative and the fervor and the euphoria of the fist riot, but Donnie felt things just weren't working. The real estate offices took hits again, but the strange ballet between the pro and anti forces among the students continued late into the night, and the bank remained intact. The cops used a new tactic. They rumbled into the loop in huge dump trucks, several cops in back. They brandished rifles and hurled tear gas canisters as they deemed appropriate, and seemed, somehow, to intimidate the rioters more than before.

Donnie stood with a group of his friends near the bank. They were considering another attempt to set it on fire when two dump trucks headed for them. A gas canister flew out and the group split up and backed off. Donnie could see some commotion over in front of the bank, but couldn't tell what was happening. Suddenly, he heard a loud crack.

"What was that?" he asked.

"Sounds like a shot!" one of his companions replied. "Shit, they're shooting at us!'

Suddenly, Donnie felt defeated. There was a saying that came to his mind: discretion is the better part of valor. That night, things just weren't going their way. It was time to retreat. He left the loop area and headed for Rebecca's apartment. A couple of times he had to duck behind a parked car or a bush as the dump trucks continued rolling through the streets near the loop. Finally he got far enough away and made it to Rebecca's place without any more incidents.

In Lancaster, Charlie and Joe relaxed in Charlie's living room, living the American dream middle class lifestyle.

"You really got it good, here, Charlie," Joe said, sipping his beer as he leaned back on the couch. "Really good. Beautiful wife, great kids, good house, you also love your job. What more could you ask for?"

"Can't deny any of that. It wasn't easy, though. I wanted to be a cop since I was 12 years old. I just kept my focus on that desire. Couldn't wait to graduate from high school and get into the Academy. You know what makes it all work? Susie. Without her, I couldn't do it. She's always there for me. She's my best friend, my ally, my supporter, and, of course, she sleeps with me. Knowing she's here waiting for me is one of the main things that keeps me from doing something stupid in the field. I got to come home to her."

"Yeah, I know I'll want to get married someday. But how do you find the right woman? How do you find a woman that will put up with all the hours we have to work at any time of day? So many cops get divorced."

"Don't give up, Joe. You'll find one. Just keep looking and be choosy. Make sure they realize what they're in for from the beginning. And let them know if they stick with it, it can really pay off."

Charlie stood up and went to the sliding glass door that led to the back yard. There he saw Tommy and Stevie playing together in the tree house. They were laughing and happy. He smiled to himself.

On that same weekend at the UCLA campus, Reggie stood near the lacrosse field sideline, speaking to the team.

"Okay, guys. First, thanks for drivin' down. I know things back in I.V. are pretty crazy right now, but think of lacrosse as our escape and therapy," Reggie said. There were a few chuckles from the group. "Where's Perry?" Reggie asked as he looked over the team.

"He told me he's quitting. Said he's tired of losing," Dominic said.

Reggie's heart sank. "Damn. Well, okay. Ryan, we need you at midfield today. Okay, Jack?" Reggie asked their player-coach.

"Unhh," Tyler grunted, seemingly disinterested.

The rematch against UCLA, played on the UCLA campus, started auspiciously enough. Once again, Ben broke out on a fast break ahead of everyone. Again, the goalie came out after him. This time, however, Ben got the shot off and avoided a collision. The ball rolled into the empty goal. Reggie was overjoyed. They were actually leading 1-0.

But it didn't last. Methodically, UCLA began to pile up the goals. By the end of the first quarter, it was 4-1. In the second quarter, the Gauchos got a chance to use the extra man play Tyler had devised. Ben and Jim both stood right in front of the crease. This was confusing to opposing teams. Reggie had never seen the formation before. Normally, on an extra man play, the defense goes into a zone and the offense passes the ball around the perimeter trying to exploit the seams of the zone for a good shot. By putting two attacks right on the crease, Tyler's scheme would seem to cancel out the extra man advantage as the crease defenseman could guard both. However, Tyler had Ben and Jim keep setting back screens on the defenseman and curling around each other. Meanwhile, he was behind the goal, bobbing and weaving in that odd style of his. Suddenly, either Jim or Ben would pop open for a split second. That was all Tyler needed as he would flip a feed perfectly on the money. The first time they tried it, Jim scored. The next time, he almost scored as the ball bounced off the goalie's chest. Then, in the third quarter, Jim scored again on the play, but it only brought the score to 10-3.

The issue was not in doubt. UCLA would win. Reggie was playing midfield. It wasn't an extra man situation, but Tyler had the ball behind the goal and Reggie was in front and to the right. The UCLA coach had changed goalies to give his back up some work. The starting goalie came out and played midfield, assigned to guard Reggie.

"Hey, Reggie, how ya doin'?" he asked. Reggie didn't answer. The UCLA goalie, now temporary midfielder, turned his head to look over his right shoulder at the goal and see where the ball was. Immediately, Reggie broke for the goal. His defender let out an "oh shit!" and seemed to slip down a little. Reggie broke clear. He was right there, open, running in at the goal. Tyler, almost without looking, faked his defenseman and fed a pass right at Reggie. It was beautiful. Time stopped. The ball hung there, a perfect feed. Reggie was moving toward it, the ball was coming toward Reggie. In less than a second, it would hit the netting of his stick. A quick flip of the wrist and he would put the ball in the upper right corner of the goal. Barring an unreal save by the second string goalie, it would go in. It was going to happen. He was going to score a goal, and against his former teammates to boot.

But right when the ball was to hit his stick, Reggie's defender caught up with him and slammed his stick down on Reggie's and the ball sailed past the two of them. Tyler swore in frustration. Reggie's best chance to score a goal in his entire lacrosse career had come and gone. He would never get another. The game ended 12-3.

It was a few days later and the three roommates were in their living room. The mood was somber. "Didja hear, Reg?" Donnie asked. "The cops finally admitted one of their guys fired the shot that killed that kid. And all along they said some 'sniper' had done it. They even had the balls to release a description of this 'sniper.' And it was their guy all along. And nothing is happening to him. No charges, no fine, not even getting fired from the police department."

"I heard he claimed his rifle went off accidentally," Reggie said.

Donnie looked at him in disbelief. He didn't say anything, but just kept looking at Reggie.

"Okay, okay," Reggie finally spoke. "I don't believe that either. But if that cop has any conscience at all, it's gonna bother him the rest of his life."

"Maybe," Donnie said, "especially considering the kid was at the bank trying to put OUT a fire, not start one. He was opposed to the demonstrators. I think he was one of the guys standing in front of the bank telling me and some other guys to get lost. The cops went and killed one of their supporters, one of their sympathizers. If that isn't fucked, I don't know what is."

"You know," Trent said, "I'm sick of this shit. We're supposed to be having a great time. This is paradise. Look at that view. Look at that beach. Look at all the chicks around here. We got good dope. We got great music. I want to go to school and party. I don't need to run around, burn banks, and get shot by cops."

"Man, his poor parents," Reggie said. "They've got to be really hurting right now. Send their kid to school and he comes home in a box. Might as well have gone to Vietnam."

"One of my cousins died in a car crash when he was only 17. My uncle never got over it," Reggie explained.

"I'm just sick of this shit. It's been such a good year. Damn it!" Trent said. Reggie had never seen him this upset.

"Well, I'm going to the Laundromat down in Goleta. Anybody want to come along?" Reggie asked.

Alone, Reggie went through his laundry ritual. There was only one other couple with their baby in the place, so he was able to find enough machines to get all his clothes started at the same time. Feeling friendly, he decided to start up a conversation.

"Do you guys live in I.V.?" he asked.

"No," the man replied, holding his baby on his shoulder. "We live down Hollister a bit in Goleta."

"Just as good. Things in I.V. have been pretty crazy lately, what with all the riots, cops, and National Guard," Reggie noted.

"It doesn't matter," the guy said. "I've given my life to Christ and I know a better life is coming, and coming soon. This entire world will pass away, so it really doesn't matter."

Reggie looked at him wearily. All the signs were there. Clean cut. The man was ridiculously clean cut. His wife was blonde, prim, and proper looking. They looked like they stepped out of a small town in Iowa, not a college town in southern California.

"Really," Reggie said, and then went to check one of the machines he was using. Mercifully, the guy did not attempt to continue the conversation. He had made a pitch to witness, and Reggie had walked away, so the man left him alone. Reggie wished more of them would be like that. He did feel thankful, though, that the fundamentalist, born again, evangelical Christians cared so little about the real world that they rarely voted. If they ever woke up and got their act together to vote in numbers, the country would be in real trouble.

Chapter Nine

MAY 1970: Nudity, a Lacrosse Victory at Last, and Jerry Rubin's Blather

Music albums making the charts:

The Beatles—Let It Be
Eric Burdon and War—Eric Burdon Declares War
Miles Davis—Bitch's Brew
The Fifth Dimension—Portrait; Greatest Hits
Jimi Hendrix—Band of Gypsies
Jethro Tull—Benefit
Paul McCartney—McCartney
Elvis Presley—Let's Be Friends
Three Dog Night—It Ain't Easy
The Who—Live at Leeds

"Hey Reggie, Trent, check it out, down at the beach by El Embarcadero," Donnie began as he came into the house.

"Yeah, what?" Reggie asked.

"They're having a nude-in," Donnie said.

"A what?" Reggie asked.

"A nude-in. People are getting naked on the beach. Some of them are already there," Donnie explained.

"Why didn't I hear about this? I mean, sometimes I think I don't even go to this school. All kinds of shit happens and I never know about it until later. People burning banks and getting naked and having demonstrations…" Reggie trailed off.

"Don't feel bad. I usually hear about these things, but I missed this one. Thank you, Donnie. I think I'll wrap a towel around me and walk along the beach till I get there," Trent said.

"So, you gonna let it all hang out?" Reggie asked.

"Sure. Need to do some prospecting anyway," he answered. "What about you, Reg?"

"I think I'll just go down on my bike and watch. Should be interesting. Donnie?"

"Saw a little bit already. Not that exciting, but go ahead and check it out."

Reggie got on his bike and headed for El Embarcadero, the street that connected Del Playa to the loop. In a few minutes, he got there, found a good vantage point, and looked down at the beach. Right there, right where he and Donnie usually smoked a joint before walking around the loop, were about 200 people. And they were naked. He looked over the crowd, but didn't recognize many. Of course, the ratio of guys to girls was about 10 to 1. So, he saw a lot of dicks, but very few pussies. Still, he was able to pick out a couple of girls who had really nice bodies. One he remembered from a girls' intramural flag football game. She could really throw the football. Her breasts were rather large and stuck out from her chest much like footballs, all firm and not at all yielding to the law of gravity.

Every once in a while he saw a crowd gathered around in a circle looking down at the sand and chanting, encouraging something to continue. He could only guess that a couple was fucking. Then he saw Trent. The towel was now draped over his shoulder and he was otherwise naked. Sure enough, after only a few minutes, he was talking to one of the prettiest girls there. She was tall, seemed to be all legs, had long blonde hair, and medium sized but very nicely shaped boobs. She was gorgeous, a real knockout. To top it off, her bush was blonde, too, so unless she took the unusual measure of dying her pubic hair, she had her proof that she was a natural blonde.

As he watched them, he began to crack up. The statuesque beauty and Trent stood talking to each other as if they were at a dorm dance. As if it was perfectly normal to stand around naked and talk to members of the opposite sex. He could just imagine the conversation. "What's your major?" Or even worse: "What's your sign?" But there they were, gesturing with their hands and talking up a storm. And completely naked.

Reggie was still watching Trent and the girl who was an excellent candidate for number 47 when the helicopters arrived. They hovered over the beach and began filming the naked throng. Someone threw a Frisbee and it almost hit the tail rotor of one of the choppers. They both pulled up and away from the crowd, and Reggie decided it was time to go back home.

The next day Reggie and Donnie sat on the deck, looking at the water."Donnie, why did you guys trash the student center cafeteria? I like to eat there sometimes. What was that all about?"

"There was a demonstration behind the student center, on the lawns by the lagoon, with speakers talking about Kent State. Some in the audience got a little carried away and broke into the cafeteria. You did hear about Kent State, I assume, four dead students?"

"Yeah, I heard. But how is trashing the cafeteria going to help? And now they want to cancel classes for a week and do some seminars about the Cambodia invasion and Kent State. Waste of time. And were you with that group who went to the freeway?"

"Yup. You shoulda been there, Reggie. Four thousand of us and we shut down 101. Stopped traffic completely."

"Thereby accomplishing....?"

"Okay, Reggie, stay on the sidelines. There'll come day when you will wish you had been part of things."

They stopped talking and looked at the view, gorgeous as usual.

"It's a nice day," Reggie said.

"Yes it is," Donnie agreed.

Back in class, Reggie was feeling inspired. "Professor Harrison," Reggie asked, "a few weeks ago we were talking about how national security was the most important job of the government. Considering some of the things that have gone on both here on campus and in Isla Vista, what happens if the steps the government takes to protect national security end up infringing on our Constitutional rights?"

"Now that's a very good question and indeed a conundrum for presidents and others involved in national security. The president takes an oath to preserve, protect, and defend the Constitution of the United States. One can assume from this that doing anything to diminish or infringe on the rights contained in the Constitution would not be allowed. Trouble is, we as a nation don't always agree on just what those rights are. During World War II, Americans of Japanese decent lost almost all their rights, not to mention their property and livelihoods. Was it necessary for the war effort to put them in camps? That's arguable. Should we ever be willing to give up those Constitutional rights in exchange for security? Some would argue yes, some no."

"But sir, if we protect the country but destroy our rights doing it, what have we preserved? America is great because of those rights. Those are the rights communist countries and right wing dictatorships don't have. If we lose them in the name of protecting ourselves, in a sense, you could say our enemies have won."

"Mr. Blake, that is a debate that will have no end."

Other students joined in the discussion, and it became a lively one. Reggie could tell that Harrison was eating it up. He really liked getting the students involved in discussion, challenging their assumptions, letting them articulate their thoughts. He was a natural teacher, and UCSB, or at least the poli sci department of UCSB, had done a great job in finding him and getting him to teach a class.

Vicky joined him as they left the class.

"Not bad, Reg. I think you made up for that LSD thing," she said.

"Damn I hope so. But I bet I still get a 'B'. That's all I'll ever get."

"You sound resigned to it," she said.

"Well, at least it's what I need. As far as grades go, I mean."

"Meaning there's something else you need?" she asked.

"Yeah. You."

She sighed. "Full time permanent or temporary?"

It was Reggie's turn to sigh. "Damn it, girl, why can't we just enjoy the moment?"

"Live for today and all that hippy shit?" she asked.

"Why not?"

By that time the elevator door opened and they walked through the main floor lobby area and out onto the campus.

"Look, Reggie, I like you. I do. You do turn me on. But my world is different from yours. And it really doesn't overlap as much as you think. I thought I showed you that. It won't work for us later, so might as well stop now."

He turned to face her. "All I can think of is that you gave me the greatest night of lovemaking I've ever experienced in my 22 years. I just don't see what's wrong with enjoying ourselves a few more times before circumstances separate us permanently."

He looked hard into her eyes, begging her with his. She stopped, held her breath for a moment, then broke eye contact, looked away, and finally exhaled.

"Damn it. Reggie, you're good, you almost got me. I had fun, too, that night. But, believe me what I'm doing is the best thing for me. Maybe not for you, but I have to look out for myself. Besides, I'm seeing someone now. And, yes, he's black."

Reggie turned back and resumed walking. "Well, okay then. Hope you're happy and all that. At least I got a fantastic memory. My bike's up here, I gotta go."

"Bye," she said.

"Bye," he said as he mounted his bike and rode off.

The nude-in along with warmer weather had sparked a spontaneous movement of people going naked on the beaches just west of Isla Vista. Except at El Embarcadero, the beach in front of the cliff line was fairly narrow, but just past Windward House the beach widened out a lot, then narrowed again going around Devereux point and the Magic Forest, then opened up again with the sand dunes stretching out a mile or more. There were steps for beach access right next to Windward House, and Reggie took to taking walks in the early afternoon when the beach still had a smattering of people.

More than half the females were sunbathing in the nude. Reggie would check them out as unobtrusively as possible. Most would smile and wave. Everybody smiled and waved in I.V., and Reggie would smile and wave back. Once at the dunes, the more secluded part of the beach, he would frequently see naked girls frolicking in the surf. That was always interesting. And, of course, every once in a while the cops would come and arrest people for indecent exposure. Reggie didn't know who complained. He sure hadn't.

The thought that bothered him was his own lack of, of "it." Why couldn't he pick up girls like Trent could? What had Trent said? He went to the nude-in to do some prospecting. That girl he met there had become number 47. And if he bothered, he could probably take the same walk on the beach Reggie was taking, and go home with the girl of his choosing. Damn. If Reggie had that power, his life would be complete.

He'd made love to Tammy and Vicky, but missed out on Maureen and Janice for the weirdest of reasons. In addition there were three other girls he'd picked up only to have them turn down his advances later. One was a skinny hippy chick he picked up in the donut shop, one was a girl he met on campus sitting on the grass by the lagoon behind the student center, and one he picked up at a party. In all cases, he had promising starts, but got nowhere with any of them. Trent would have fucked them all. Life wasn't fair. And why did he keep hanging around the girls' house then? Maybe because he still had a shot at Janice.

"I need to talk to you Reggie," Janice said while letting him in the door.

They went out on the deck and Reggie had this foreboding in his gut.

"Now," she began, "I know we almost did something again the other night. I do like you, Reg, but I gotta stop doing things with you; I gotta stop making out with you and almost fucking you."

"Why?" he asked sternly. "You owe me an explanation at least."

She looked away from him and folded her arms across her chest. It was late afternoon, but daylight savings had kicked in and the sun wouldn't be setting for a while, so the evening crowd of sunset watchers hadn't assembled in the area between the houses. He looked down on her. She was so petite, so tiny, but had such a dynamite bod. He could envision himself making love to her standing up, holding up her tiny body impaled on his dick. She wouldn't weigh anything at all.

"When you first came over here, the first time you visited us, I told you I didn't have a boyfriend," she began.

"Shit, here it comes," Reggie whispered.

Janice turned and looked at him. A tear was in her eye, spilled out of the corner, and rolled down her cheek.

"That was the truth, really it was," she said, choking up. "But I did have a boyfriend before; we just broke up when I came here.

Well," she hesitated.

"Go on," Reggie requested.

"I've gone home three times this year, and the last time we got back together again. He's gonna join me here for the summer. I'm sorry, Reg. But I gotta stay away from you. I like you too much."

"Wait a minute, wait a minute," Reggie said. "What about the first time we almost made love? You got off as I recall, and I was left hanging. Why did you push me away after that? You hadn't decided to get back with your boyfriend at that time."

"No, you're right. But I was still carrying the torch for him. And I do have a problem when I drink too much. I do things I don't really want to do, like let you make love to me with your hand."

"Well, if you ask me, you do things you really want to do," Reggie pointed out.

"Okay, yeah maybe. There is a part of me that wants to make love to you real bad, and a part of me that says that would be wrong for various reasons, boyfriend or no. You don't need me anyway because I'm pretty sure you've been with other girls while you've been up here. And I just think it would be better for me if I stayed away from you."

With that she hugged him quickly, holding him very tight, then dropped her arms, pushed away, and went back into the house. Reggie stayed out on the deck, watching a pelican turn and dive like a plane that stalled out, rolled over, and crashed into the sea. He wondered if the bird had caught anything.

Down in the desert, Charlie was in the back yard, standing at his barbecue, nursing the steaks. Joe stood nearby, beer in hand. Susie and Veronica, a young friend of hers, were in the kitchen and Charlie's kids were out playing somewhere. The weather had warmed up considerably over the last few weeks. Summer would soon be on them along with its triple digit temperatures. But right now was the perfect time. Life was good. The steaks would soon be done and they could eat their meal outdoors as the soft desert night enveloped the valley.

"Things are getting real dicey," Joe said.

"In what way?" Charlie asked.

"Well, there was another riot up at Santa Barbara last month, and a kid was killed by a cop. Then there were the Kent State shootings, with four students killed. Finally, there was Jackson State, with the cops shooting two students dead in their dorm rooms. Is it happening? Is this a revolution or something?"

"I think it's just the inevitable consequence of an ever escalating clash between the government and the anti-war demonstrators. It's not at all a good thing, Joe. It could get much uglier."

"Yeah, hey, did you hear about that one demonstration in New York, where the hard hat construction workers attacked the peace marchers? Beat the shit out of a bunch of them."

"Look, I, as much as anybody, hate the anti-war demonstrators. I mean, what is the big reason for the current spate of demonstrations? The invasion of Cambodia. And why did we invade Cambodia? Because the Viet Cong and the North Vietnamese use Cambodian territory to get away from our troops. Hell, the Ho Chi Minh Trail goes right through both Laos and Cambodia. In Korea, we couldn't chase Chinese planes across the Yalu River. That was stupid. And it would be stupid now not to go into Cambodia right after those bastards. Who knows, maybe we can find their main headquarters and take them out and end the fuckin' war," Charlie said. He reached down with his fork and flipped the steaks. "Still, as much as they piss me off, we shouldn't be shooting the demonstrators. That won't accomplish anything."

"Well, if there's any more trouble in Santa Barbara, we'll probably be called in. And maybe we won't shoot them, but it sure would feel nice to crack some heads and kick some ass," Joe said.

"Maybe it won't come to that," Charlie said. "But I could see myself feeling real good about messing some of them up. And that feeling bothers me."

Just then Susie and Veronica came out of the house with plates of food. "Check her out, Joe," Charlie whispered. "She may be the one."

"Sure is pretty enough, that's for sure," Joe answered.

Joe, slightly nervous, moved quickly to help, taking a heavy plate from Veronica as she smiled sweetly at him. For a few hours, they forgot about Santa Barbara.

Back in Isla Vista, this would be it. Their last game, their last chance to get a win. They were at the soccer field, the same place they had lost to Claremont 4-3 in their first game. But it was sunny and dry, unlike the Claremont game, perfect weather for lacrosse. They would be playing against one of the weakest teams in the league, the San Fernando Valley Lacrosse Club. Looking over their players as they warmed up on the field, Reggie noticed they seemed to be either older men in their 40s or young kids maybe still in high school. They would be playing against a father-son team.

"Okay, gather round," Reggie called to the players. "Jack, got any last minute instructions?"

"It's John," the former Maryland player said.

"What?" asked Reggie.

"My name's John, John Taylor," he answered.

"You told me your name was Tyler, Jack Tyler," Reggie countered.

"No I didn't. You musta misheard me," he replied.

"I've been calling you Jack Tyler for two months, and you only now correct me? I don't get it."

"Not my problem you can't hear," Taylor said with a scowl on his face.

Reggie just stood there, confused. He remembered clearly that he said his name was Jack Tyler, the note he had left in the recreation office said Jack Tyler, and he had even talked to the LA Lacrosse Club players as Jack Tyler. But Reggie didn't want any distractions, so he let it go.

"Well, do you have any last minute instructions?"

"No. Just everybody make good use of my feeds."

They broke to go on the field. Reggie was going to anchor the second midfield, so he wasn't starting. Dominic, the team's best midfielder, held back as the others took the field.

"Hey Reg," he said quietly. "The name thing is not all that's weird about him. He's not staying in the frat house any more. He owes them money and they found out he really wasn't a member from their Maryland chapter like he said. Who knows, maybe he didn't even go to Maryland."

"Well," Reggie replied, "he learned some good lacrosse from somewhere. And right now I don't care who he is, if he helps us win this game."

And help them he did. And make use of his feeds they did. As the game wore on, Reggie began to feel the excitement of the distinct possibility they would win. They scored twice in the first quarter and once in the second before Valley scored, and they led 5-1 at halftime. Jim had scored twice and Ben had scored once as well as Dominic and a new guy called Mike.

But Reggie was nervous. Something still could go wrong. Indeed, in the second half, Valley seemed to control possession. Russ made save after save, but finally Valley broke through to make the score 5-2. From that point, Reggie played possessed. He slammed one of the opposing players who had just caught a pass. He was young and small, but the rules say you can hit someone who has the ball. Hit him Reggie did. The kid hit the ground and coughed up the ball. Reggie got it and passed it up to clear. He turned back to see the kid still lying on the ground. The ref blew the whistle to stop the clock and a Valley player was leaning over the kid. Reggie felt a sudden panic that he may have hurt someone. He went over to check.

"Hey, you okay?" he asked.

"Yeah," the kid answered, getting up to a knee. "Had the breath knocked out of me, that's all. You hit really hard."

"This is my son," the other Valley player said.

"Sorry sir," Reggie said, "I didn't mean to hurt him."

"It's okay," the Valley player said, "I saw the hit, it was legal. He needs to learn to take those if he wants to play lacrosse."

The game continued. Another new player, Terry, got loose on a fast break and beat the goalie with a hard shot on the ground to make it 6-2. Then, Jim scored his third goal on a feed from Taylor, and

Dominic scored on a give and go from Lance. It was now 8-2. Reggie just wanted to make sure they ran out the clock. The last three minutes took forever as Valley scored once to make it 8-3. But they won the ensuing face off, Reggie picking up a ground ball and getting it to Taylor. He settled it down, keeping it away from the defenseman, until the clock ran out. Wonder of wonders, they had won.

"Yeeeeha!" Reggie screamed at the top of his lungs. He jumped in the air, threw up his arms, and yelled like a maniac. The other players were all cheering as well, everybody had a smile. Except Taylor.

"Party at Windward House but BYOB or J as the case may be," Reggie announced. Turn in all your equipment. That's it for the year. No more practice; no more games. We're done."

They all gathered around, smiling and breathing heavily. Their heavy breathing was not so much from the game but from the exhilaration they felt. It was a huge sense of relief. For Reggie, his work had not gone unrewarded.

Sandy, Maureen, Joyce, and Janice came up to him.

"Way to go, Reggie," Maureen said, giving him a hug.

"Hey, I'm all sweaty," Reggie protested. But Janice hugged him ,too. "Now this is the game I wanted you to see." The girls moved off to their car. Trent, Donnie, and Rebecca came up to him.

"Good job, Reg," Donnie said, "you finally broke into the win column. Guess it was all worth it."

"Thanks for coming, guys. Really glad you saw our only win," Reggie said. They too, after some high fives and back slaps, then left for their cars. Reggie turned to the players, still standing around, enjoying the euphoria.

"Hey Reggie," Jim asked, "who's gonna run the team next year? You'll be gone, right?"

"Yeah, I'll be gone. But Ryan and Russ will still be here, hell most of you will still be here. Someone will step up. There're plenty of you who could do what I did. Find some more players, and hey, one day you could have a really good team. I really want to thank all you guys for your dedication and for putting up with my nagging phone calls."

"Thank you Reg," somebody said from the crowd.

"I had fun, even with the losses," Dominic said. "I'm glad you kept nagging us."

"Well," Reggie said, "maybe lacrosse provided some tension relief. It's been a heavy year here, I'm glad you guys all hung in there. You'll be fine next year. Help me load up the Ford, will ya? And be sure and come by the house tonight."

With that, some helped Reggie with the equipment and the rest headed for their cars. Reggie noticed that Taylor was apart from all the players, not talking to anyone. He wasn't smiling either, like he didn't feel any gratification that they had finally won. Much of his anger, for some reason, seemed to always be aimed at Reggie. He didn't know why, but he didn't care. Taylor had helped them get better and win a game. Next year, he'd be someone else's problem. Reggie didn't have to deal with him at all anymore. And he wasn't going to let Taylor ruin the moment. They had won. They had actually won a game in the league. An official game. It was in the books. It could never be taken away. Reggie didn't know which would be his bigger accomplishment:

his master's degree, or starting the UCSB lacrosse team.

A few days later the three roommates walked toward the campus stadium.

"So let me get this straight," Trent asked. "They didn't let this Jerry Rubin guy speak because they thought it would start another riot like what happened after his lawyer spoke; however, because they didn't let Rubin speak, it actually caused a riot and a student was killed, and now they're letting Rubin speak."

"You got it," Donnie answered.

"A little bit of Alice in Wonderland would be appropriate here I think," Reggie offered.

"Well I don't know," Trent said, "but this Rubin guy better have something interesting to say."

They continued walking, following the crowd as people began to stream toward the stadium. The same stadium where Reggie's lacrosse team had been shut out 11-0 by UCLA. Reggie noticed a group of blacks in uniform and in formation standing just outside the entrance. Their jaws were set in angry, defiant determination. Their eyes were straight ahead. He saw one of the guys from the apartment Vicky had taken him to standing in the ranks. Reggie nodded at him. Very slightly, imperceptibly almost, he nodded in return, and then looked straight ahead. Reggie assumed they were Black Panthers. Whatever they were, they looked militant and scary.

They walked into the stadium and up into the stands to find seats. The place was filling up in front of a stage that had been erected on the field. Just then Reggie, Trent, and Donnie noticed another group. There were 20 or 30 guys and maybe girls dressed in brown hooded robes and carrying long wooden staffs. They filed into the stadium, did not speak to anybody, and climbed up to the top row of the stands. There they encircled the stadium evenly spaced apart. Reggie shook his head. What kind of a kook cult was this? Everybody ignored them, even the master of ceremonies.

The warm up speakers soon began and it was the same old tripe. Reggie was quickly getting bored, but Donnie was eating it up.

"Donnie," Reggie said in the middle of a particularly long and predictable anti-U.S. diatribe, "will you listen to this shit? I mean, really listen. It's crap, pure and simple."

"Reggie, leave me alone and let me listen to it," Donnie said, perturbed.

Reggie shook his head. The speaker droned on and on about imperialism, capitalism, the military-industrial complex, the immorality of war, and used every catch phrase Reggie had ever heard. Suddenly, at a point where the speaker was catching his breath, someone in the audience yelled out "Yay, rhetoric!" Many in the crowd laughed. Others scowled. The strange people in the brown robes said nothing, did nothing.

Jerry Rubin finally arrived and ascended the stage. Someone offered him a joint and he made a big show of smoking it in front of everybody. Reggie looked around but he saw no cops in the stadium. Maybe the administration was finally getting smart. Fat chance of that.

Rubin's speech was more of the same. Reggie took an instant dislike to him. He seemed a hyperactive little man, full of himself and the place he thought he had in history. After about 20 minutes of his speech, people began leaving. First it was only a trickle, but then quite a few began filing out the rows and down the steps to get out of the stands.

Noting the exodus, Rubin gave his funniest line of the day. "Don't worry," he said, pointing to those leaving, "there will always be some who will watch the revolution on television."

The remaining crowd laughed. Others got up to join those walking out. Rubin went on for a while, losing more audience. But Reggie wanted to hear him out. Then Rubin said something that Reggie couldn't stomach.

"You can't be part of the new order, you can't help the revolution, unless you're ready to kill your parents," he said.

Reggie and Trent looked at each other.

"That's it!" Trent proclaimed. "I'm outa here."

"Me, too," Reggie agreed.

They both looked at Donnie. "I don't agree with everything he says, but I still want to hear it all," Donnie said.

"Well, I like my parents, and Reggie likes his parents, and I bet even you like your parents. I like them a lot more than listening to this freak," Trent said.

"Let's go, Trent," Reggie said, "I think the revolution is on Channel 3."

Chapter Ten

JUNE 1970: LA County Sheriffs, Oral Exams, and a Poco-aided Pick-up.

Music albums making the charts:

Johnny Cash—The World of Johnny Cash
The Grateful Dead—Workingman's Dead
The Jackson Five—ABC
Poco
Elvis Presley—On Stage 2/70

"Well, it's just all adding up, that's all," Donnie said, fresh out of the shower and dressing himself, as if for combat. "Nixon invades Cambodia, four students are killed at Kent State and I believe a couple of them weren't even demonstrating, they were just on their way to class. Then two black students are killed in their dorms at Jackson State. You've got at least 100,000 people who marched against the war in Washington and it does nothing. Nothing. Someone has to stand up." He tied his shoe with emphasis, staring at Reggie with determination.

"And now?" Reggie asked.

"Well, if you haven't heard, they indicted 17 people for burning the bank. And here's the joke: two of them were in jail the night the bank was burned. Actually in jail and they indicted them. How stupid is that? And if those guys were in jail and couldn't have burned the bank, chances are most, if not all, of the others are innocent, too."

"You were there, Donnie, do you know who burned the bank?"

"Lots of people. But I don't know many names. I watched a flaming trash bin being pushed up into the bank. But the Boy Scouts, the frat rats and jocks, pulled it out and put the fire out. Later, a few guys went into the bank with gasoline. That's when the big fire started. I knew a couple of them," he explained.

"You could earn $25,000 from the Bank of America if you told the cops what you know," Reggie said.

Donnie sat on his bed and stared at Reggie.

"I can't believe you think I would even consider that. You are kidding, aren't you?" Donnie asked.

"Sort of. It's just all pretty weird. They don't even bother to check alibis. If they had, they wouldn't have indicted the two who were in jail. It's kinda like that old Bogart movie, 'Casablanca.' There's a scene in there where the Vichy French cop is dealing with some problem and he says to his men: 'round up the usual suspects.' Seems like that's what they were doing. So what are you gonna do?"

"I'm goin' down to the loop. There'll be more shit happening tonight. We're not gonna take this anymore. Maybe we can burn down the new temporary bank."

"You tried that a couple of months ago," Reggie said. "You know the cops improved the efficiency of their tactics then. I bet they have some contingency plans if you guys start another riot. It could get real nasty."

Donnie stood up and headed for the bedroom door, picking up his jacket off the end of his bed.

"You should come with me, Reg, it's the right thing to do."

"Donnie, the cops may be wrong and the admin of UCSB may be wrong and President Nixon may be wrong and Governor Reagan may be wrong, but burning cop cars and banks and real estate offices is not right. It's just not."

"You should go. You'll wish you had. Where's Trent, still celebrating his birthday that gave him the magical 366? He should go to, just to make up for his draft lottery number."

"I don't know where Trent is. Maybe he went to the movies with number 47."

"Who?"

"Uh, I think her name is Terry or Tracey or something. The one he met at the nude-in."

"Better not be the Magic Lantern, there'll be too much action around it tonight. And I hear a curfew is being imposed, starting at dusk. So he might not be able to get back into I.V. if he went to Goleta or Santa Barbara. And Reggie, you should go." With that he turned, walked out the door, and headed down Del Playa toward the loop.

Reggie just sat there, thinking of all the implications. What was the right thing to do? If the right thing was to demonstrate, then Reggie was convinced that the demonstrations had to be peaceful. And the demonstrations in I.V. had not been peaceful. Thus, they had been wrong. But it wasn't right for cops to beat people up, either. So what was the right thing to do?

Charlie and Joe stood with at least a few hundred other LA County Sheriff Deputies, all members of the special tactical task force, as they staged themselves in a field just outside of Isla Vista. An officer began to address them.

"Okay, here's the deal. The Santa Barbara cops are going to take control of the loop area, that's the downtown part of Isla Vista where the bank and stores and restaurants are located. They're moving into position now to secure it. The Highway Patrol will block off the roads into Isla Vista. There's really only three including one that goes through the campus. I believe they've already set up. Our job will be to enforce the curfew throughout Isla Vista. That's about a half a square mile full of apartments and houses where the students live. Now hey, Santa Barbara cops have been injured by rocks and bottles. So be careful, protect yourselves at all times. Some of you will stay on foot; some of you will ride in these dump trucks. All right, saddle up and let's go!"

"Hey Charlie," Joe said, "these flak jackets…"

"Yeah?"

"Well, when we have them on they cover over our badges and name tags. No one can see our names or our badge numbers. And with a helmet and visor, well, we're gonna all look the same."

Charlie stopped a minute as he was about to put on his helmet and looked at Joe. Then he looked around at the deputies and realized Joe was right. They would have the cover of anonymity. They could do damn well pretty much what they wanted to. Charlie struggled against his growing anger at the students. They were just so wrong about everything and had no respect of America or American values. He wanted to hurt them, but he knew that was wrong, too.

At another order from a captain, they broke into groups of about 50 and began moving into Isla Vista.

Donnie stood with some of his friends by a burning trash dumpster that had been pushed into the middle of Seville about a half a block from Embarcadero del Mar, the other half of the loop. They could see down to part of the park area behind the bank, and it was filled with tear gas that was rapidly dissipating. They couldn't see many demonstrators, as it appeared the cops had pretty much managed to secure the loop. They saw a few of the dump trucks moving continuously around the loop, tossing tear gas at anybody caught outside. Suddenly somebody shouted.

"Behind us!"

They turned in time to see a mass of about 50 cops come around a corner and head straight for them. A few of the demonstrators picked up rocks and began throwing them. The cops charged and Donnie's group began to scatter in all different directions.

"Fuck, Charlie, that was close," Joe said, "that bottle hit my helmet and could have taken out my eye!"

"Let's get'em," Charlie said. It was time for combat. Their lives were in danger; they were threatened by people not listening to the proper authorities, by people who were breaking the law. They had to be stopped by any means.

The rush of cops caught up to a couple of the guys who had been by the dumpster. Soon, they were both on the ground as four or five cops each took turns beating them with their batons.

"I saw one run in there," Joe said, pointing to an apartment.

He, Charlie, and three others rushed up and into the apartment complex.

"Which one?" one of them asked.

"This one, I think," another said. They kicked in a door and rushed inside. A student was sitting at his table with a textbook open. It was, after all, finals week. The kid stood up.

"What's wrong?" he asked.

Joe picked up the table and overturned it while another cop slammed the butt of his baton into the kid's stomach. He dropped to the floor allowing Joe the opportunity to give him a good kick in the ribs. The kid rolled on the floor, trying to get his breath.

"Maybe it wasn't this one, let's try another," one of them said.

They went outside and saw another kid standing by an open door.

"Officers, what's going on?" he asked innocently.

One of the deputies ran up to him and hit him on the shoulder with his baton. A second deputy grabbed the kid, throwing him to the ground while Charlie and Joe went into the apartment. It was empty. When they emerged, they saw the other two deputies continuing to beat on the kid.

"Enough," Charlie said. "He doesn't know anything. Let's go find some rioters."

They went back to the street and discovered that their group had successfully cleared the avenue of demonstrators, though the dumpster was still burning now at the side of the road. Just then, a car came down a cross street. Ten deputies surrounded it and began beating against the windows with their batons. There was the sound of breaking glass held together only by the laminating process that prevented shattering in car windows. The driver yelled out at them to stop, but they only hit it more. He turned a corner to get away and sped off down the street, all his windows broken.

A group of students approached and began throwing rocks at Charlie's group. They were instantly charged and literally beaten back.

"Aren't we gonna arrest anybody?" Charlie asked.

"Arrest, hell. We're gonna beat 'em off the streets. We'll chase them into their houses. We'll enforce the curfew. To hell with arresting them," a sergeant answered.

Donnie sat behind a large bush next to a house on Sabado Tarde, a street that paralleled Del Playa. He had managed to stay under cover as two dump trucks full of cops passed by. Fortunately, he hadn't been seen. He needed to find other demonstrators so they could regroup and consider their next moves. But this time, the cops appeared to be everywhere. He finally got up the nerve to leave his hiding place and ventured back out onto the street. He once again headed toward the loop, looking for potential confederates and keeping an eye out for cops.

At the same moment, Charlie, Joe, and about ten other cops had entered the fraternity house down the block thinking it was another apartment building. A huge kid, a football player, stood in one of the main rooms downstairs. Joe and three of the deputies immediately knocked him down and began beating him. Another fraternity member appeared at the stairs.

"Hey, what are you guys doing?" He demanded. "We're on your side, we're not…" He didn't get a chance to finish as Charlie put him down with a baton jab to the solar plexus.

"We saw rock throwers run in here, where are they?" Charlie demanded.

The kid tried to catch his breath. "No rock throwers came in here, they wouldn't come in here. We've been fighting them ourselves, trying to protect the bank." Still angry, Charlie hit the kid again for good measure.

"Bullshit," Charlie said.

Back out on the streets arrests were, in fact, being made. Those arrested were secured with plastic handcuffs, usually put on so tight the circulation was cut off and their hands began to go numb and turn blue. They were all taken to a place by the park where a bus was waiting to take them to the jail.

"Hey Joe," one officer shouted. "Come on over and help us check these kids for weapons." Joe turned and saw three girls with their hands leaning against a wall. He walked over to see what was happening.

"Here's how we do it," the one cop said. He began to pat down one of the girls, running his hand up under her shirt to squeeze her breasts and then down along her legs, moving his hands back up to grab her crotch and hold it there. The girl said nothing but cried softly, tears running down her cheeks.

"Let go of her you fucking pig, you can't do that," another said.

"Oh yeah?" Joe responded. "Watch this." He proceeded to grab both her breasts from behind while he pushed his pelvis against her ass. She began to squirm and take her hands off the wall. "Better not," Joe warned, "don't want to resist an officer of the law."

"What law," she answered as he dry humped her from behind, "damn you. You can't get away with this."

His right hand left her breast and went down to her crotch. He rubbed her there, trying to find and trace her outer labia. She wiggled her ass to try to break free. He grabbed her crotch tighter.

"I won't let go until you stop resisting," Joe said with a smirk.

She stopped moving, bit down on her lip, and waited. He stroked her crotch a couple more times and then he finally let go and backed away.

"Hey Charlie, there's one more over here that needs to be searched."

Charlie had watched the scene play out from across the street. He hadn't really liked what he saw but he did nothing, said nothing. He shook his head and turned away.

Charlie, Joe, and about 20 others moved away from the loop and began patrolling down the streets of I.V.

Donnie came around a corner and saw the group of cops approaching. He immediately picked up a rock and threw it. The rock hit Charlie square in the chest, but the flak jacket diminished its effect. However, it did make Charlie even angrier. Both Charlie and Joe began to run at Donnie.

Donnie turned to run away. The cops were shouting at him. He sped around a corner and ran right into the path of one of the big dump trucks. He stopped and tried to pivot out of the way of the truck, but he slipped on some gravel and fell. The front tire of the truck ran over his left foot, crushing the bones. Donnie screamed.

Joe, by this time, had caught up to where Donnie lay on the

street. Ignoring his screams, Joe began kicking him in the stomach. Donnie just writhed on the ground, unable now to even scream.

"Get up, asshole!" Joe yelled. He reached down and grabbed Donnie by the arm and tried to pull him up.

Donnie, breath somewhat recovered, screamed out again.

"My foot!" he yelled, "my foot!"

By this time Charlie had come up. He was about to kick Donnie in the ribs when he looked at the foot. There was a mass of blood soaking Donnie's shoe and the foot seemed to be pointing backwards.

"Hold on, Joe, hold on. His foot really is messed up, take a look."

Joe stopped and looked down. "Jesus," he said. "We better get him an ambulance."

A couple of days later, Trent, Reggie, and Rebecca were visiting Donnie at the hospital.

"It was just as bad last night as when you got hurt," Trent said, sitting in a chair in Donnie's hospital room. "I mean, I couldn't believe it. They were not only beating up the demonstrators and rioters, but they were beating up everybody. People who tried not to get involved and even football players, other jocks, and frat rats who had gone out to try to stop the demonstrators and put out fires. I couldn't believe some of the stories my friends told me. They busted into houses and apartments and fraternities, beating everybody they came across."

"It was like Vietnam in a way, I guess," Reggie added. "They saw everybody, absolutely everybody in Isla Vista as the enemy. They thought they were on search and destroy missions or something. And it was all the LA county sheriffs, that special tactical squad of theirs."

"Now even the frat houses have hung out signs on their walls telling the LA sheriffs to go home," Trent noted.

Donnie tried to sit up a little, and winced in pain.

"What did the doctors say?" Rebecca asked.

"Well," Donnie began, "they operated on the foot for, I don't know, five or six hours. It was all mangled and crushed. They almost took it off, but they managed to save it. They had to do some creative work, I guess, fuse some bones together and put some stainless steel rods in or something. The doc was explaining it to me but I was still woozy from the great stuff they gave me. He just left before you guys came. I guess I'm going to need some more operations. But, he said I'd be able to walk on it, even though I'll probably always have a limp."

"You're gonna walk with a limp for the rest of your life?" Reggie asked.

"Yeah, I guess," Donnie replied. "If I just hadn't slipped…"

"If you just hadn't gone down there," Rebecca said.

"Donnie," Reggie injected, "you're going to walk with a limp for the rest of your life. Don't you realize what that means?"

Donnie thought for a moment, then his face lit up and his eyes grew wide.

"IV-F!" he shouted.

"That's right," Reggie said. "You'll never have to worry about the draft again. You'll be IV-F. You're free of the threat of going to Vietnam."

"Why, why didn't I think of that before? Of course I'll be IV-F. I'm safe!"

He lay there, smiling and choking back tears. "I'm safe; I'm safe," he kept repeating.

"Well, we got to go soon. Monday our lease is up. Your parents are at the house now, packing up your stuff," Trent said.

"You know," Reggie said, "I told them they could sleep in the room and I'd sleep in the living room, but they insisted on going to a motel."

"Yeah, they would," Donnie said. "My dad doesn't like imposing and it's not like they can't afford a motel in Santa Barbara for a few nights."

"When are you going to be released? Did you finish all your finals? Are you under arrest?" Reggie asked.

"No…well, I mean the cops just threw me in the ambulance without paperwork and without any cop coming along, so I guess they're not pressing charges. I finished two of my finals. In two others. they're going to give me incomplete's and I'll come back during the summer to take the tests. My dad arranged it all. I think they're letting me out of here on Sunday. But I can't put any weight on this for many weeks yet. Our lease is up when?"

"Monday. Think you can make it over to Windward House before you head back to the Valley?" Trent asked.

"Yeah, I'll get my parents to bring me by on Sunday. Got to get my car anyway. Jeez, has the whole year gone by already? It seems like we just moved in," Donnie said.

"Well, I'd like to keep the place for a little while longer, but it just won't work out." Trent mused. "I've got something planned for the summer, a long trip to Asia and I've been accepted to UC Irvine for grad school. So I'll be moving home. No more Isla Vista for me, as interesting a four years as it has been. Especially this year."

"What are you gonna do, Rebecca?" Reggie asked.

"Donnie and his parents have invited me down to LA for a couple of weeks, but I'll be back up here for summer school. I want to get some gen ed classes out of the way. What about you, Reg?"

"Oh, like I always thought, I'll go back to LA and start my career somewhere," Reggie said.

Donnie began to smile.

"Teaching," Donnie said. "You'll end up teaching. Just wait and see."

"C'mon, Donnie, don't say that. You'll put a curse on me," Reggie pleaded.

"I'm just sayin' what the truth is, Reg. Poli sci will get you nowhere."

"Hey Donnie, you know what?" Reggie asked, deliberately changing the subject. "You shoulda paid more attention to that Mayall song, the first one on 'The Turning Point'."

"I don't remember, what is it?" Donnie asked.

"It's called 'The Laws Must Change.' The last line is very appropriate. He says 'Don't throw rocks at policemen, but get the knots of law untied.' You shoulda listened to that instead of the Stones' 'Street Fightin' Man.' You all should have listened to that. Thoreau, Gandhi, and Martin Luther King all advocated peaceful demonstrations, non-violent demonstrations. Gandhi freed a whole nation that way, and King helped his people get out from under legal segregation and discrimination."

"Speaking of that, what's going on now with this last riot? What's happening tonight? Are the LA cops going to go wild again?"

"Actually," Trent began, "we're going to have a peaceful demonstration. We're going to meet in Perfect Park just before the curfew starts and just sit there. No rocks, no fires. Just a peaceful protest. Breaking the law to be sure because we'll violate the curfew, but peaceful nonetheless."

"We? You mean you're actually going, Trent? You're going to demonstrate?" Donnie asked incredulously.

"Too many bad things have happened to too many of my friends. Now, Donnie, don't take this wrong, but I don't count you. You were out there to fight with the cops and you got hurt. But many people were minding their own business and got hurt. I'm demonstrating for them and the rights we all have."

"I never would have believed it. Trent Foster, activist. Amazing. Are you going, too, Reg? Does breaking the law by sitting in a park past curfew qualify as a method you could approve of?"

"Sure does. It's classic civil disobedience. That means you break the law, but you expect to get arrested…in fact, you want to be arrested to call attention to a bad law."

"So," Donnie asked, "you're going, too?"

"Can't. My master's oral exams are tomorrow. I can't take a chance of getting arrested and missing them."

Donnie looked at him and shook his head.

"Now…damn it, Donnie, don't go judging me. You know how focused I am. I'm not throwing away this whole year. I came here for a master degree and I'm gonna get it."

Later that day, Trent stood with all the people in the park at the loop. There must have been a thousand or more gathered peacefully as the sun began to dip to the west. There seemed to be just as many cops as well, ringing the loop and watching the crowd.

"Trent, hey, you came here, too?"

Trent turned to see Maureen standing in front of him. She looked beautiful. She wore a tube top straining heavily to hold everything in and a big unbuttoned work shirt over that. Tight jeans completed her wardrobe. Trent had spent so much time avoiding her, he'd forgotten how deadly foxy she was.

"Maureen, what are you doing here? Things will get bad here pretty soon, go on back to your house," he said protectively.

She smiled slightly. "No, I'm staying right here. The cops are wrong and they've hurt some of my friends. I'm staying right here."

Trent took a deep breath and exhaled slowly. "Well, okay," he said, "stay close to me. And you better button up your shirt. Don't show the cops that much skin. Let's sit down; we'll all be sitting soon."

With that, they sat down and, as if by a signal, everybody sat down on the patchy grass of the de facto park. They sat and waited as the sun began to set.

"So, now you want me close to you?" Maureen noted sarcastically.

Trent looked at her. "What can I say, Maureen? I'm a cad. I change women like most men change socks. You might be the right girl, but this is the wrong time."

"Why?" she asked, truly curious.

"Because I have this gift, at least to me it seems like a gift. I can get almost any girl I want to go to bed with me. And I feel as long as I have this gift, I should use it. I can't commit to one woman for the rest of my life or even for the rest of the year."

"At some point, doesn't that get old: screwing one pretty girl after another?"

Trent laughed. "I dare you to ask any guy if that would ever get old. No, it doesn't get old. It never does. You shouldn't be going after guys like me. You would have been much better off with Reggie."

"He fucks around, too. I mean, he goes through women, too, just not as often as you I guess."

"Only from necessity I think. I mean, knowing Reggie as I do, if either you or, what's her name, the Asian girl?"

"Janice."

"Yeah, Janice. I know he likes both of you. If either one of you had latched on to him, then you could have built a serious relationship. He wouldn't have dropped either one of you to go find another girl like I always do. He would be different, I think, in that way. Maybe you wouldn't end up getting married, but you might have had a long term relationship with him. More so than with me."

A bullhorn began to blare. "You are all in violation of the curfew. If you don't leave in the next five minutes, you will all be arrested."

Trent and Maureen looked around. Nobody was moving. Everybody continued to sit and await their fate.

"But Trent," Maureen continued, "don't you ever want to settle down, get married, raise a family?"

Trent looked into her eyes. "Someday, yes. But not until I finish my Ph.D., which I plan to have in three more years. Then, I want to work for a while, figure out what I'm doing. I'm thinking by the time I'm 28 or so, I'll be ready. But there'll be a lot of women between now and then."

Their conversation was interrupted as the police moved in and began forcefully picking people up and dragging them off. Everybody remained calm however. Trent pulled Maureen over close to him. She sat right next to him, holding his arm. The police kept dragging demonstrators off, but there were just too many. It took a long time, but eventually they hauled off the people sitting next to Trent and Maureen. Finally a couple of big, burly cops grabbed Trent, jerked him to his feet, and put tight plastic cuffs on his hands.

"Trent!" Maureen shouted.

"Stay calm; stay calm. Do what they tell you to."

She, too, was picked up with the cop making sure his hand grabbed a lot of boob as he lifted her. They both were hustled over to the busses where the other arrestees had been taken. Trent and Maureen were the last ones loaded on the last bus.

Again the bullhorn blared out. "You are all in violation, go home now!" Nobody moved. About 300 had been arrested, but another 700 or so still occupied the park. Suddenly, a huge tear gas machine began spraying the crowd with pepper gas. At the same time, cops charged in, swinging their batons. At that, the demonstrators began to run away from the park and the cops. This time, no one chased them into I.V. Trent and Maureen watched the melee as the bus pulled out and headed away from the loop. They wondered what kind of treatment awaited them at jail.

Meanwhile, Reggie felt weird being alone in the house. True, Donnie had spent a lot of time at Rebecca's, but Trent had usually been home. Now, Donnie was in the hospital and Trent may have been arrested. And Reggie's orals were tomorrow.

He looked at his pile of notebooks. There were nine of them, one for each class he had taken at UCSB. One by one, he picked them up and began to peruse them. He tried, even, to study them. But it was impossible to know how to prepare. He'd never had oral exams before. Who knew what they would ask? He'd have to study everything.

An hour and a half later, he felt drained. He also felt like he hadn't really accomplished much. Feeling frustrated, he put on the Stone's "Let It Bleed" album and walked out on the deck to stare at the ocean. Night had fallen and the lights from the oil platform reflected off the water, forming lines that pointed right at him. He sat out there, listening to "Gimme Shelter" and watching the lights on the water. Then, as the song was about to finish, he got up and re-entered the house. He shut off the stereo and went into his room, opening a dresser drawer. There lay two notebooks he had brought up from home earlier in the year when he had Palmer's law class. They were the notebooks from his two constitutional law classes he took in his senior year at UCLA. He had thought they might be useful in Palmer's class, but they hadn't been. He picked them up, brought them to the table, and began to look them over.

He was up in the morning, but Trent was still not back. Reggie hoped he was okay. His exam wasn't until two, so he still had time to study. Once again, he leafed through his notebooks from his UCSB classes. Once again, he gave up and began going over his two UCLA notebooks. They just seemed so much more organized. He would be tested mostly in two areas: international relations and public law. At least, he could prepare for law.

By one, Trent had still not returned and Reggie left on his bike headed for campus. He rode leisurely through Isla Vista, savoring the atmosphere that, in spite of the riots, was still there. The loop was peaceful and he saw no cops. He biked over to the student center and had an omelet. He sat on the grass and looked at the placid little lagoon. Finally, it was time to go to the building where all his classes had been and face the inquisition. Or whatever it turned out to be.

Edwards met him at the poli sci office.

"Your panel is supposed to consist of myself, Dr. Chang, and you requested Dr. Harrison, right?"

"Yeah, that's right. Was that okay?"

"Well, he confirmed for today, but he's not here yet. We'll give him a few more minutes, but we really need to start your exam. We have others scheduled all day today."

"Well, can we go ahead and start? I mean, can't he join us later?"

Edwards thought for a moment.

"Tell you what. The rules say there have to be three of us. Let me see who's around and can fill in. That way, if Harrison doesn't show up, it doesn't matter, and if he does he can just join us in progress."

"Okay," Reggie answered, "that sounds fine."

Reggie waited in the hallway. He saw Chang go into the conference room. A few minutes later, Edwards appeared. With him was—Baer!

"Mr. Blake," Edwards began, "Dr. Baer has graciously agreed to sit on your panel. Hope you don't mind; he was the only one available."

"No, not at all. I don't mind at all; that will be fine. Thank you Dr.

Baer," Reggie lied. Baer nodded and walked on into the conference room.

"In a minute, I'll call you in," Edwards said, before disappearing into the room. Reggie stood in the hallway, cursing his luck. Maybe he should have gotten arrested last night instead. All Reggie could think about was focusing on the moment. Baer or no Baer, he would take care of business. He was soon brought in and sat at the table. The three of them sat across from him like some kind of tribunal. They started with questions on international relations. Reggie bobbed and weaved as best he could without overtly bullshitting, but he didn't feel comfortable. Baer seemed okay, not asking any off the wall questions. Then Harrison arrived, and he was dealing with four professors.

Edwards decided to dip into theory.

"Can you explain the controversy in social science as raised by Peter Winch?"

"Yes I can. The controversy seems simple enough. Is social science different in kind from other natural sciences, or only in degree? If only in degree, then eventually everything in social science could be quantified and computerized. But Winch says that social science is a different kind of science and can not be reduced to formulas and numbers entirely."

"Which do you think is true?" Baer asked.

"I agree with Winch. If he's wrong, then eventually we'd be able to, for example, build a computer that functions exactly like a human brain. If that ever happens, there will be ethical and control issues like you wouldn't believe, but I don't think it will. I don't think social sciences will ever be able to be examined the way one examines hard sciences, with math and experiments and hard data all fitting into formulas. They can't even build a computer that can beat grand masters at chess. The problem is, in my opinion, the social sciences, especially political science, well, they're spending too much time arguing on how to study the field instead of actually doing the studying. They're focusing on the process and not the content."

"Interesting point," Chang said. He then asked Reggie about some obscure political science philosopher. Reggie searched his brain.

"He was pretty libertarian. He didn't believe that victimless crimes like prostitution and drug use should be illegal. He felt the government was wrong in proscribing those kinds of activities," Reggie answered.

"What about gambling?" Edwards asked.

"Well, he would have been opposed to making it illegal," Reggie answered.

The four professors looked at each other.

"Actually, he makes an exception for gambling. He believes governments should make gambling illegal. Do you know why he makes that exception?" Edwards asked.

Reggie sat back in his chair and looked at the ceiling. He then leaned forward, drummed his fingers on the tabletop a few seconds, and finally answered.

"Now that you mention it, I do remember that he made an exception for gambling. But I don't remember his reason; I can't recall his rationale, his argument. I just don't remember."

Again, the four professors looked at each other.

"Well, okay, let's turn to law then," Edwards said.

Reggie was ready. He'd been waiting for this. Edwards framed a question that gave him a perfect launching pad. He started with Schenck vs. US and began rattling off a list of key Supreme Court cases on the first amendment. West Virginia Board of Education vs. Barnette, New York Times vs. Sullivan, Ginsberg vs. New York, Cantwell vs. Connecticut, Marsh vs. Alabama, Gitlow vs. New York. He went on and on, listing the cases, outlining the issues, explaining the court's finding, and expounding on the precedents set. They asked more and more detailed questions and he answered them all. That part of the exam, he knew, he had excelled.

"Well, Mr. Blake, that completes the exam. If you would wait outside, we're going to deliberate for a few minutes and I'll come out and tell you the result of your exam," Edwards explained.

Reggie waited nervously outside in the hall. There was no place to sit, so he just walked back and forth. There were, technically, four grades they could give him. The best was "excellent." With that, they would accept the student into their Ph.D. program at UCSB. Next was "good." A "good" meant that the student got the master's and the UCSB poli sci department would give him a recommendation to go to a Ph.D. program somewhere else, but not UCSB. Then there was "pass." That meant the student would be granted the master's, but given no recommendation to other schools or, of course, UCSB. Finally, they could give a "fail," which would mean no degree. The rumor was, however, that they wouldn't let someone get to the oral exams unless they had already decided to grant the degree. They would flunk them out with a "C" somewhere. Like Reggie's almost "C" from Baer. That had been close, but maybe they intended all along to give him the degree.

"Congratulations, Mr. Blake, you have your master's degree in political science," Edwards said, holding out his hand.

"For the record, we were a bit concerned at the start of your exam. You were a lot weaker on the international relations questions than we expected. We were, however, gratified that you weren't afraid to admit you didn't know something, like with the gambling question. You could have tried to fake your way through it, but you admitted your lack of knowledge and that was good. But we were really impressed with your knowledge of constitutional law. You had those cases at your fingertips, almost as if you had briefs in front of you and were reading from them. Good job, Mr. Blake. We're giving you a 'good,' which means you get your degree and we'd be happy to give you a recommendation if you apply for a Ph.D. program at any other school. Good luck in the future," he held out his hand again. Reggie shook it, and walked out of the building feeling light and free.

As he biked through the loop, he saw the strangest sight. Though it was only mid-afternoon, and the sun wouldn't be setting for another four hours or so, the loop was lined with cops. There was one every hundred feet or so, standing on the sidewalk, all the way around the loop. Groups of students were knotted around some of them, engaged in conversation. Little mini-debates. The cops remained cool and expressed their viewpoints as well as they could. And it was peaceful. Reggie felt it was a good idea, indeed if it had been someone's idea, to get the cops talking to the students. Make each other human and it's harder to hate. These were Santa Barbara cops. The LA County Deputy Sheriffs had gone home.

He saw Vicky standing in the park and rode over to her.

"Hey Vicky, I just passed my orals!"

"Way to go, Reg. What'dja get?"

"They gave me a 'good'," he said. "So I won't be staying here. Have to go back to LA and start my life. I didn't want to continue school anyway. I'm kinda burned out on school, especially poli sci."

She stood there as he straddled his bike, feet on the ground. She smiled.

"Do you have any idea of what you might do?" she asked.

Reggie looked at the strange scene around them with dozens of non-violent confrontations of police and students talking to each other.

"You know, maybe I could become a cop," he said. "They need some liberal blood in their ranks, keep them more honest."

Vicky's smile disappeared, replaced with a menacing scowl.

"Reggie Blake, don't you even think about bein' a cop. Don't even consider it. If you want to become a cop, I'm gonna have to get some of my friends and visit you," she said.

Reggie was taken aback.

"Are you threatening me?"

"Damn right!" she answered. "You don't want to become a cop."

"But look at what's happening out here, they're talking. Isn't that better than throwing rocks and swinging night sticks?"

"Well, so far so good, that's fine. But you don't want to be a cop."

"Don't you think a few guys like me could change the cops and make things better?"

"Are you serious? You won't change them, Reggie, they'll change you. Now I'm telling you, that is not something you want to aspire to be with your new master's in political science."

"Okay, relax already, I was just thinking out loud. I'm not gonna be a cop. By the way, did you take your orals yet?"

"Yes, already this morning," she said, becoming more relaxed.

"Well?"

"I passed," she said.

"Yeah but with what?"

"Excellent. They want me to do my Ph.D. here."

Reggie sat there on his bike, his mind churning.

"Well, did you, I mean, did you get some 'A's in your classes?"

"Yeah," she answered, a sly smile forming on her lips.

"How many?"

"All of them," she answered matter of factly.

"You got 'A's from Gupta and Harrison and in every class you took?"

"Yeah. So what, you don't think a black woman can get straight 'A's, or are you surprised I got straight 'A's because I'm a black woman?"

Reggie looked at her and shook his head.

"No," he said quietly but firmly, "No. It has nothing to do with you being black, I wasn't thinking that. It's not the 'black doctor syndrome', so don't try to make it that. I just realized that I'd never asked what kind of grades you were getting and I just assumed you were struggling to maintain a 3.0 just like me. I know you got your bachelor's here, and now your master's and soon your Ph.D. I'm impressed not because you're black, but because you did it."

Vicky looked at him and shook her head.

"Yeah, sure."

He looked back at her. "I'd make love to you right now if you'd let me, miss Ph.D. candidate."

"Good bye, Reg," she said. "Good luck with your life."

He leaned over to give her a kiss, but she moved her head back just enough to keep away. He stopped, looked into her eyes, shook his head, and then rode off without saying goodbye.

Reggie walked in Windward House only to find Trent and Maureen sitting in the living room.

"The judge let us go," Trent explained. "He let everybody go who was arrested at the park and then he blasted the cops."

"Great, then you're okay?"

"Yeah, but Reggie, I've never been so humiliated," Maureen said. "These old hard looking female cops stripped me down and hosed me off, like I was covered in vermin or something. They poured some kind of smelly medicine on me. They said it was to kill lice. I don't have lice. They didn't have to treat me that way."

"And my hands are still a little numb from those plastic handcuffs," Trent explained, holding up his hands.

"Shit, that's really screwed up," Reggie said. "Well, there're cops in the loop right now, but the feeling is different. They're standing around talking to people. I think the LA sheriffs are gone. Maybe things will get back to normal."

"How'd your exams go?" Trent asked.

"About like I expected. They'll give me the degree, but they don't want me in their Ph.D. program, which is okay because I don't want any more school right now. But you know the weird thing? They told me after the exam that I had really impressed them with my knowledge of constitutional case law. Last night, I studied my notebooks from two con law classes I had at UCLA last year. That's what pulled me through, that's what I excelled in. Nothing that I learned here, certainly not from Palmer or Baer or even Edwards."

"Hey Reg," Trent said, "Did you ever think of law school?"

"Hell, no!" Reggie answered. "That's three years and a bar exam at the end. No thanks. I don't want to be a lawyer."

"Yeah, but lawyers can make a lot of money and…it's not teaching," Trent added, smiling.

Reggie sat for a second.

"I'm just burned out from school. I need to work for a while. I'll find something down in LA."

"When are you guys leaving?" Maureen asked.

"Our lease is up on Monday. We've got some cleaning to do; luckily Donnie used the kitchen the most and always kept it really clean. Reg, you gonna stay until Monday?"

"Yeah, might as well. Got some goodbyes to say. Donnie should be here on Sunday, I want to get some pictures."

"Hey Reg," Maureen asked, "walk me home, will you?"

"Okay," Reggie said.

The Lancaster spring would soon turn into summer. Charlie and Joe sat parked in their cruiser feeling the gathering heat while waiting for potential speeders. It would soon be too hot and they'd have to drive around.

"We did wrong, Joe," Charlie said.

"Huh? What do you mean?"

"Up at Santa Barbara, we did wrong."

"Bullshit if we did. We did what we had to do. What's wrong with you? You hate the anti-war demonstrators. What's wrong?"

"I do hate the demonstrators with their America-bashing rhetoric and their North Vietnamese flags and their total disrespect and lack of appreciation for the greatness of our country. We're not the bad guys. But, but, we did wrong."

"How? Explain to me. We had to protect ourselves. Hell, I almost got my eye put out by a fuckin' broken bottle. They threw rocks, they threw bottles, they trashed those real estate offices, they burned cop cars, and they burned a fuckin' bank. I feel no remorse at all for anything I did up there, it was necessary."

"Don't you see," Charlie explained, "we were so full of our own hatred for hippies and protestors that we crossed the line. We hurt innocent people."

"It happens. Fortunes of war," Joe countered.

"No, Joe. We're supposed to protect the innocent. Hell, remember that one kid, the one in the first apartment we went into. He was studying. You know why? It was finals week. Did you know it was finals week?"

"No, I didn't know that."

"So here's this kid, minding his own business, doing what he had gone to Santa Barbara to do, studying for some final, and we bust in his door and beat the shit out of him simply because he was there. Then, we go into a fraternity house and beat up guys who were actually on our side. Not just trying to be neutral and mind their own business, but actually on our side opposed to the demonstrators. We beat them up, too. How are all these people we beat up gonna feel about cops now? We did wrong. Maybe that's what our troops in Vietnam think they have to do, only they're not just beating people up, they're killing them."

"Don't beat yourself up over it, Charlie. We took control of the situation and quelled the riot. We did what we had to do."

"Like you feeling up that girl? No, we did wrong. Fuck, I hate this war," Charlie said.

The night after his oral exams, Reggie headed on over to campus, on foot, to check out a free concert being put on near Storke Tower by a new country-rock group called Poco. It was supposed to be some kind of gift to the students to help them uplift their spirits after the turmoil of the third riot. Reggie was interested in Poco because they included two members of the defunct Buffalo Springfield: Richie Furray and Jim Messina. Neil Young and Steve Stills had also been in that band. Reggie had really liked the Springfield. Their sound was fresh and clean.

Students were crowding around as there was no real seating. The band set up in a recessed plaza. Students were sitting along walls above them and on the steps down to the plaza. Or not sitting at all. Reggie had to stand and found himself next to a girl with long black hair. She smiled at him, he returned it.

"Do you like these guys?" she asked.

"Haven't heard them yet. But two of them were in the Buffalo Springfield, a band I really liked."

"Oh yeah," she said, "which two?"

The band, having finished a couple of interesting up-tempo

numbers, broke into "Kind Woman."

"There, the guy singing. That's Furray, that's his song from the Buffalo Springfield. And I think that's Messina over there on guitar. Well, of course, they all have guitars except the drummer."

She laughed and smiled broadly. It was a very pretty, inviting smile. They stood listening to the music. Reggie liked it. He thought the relatively new genre of country-rock showed promise. The Byrds had done some, and the Buffalo Springfield itself had a country feel. And there was the Band. Poco's songs were light and hopeful with interesting guitars and clear vocals. He thought they might last a while, but he didn't know if they'd ever get very popular. He could not, however, stomach much of main stream country music. Johnny Cash was good, but to Reggie, most country songs were corny and had a twang to them that really put him off. Singing about cigarettes and trailer courts and beer and truckers and waitresses. Not much depth in most of it.

After a while standing was not cutting it. And free concert or not, Reggie felt it was time to go.

"Wanna split?" he asked.

She turned to him and smiled. "Sure!"

He grabbed her hand and pulled her away from the crowd. Trying to find a pathway through to Isla Vista, they ran into a big pickup truck parked to block their exit. There was no way around either end. Impulsively, Reggie opened the door and slid across the seat, opened the other door, and stepped out. The girl followed him, laughing happily.

"My name's Reggie, by the way."

"Hi, I'm Stacie," she said.

They walked down the street in Isla Vista, and soon they were on Del Playa.

"Where do you want to go?" he asked.

"I don't care; it's up to you."

"My house is down here on Del Playa, all the way near the end. We could go there, get something to drink, smoke a joint if you want."

"Can we fuck?" she asked and then began to laugh.

"Uh, yeah, we can do that," he answered.

"Okay," she said, then put her arms around Reggie and kissed him. He held her close to him. She was taller than Janice, but only a little. Her body appeared just as compact and Reggie had noticed she had a great ass. They broke their kiss and looked each other in the eye. She was all long hair and pretty smile. He didn't notice much in the boob department, but at the moment he didn't care. He wondered what it would feel like to have that ass of hers under him.

For guys, the game of the constant search for sex was just completely crazy. Sometimes it was impossibly hard to find any, sometimes ridiculously simple.

Soon, after smoking a joint, they were naked on his bed. Santana was on the stereo. She told him she was on the pill and trusted that he had no diseases. They could all be cured anyway. Soon he was on top of her and her shapely legs were wrapped around him. As he thrust in and out, she kept smiling and kept rubbing her legs against his side, back, and butt. The dope intensified everything. He couldn't believe it was happening, her legs felt so good. Then she got close to climax and began to squeeze him with those legs.

Damn but he loved sex. He was there, his dick was sliding in and out of a pretty girl's pussy, it just felt so ridiculously good, and the dope made it all that much more powerful. Soon, they managed a simultaneous climax. He spurted his life into her, and she accepted it without question.

They showered together. He soaped up her pussy, fingered her to pull out any residue semen, rinsed it all off, then went down on her. She leaned against the shower wall, her long hair all wet and draped over everything, and spread her legs apart to allow him easier access. The shower floor tiles were a little hard on his knees, but he was too into it to stop. He licked her up and down her slit, and stuck his tongue in her. Before he knew it, she grabbed the back of his head, pushing him down even tighter into her bush, and shook all over. As she was in the throes of her climax, she brought one of her legs up and wrapped it around his back.

They dried off and she immediately pushed him down on the bed. Soon, he was watching her pretty face move up and down on his dick. The sensation was intense. Though he had already cum, he quickly felt his orgasm building again. Soon, he was spurting into her mouth, filling her up with his essence, and supremely satisfied.

She lay with her head on his shoulder, rubbing his chest hair with her hand.

"I'm not a slut, you know," she said out of the blue.

"What? Why did you say that?"

"Well, you might think I' m a slut because I made love to you the first night we met."

"It's happened to me before. I certainly don't disrespect any girl for doing what I want her to do. I love the sexual revolution. I wish all girls were more open about sex."

"Well, I don't know if you believe me, but you're the first guy I've been with this whole school year. I know who you are; I've seen you around."

"You've seen me around, where?"

"On campus, and you play lacrosse, I actually watched one of your games."

"Wait a minute. You've seen me on campus and watched a lacrosse game. Why didn't I notice you? Believe me I would have. With that ass, and that hair, I would have noticed you."

"No you wouldn't. I always wear my nerdy bookworm wallflower outfit. I put my hair in a bun, wear a long work shirt to hide my shape, I don't have big boobs sticking out anyway, I wear big ugly glasses, and I walk slouched over. I look completely nondescript. Nobody notices me."

"Why do you do that?" he asked.

"Probably because my high school sweetheart, the one I gave my virginity to, well, I caught him in bed with my best friend. It turned me off for a long time. Plus, I'm actually shy and afraid of boys. I was so nervous standing next to you at that concert. My knees were shaking. I almost ran away."

"Well," he said, leaning over to kiss her, "I'm really glad you didn't. Why did you decide to come out of your shell tonight?"

"Some of my friends got beat up by the cops, including this thing that happened right in my apartment building. And I realized I had wasted the year trying to be ugly and unnoticed. I don't know why. I, I don't know why my friends getting beat up made me want to have fun. But I let my hair down and went to the concert. I saw you there and decided I wanted to have you."

"You decided you wanted to have me?"

"Yeah. You never had a chance, really. Nervous or not, I was determined."

By this time, he was hard again. She squeezed his dick with her hand, smiled broadly, and then climbed on top of him. Soon he was buried inside her, and he scooted over to the edge of the bed, put his feet on the floor, and sat up.

"Ooh, hi," she said, smiling sweetly and putting her arms around his neck.

"Hi," he answered, and then stood up, holding her completely off the ground, her chest with her medium tits pressed next to his, his dick inside her, his hands holding her up by her beautiful, round, firm ass cheeks as she wrapped her legs around him. She smiled and giggled, and he thrust in and out, up and down. They kissed with their tongues taking turns in each other's mouths. It wasn't long before she began again to shake all over. He, however, was having a hard time reaching the point of no return. He thrust and thrust, and she came two more times smiling all the while. Finally he erupted, spurting his life into her once again.

"Feel better?" she asked between kisses as they still stood in the middle of the room, he still imbedded in her. "That was fun. Can I sleep now?"

In the morning, he woke up with her standing at the foot of his bed, naked. He looked at her body up and down. The boobs were not large, but more than a mouthful and very nicely shaped. Her bush was a deep black and very thick, which he liked. Her ass was wonderfully round and tight. Those legs were fantastic, the hair great, and the smile disarming.

"Do you want to do something again?" he asked.

"No, sorry, I have to go. But I had a really great time," she said, smiling. "Uh, you said you're moving back down to LA?"

"Yeah, our lease is up on Monday."

"Well," she sighed, "I guess we won't see each other again. Do you like my body?" she asked, changing the subject and twirling around with her hands in the air and her long hair flying out.

"You sure you don't want to make love again?"

She stopped and thought for a moment.

"Okay," she said, as she jumped back into the bed.

On Sunday, Donnie and his parents returned to Windward House.

"Mr. Johnson," Reggie asked, "could you take our picture? We'll do it out on the deck here."

The 40 plus man took the camera, listened to Reggie's instructions, then walked out in front of the deck. Trent, Reggie, and Donnie on crutches all sat on the end of the deck. The camera clicked away, and soon the photo session was over.

"Donnie," Mr. Johnson said, "we gotta get going. We'll wait for you in the car. Nice meeting you Trent, Reggie. And thanks for all you did for Donnie, we really appreciate it."

The three were alone in the living room. No music was on as Trent had already packed up his stereo.

"Man, I'm glad I walked into that real estate office when I did.

You guys are great. I'm really gonna miss both of you," Reggie said seriously.

"You mean after all the arguments about the war and demonstrations and the monkey and all that?" Donnie asked.

"Yeah, even after all that,"

"And even after I fucked a girl you were shooting for?" Trent asked.

"Yeah," Reggie said, "even after that."

Donnie leaned on his crutch to get up from the couch. "I gotta go, my parents will get antsy. My mom has to drive my car and she doesn't like it."

Reggie shook his hand, as did Trent. Donnie turned and hobbled out the front door. They went out with him to the parking area. Donnie turned to face them.

"You know what?" he asked. "Del Playa is wrong. It's not correct Spanish grammatically. It should be De La Playa. Means 'of the beach'."

He then got in his dad's car and they drove off, waving one last time. The mom followed in Donnie's car. Reggie wondered if he would ever see him again.

"I'm goin' over there," Reggie said, nodding at the girls' house. "Take some more pictures, say some more goodbyes."

Sandy opened the door to let him in.

"You're leaving tomorrow?" she asked.

"Yup, is everybody here?"

"Yeah, we're all here."

"Call everybody up to the deck; I want to take some pictures."

Soon they all had gathered in the living room and some went out on the deck. Reggie noticed a beautiful, tall blonde wearing cut off shorts and a half t-shirt with most of her midriff exposed and her tits pushing out seductively, holding the bottom of the shirt out away from her body.

"Who's this?" he asked.

All the girls immediately cracked up.

"That's Mary," Joyce said. "She lives here, too,"

They all burst out laughing again.

"I've been coming over to this house since October, and I'm only now meeting you?" he asked.

"Well, I've really been staying with my boyfriend, so I didn't come over here much."

"I guess so. Well come on, I want you in the picture, too," Reggie said.

"Why?" Mary asked

"Cause your too damn foxy, just like every girl in this house. You guys," he addressed them all, "do you realize how absolutely beautiful you all are? This is incredible. Playboy could do a spread just on the girls of this house."

"Thank you Reggie," Sandy said.

"Okay, everybody on the deck, against the railing."

And the five of them went out and he took pictures. He took pictures of them smiling sweetly, he took pictures of them acting silly, and he took pictures of them looking sexy. Then, John took pictures of Reggie with the girls. In one, they all hugged and kissed him at the same time.

"Well," he said, "I gotta go. Tomorrow it's back to Santa Monica and the start of my life."

Joyce came up and gave him a quick hug with a kiss on the cheek. "Bye Reg," she said. "Thanks for the cool times."

Sandy gave him a big hug and a kiss on the lips. "Take care, Reg, it's been fun."

"Are any of you guys keeping this house?" Reggie asked.

"Janice will stay along with me and Maureen, some more people will come down from Menlo," Sandy answered.

"Well, nice meeting you, Mary," he held out his hand.

"To hell with that," she said, "I want a hug and a kiss, too."

She pressed her fantastic body against his, put her arms around his neck, and kissed him softly. Then, she stepped back, holding his hand. "Not bad," she said, smiling.

"Okay," Reggie said.

Maureen was next. She said nothing, but looked into his eyes and hugged him long and hard. He felt her full breasts against his chest. She kissed him, with tongue, and they stood for several minutes holding each other and kissing. Then, she broke it off and stepped away.

Janice came up to him. He put his arm around her and looked down into her beautiful Korean eyes.

"So, I'm gonna stay stuck on third?" he asked.

"Looks like it," she answered.

"What about a sacrifice fly?"

"Already two out, won't work."

"And that leaves out a suicide squeeze, too, doesn't it?"

"Sure does."

"What if I steal home?"

"Not gonna happen. The pitcher is right handed. You'll never make it."

"Any chance for a passed ball or wild pitch?"

"I don't think so."

"What are you guys talking about?" Sandy asked, laughing.

With that, Reggie and Janice kissed for the last time. She hugged him and began to cry. He broke off from her, waved to them all, then went out the side door, the one he had come in all those months ago, and walked back to Windward House.

The next morning, he and Trent packed up their cars and locked up the house. "I'll drop your keys off at the real estate office," Trent said.

"Thanks," Reggie said. "Hey, I meant what I said. I wouldn't change anything. It was a great year."

"Yes it was," Trent said and stuck out his hand.

They shook hands, and Trent got into his car. Reggie took a deep breath. The sea air felt good, but the oily smell was still there. He got into his car and followed Trent out of the parking area. They drove off, leaving Windward House forever.

Epilogue

The Bank of America built a new riot-proof fortress of a bank in the spot where the old bank had been burned. By the 1980s, however, the branch was closed and the building became a popular bar. That closed down in the 1990s and the University bought both it and the Magic Lantern Theater, turning them into lecture halls for classes to be held in I.V.

The UCSB lacrosse team flourished, getting better and better until by the 2000s they were winning national titles for college club lacrosse.

The draft ended in 1973 and by 1975 all our troops were out of Vietnam. The counter-culture movement quickly evaporated and for most, life continued as always.

Thanks to the 26th Amendment to the Constitution, 18 year-olds got the right to vote. Since then, they have stayed away from the polls in droves. Evangelical Christians, on the other hand, finally realized that control of the political process could help them push a social agenda favorable to their views and they have influenced many elections since.

Computer scientists eventually constructed a machine that could and did defeat grand masters at chess.

The Blind Faith album was released in the United States by Atco originally with the naked pre-teen girl on the cover, but they soon replaced that with a different cover showing a picture of the band.

Vicky married a black grad student, completed her Ph.D., and returned to Watts to work on community action programs for which she wrote grants.

Sandy married John and they stayed in the Santa Barbara area. They both eventually completed degrees at UCSB and opened day care centers.

Joyce took a trip to Europe and never returned. It was rumored she married a Dane and stayed in Copenhagen.

Maureen ended up marrying a skinny, short, glasses wearing, socially awkward, nerd. He became a doctor and developed a successful practice in Ojai, where they lived. He was completely devoted to her and she loved him madly. They had four kids.

Janice returned to the Bay area where she finished a degree at

San Francisco State. She married and divorced three times, having a kid each from three different husbands. She often thought of Reggie. She finally found some comfort and satisfaction with her fourth husband, an engineer for the city of San Francisco. She never went to Korea.

Rebecca discovered that she liked girls as much as boys and left Donnie for her girlfriend. After getting degrees at UCSB, they moved to San Diego where they worked at the Zoo. Rebecca ended up in charge of the monkey house.

Donnie Johnson did get his IV-F and did walk with a limp the rest of his life. How much the IV-F saved him is not clear, for the draft ended in 1973, the year he should have been protected to by his II-S deferment. The war ended about then, too. Donnie stayed in the Santa Barbara area, becoming relatively comfortable in real estate. He even dealt with property in Isla Vista, and ended up purchasing Windward House which he always rented to students. He married a girl he met in his junior year and they had two kids.

Trent Foster got his master's in math at UC Irvine then went to UCLA for a Ph.D. in computer science. He completed that and was hired by UC Santa Cruz to teach math to undergraduates. He was dismissed after only three semesters when it was discovered he had sex with eight different coeds. He was picked up by a computer company near San Jose in what would become known as Silicone Valley. He took advantage of stock options and eventually became worth tens of millions of dollars when his company became outrageously successful. He finally married and settled down, having three kids.

Reggie Blake returned to the LA area and could not find work except for minimum wage jobs. After a year of that, he went into the Peace Corps. Stationed in Thailand, he taught English. He also took the opportunity to frequent the sex clubs in Bangkok, looking for tiny girls who reminded him of Janice. By the end of his two years, he was fluent in Thai, had made love to about 50 different Thai girls, and had contracted a drug resistant strain of gonorrhea that took him a year to shake. He eventually moved to the Big Island of Hawaii where he married a tall, statuesque Chinese-Hawaiian fitness nut with big boobs and long hair. They had four kids. He never played lacrosse again. Reggie spent 30 years teaching in a local high school.

Other Books by Reilly Ridgell

Green Pearl Odyssey. Tokyo: Blue Ocean Press, 2010.

Pacific Nations and Territories, the Islands of Micronesia, Melanesia, and Polynesia, Fourth Edition. Honolulu: Bess Press 2006. (Textbook for secondary.)

Pacific Neighbors, The Islands of Micronesia, Melanesia, and Polynesia (with Betty Dunford), Second Edition. Honolulu: Bess Press 2006. (Textbook for elementary.)

Bending to the Trade Winds, Stories of the Peace Corps Experience in Micronesia. Guam: University of Guam Press 1991.

About the Author

Reilly Ridgell graduated from Palisades High School (LA) in 1965, got his BA in political science from UCLA in 1969, and an MA in the same field from UC Santa Barbara in 1970. In 1971, he joined the Peace Corps, teaching English in the outer islands of what is now called Chuuk State in Micronesia. After his Peace Corps service and a teaching contract, he left Chuuk in 1975 to teach in Guam. In 1980, he became an assistant professor at Guam Community College and in 2001 moved into administration as Dean.

He is the author of the widely used textbook, Pacific Nations and Territories, which has been in print continuously since 1983, and co-author of its elementary level version, Pacific Neighbors. He also authored the anthology of Micronesian Peace Corps stories, Bending to the Trade Winds, and in 2010 his first novel, Green Pearl Odyssey, was published by Blue Ocean Press.

If you enjoyed *The Isla Vista Crucible* consider these other fine books from Savant Books and Publications:

Essay, Essay, Essay by Yasuo Kobachi
Aloha from Coffee Island by Walter Miyanari
Footprints, Smiles and Little White Lies by Daniel S. Janik
The Illustrated Middle Earth by Daniel S. Janik
Last and Final Harvest by Daniel S. Janik
A Whale's Tale by Daniel S. Janik
Tropic of California by R. Page Kaufman
The Village Curtain by Tony Tame
Dare to Love in Oz by William Maltese
The Interzone by Tatsuyuki Kobayashi
Today I Am a Man by Larry Rodness
The Bahrain Conspiracy by Bentley Gates
Called Home by Gloria Schumann
Kanaka Blues by Mike Farris
First Breath edited by Zachary M. Oliver
Poor Rich by Jean Blasiar
The Jumper Chronicles by W. C. Peever
William Maltese's Flicker by William Maltese
My Unborn Child by Orest Stocco
Last Song of the Whales by Four Arrows
Perilous Panacea by Ronald Klueh
Falling but Fulfilled by Zachary M. Oliver
Manifest Intent by Mike Farris
The Mythical Voyage by Robin Ymer
Hello, Norma Jean by Sue Dolleris
Richer by Jean Blasiar
Charlie No Face by David Seaburn

Number One Bestseller by Brian Morley
My Two Wives and Three Husbands by S. Stanley Gordon
*In Dire Strait*s by Jim Currie
Wretched Land by Mila Komarnisky
Chan Kim by Ilan Herman
Who's Killing All the Lawyers? by A. G. Hayes
Ammon's Horn by Guerrino Amati
Wavelengths edited by Zachary M. Oliver
Almost Paradise by Laurie Hanan
Communion by Jean Blasiar and Jonathan Marcantoni
The Oil Man by Leon Puissegur
Random Views of Asia from the Mid-Pacific by William E. Sharp, Jr.

Scheduled for Release in 2012:

Blood Money by Scott Mastro
In the Himalayan Nights by Anoop Chandola
Perverse by Larry Rodness
On My Behalf by Helen Doan
Rules of Privilege by Mike Farris
Light Surfer by David Allan Williams

http://www.savantbooksandpublications.com

www.ingramcontent.com/pod-product-compliance
Lightning Source LLC
Chambersburg PA
CBHW071134260626
47162CB00003B/778
* 9 7 8 0 9 8 3 2 8 6 1 6 5 *